*Abide with Me*

 RANDOM HOUSE | NEW YORK

# Abide with Me

A NOVEL    *Elizabeth Strout*

Published in the United States by Random House,
an imprint of The Random House Publishing Group,
a division of Random House, Inc., New York.

RANDOM HOUSE and colophon are
registered trademarks of Random House, Inc.

LIBRARY OF CONGRESS CATALOGING-IN-PUBLICATION DATA

Strout, Elizabeth.
Abide with me: a novel / Elizabeth Strout—1st ed.
p.   cm.
ISBN 1-4000-6207-1
1. Clergy—Fiction. 2. Widowers—Fiction.
3. New England—Fiction. 4. Bereavement—Fiction.
5. Mute persons—Fiction. 6. Single fathers—Fiction.
7. Fathers and daughters—Fiction. I. Title.
PS3569.T736S73 2006
813'.54—dc22        2005050380

Printed in the United States of America on acid-free paper

www.atrandom.com

2 4 6 8 9 7 5 3 1

FIRST EDITION

*Title-page photograph by Daniel Menaker*
*Book design by Barbara M. Bachman*

*To the memory of my father,*

*R. G. Strout*

*Book One*

# ONE

Oh, it would be years ago now, but at one time a minister lived with his small daughter in a town up north near the Sabbanock River, up where the river is narrow and the winters used to be especially long. The minister's name was Tyler Caskey, and for quite some while his story was told in towns up and down the river, and as far over as the coast, until it emerged with enough variations so as to lose its original punch, and just the passing of time, of course, will affect the vigor of these things. But there are a few people still living in the town of West Annett who are said to remember quite clearly the events that took place during the wintry, final months of 1959. And if you inquire with enough patience and restraint of curiosity, you can probably get them to tell you what it is they claim to know, although its accuracy might be something you'd have to sort out on your own.

We do know the Reverend Tyler Caskey had two daughters at the time, but the littler one, really just a toddler then, lived with Tyler's mother a few hours away, farther down the river in a town called Shirley Falls, where the river got wide and the roadways and buildings more frequent and substantial, things taking on a more serious tone than what you might find up near the town of West Annett. Up there, you could drive for miles—and still can—on twisting back roads, not passing by anything more than the occasional farmhouse, acres of fields and woods all around. In one of these farmhouses, the minister and his little girl Katherine lived.

The place was at least a hundred years old, built and farmed for decades by the family of Joshua Locke. But by the end of the Depression, when the farmers had no money to pay for hired hands, the farm had fallen into disrepair. Their blacksmith business, started before the First World War, also dwindled away to nothing. Eventually the house was occupied, and remained so for years, by the sole inheritor, Carl Locke, a man who seldom came into town, and who, when called upon to pull open his door, did so holding a rifle. But in the end he had left the entire place—house, barn, and a few acres of fields—to the Congregational church, even though no one seemed to remember him being inside the church more than twice in his life.

At any rate, West Annett, even containing as it did the three white buildings of Annett Academy, was a fairly small town; its church coffers were small as well. When Reverend Smith, the minister who had been there for years and years, finally got around to retiring, hauling his deaf wife with him off to South Carolina, where apparently some nephew waited to look after their needs, the church board waved them good-bye with a tepid farewell, then turned around enthusiastically and made a very nice real estate deal. The parsonage on Main Street was sold to the local dentist, and the new minister would be housed at the Locke place, out there on Stepping Stone Road.

The Pulpit Committee had made their recommendation of Tyler Caskey with this in mind, counting on his youth, his big-boned, agreeable nature, and the discomfort he had shown right away in discussing matters of money, to prevent him from complaining about being housed in a field two miles from town; and on all these points they were right. The minister, in the six years he had lived there now, had never once complained, and except for permission to paint the living room and dining room pink, had never asked the church for anything.

Which is partly why the house remained a bit ramshackle, inside and out. It had a broken porch railing and tilting front steps. But it offered those pleasing lines you find in old houses sometimes; a tall two-story, with generous windows and a nice slope to the roof. And if you studied the place for a moment—the southern exposure it got on the side, the way the mudroom faced north—you realized the people who built it years before had possessed a fine sense of what they were doing; there was a symmetry here that was unadorned, kind to the eye.

So begin with a day in early October, when it's easy to think of the sun shining hard, the fields surrounding the minister's house brown and gold, the trees on the hills sparkling a yellowy-red. There was—there always is—plenty to worry about. The Russians had sent up their Sputnik satellites two years before—one whirling around right now with that poor dead dog inside—and were said to be spying on us from outer space, as well as right here in our own country. Nikita Khrushchev, squatty and remarkably unattractive, had even arrived a couple of weeks before for a visit to America, whether people liked it or not—and many did not; they were afraid he'd be killed before getting home, and then what horrors might ensue! Experts, whoever they were, and however they did it, had determined that a guided missile from Moscow to New York would fall within 7.3 miles of its target, and while it was a comfort to live outside this radius, there were three families in West Annett who had bomb shelters in their backyards anyway, because after all, you never knew.

Still: This happened to be the first year in many where country-wide church membership had not increased at a greater rate than the general population, and that, if you thought about it, had to mean something. Possibly it meant people were not panicking. Possibly it meant people wanted to believe, and were apparently believing—particularly here in the northern reaches of New England, where the same people had lived for years, not many communists among them (although there were a few)—that after half a century of colossal human horror, the world really could perhaps be finally decent, and safe, and good.

And today—the one we've chosen to start with—was lovely in its sunny brightness, the tops of those distant trees a brave and brilliant yellowy-red. Even keeping in mind how this kind of autumn day can be an awful thing, harsh and sharp as broken glass, the sky so blue it could break down the middle, the day was perfectly beautiful, too. The kind of day where you could easily imagine the tall minister out for a walk, thinking, *I will lift up mine eyes unto the hills.* It had, in fact, been Reverend Caskey's habit that fall to take a morning walk down Stepping Stone Road, then turn back up around Ringrose Pond, and there were some mornings when he continued on into town, headed to his study in the basement of the church, waving to people along the way who tapped their horns, or stopping to talk to a car that pulled over, leaning his large body down to peer into the window, smiling, nodding, his hand lingering on the car door until the window was rolled up, a wave good-bye.

But not this morning.

This morning the man was sitting in his study at home, tapping a pen against the top of his desk. Right after breakfast, he had received a telephone call from his daughter's school. His daughter's teacher was a young woman named Mrs. Ingersoll, and she had asked the minister in a remarkably clear voice—though it was somewhat too high-pitched for his taste—if he would come to school in the late afternoon to discuss Katherine's behavior.

"Is there a problem?" the minister had said. And during the pause that followed, he said, "I'll come in, of course," standing up, holding the black telephone while he looked around the room as though something had been misplaced. "Thank you for calling," he added. "If there's any kind of problem, of course I want to know."

A small, stinging pain below his collarbone arrived, and, placing his hand over it, the man had the odd momentary sense of someone about to say the Pledge of Allegiance. Then for some minutes he walked back and forth in front of his desk, his fingers tapping his mouth. Nobody, of course, wants to start a morning this way, but it was especially true for Reverend Caskey, who had suffered his share of recent sorrows, and while people were aware of this, the man was really far more worn down than anyone knew.

THE MINISTER'S STUDY in the old farmhouse had been for many years the bedroom of Carl Locke. It was a large room on the first floor, with a view of what must have been, at one time, a very nice side garden. An old birdbath still stood in the center of a circular design of now mostly broken bricks, and vines grew over a tilting trellis, beyond which could be seen part of a meadow and an old stone wall that wobbled its way out of sight.

While Tyler Caskey had heard stories of the cantankerous and, some said, filthy old man who had lived here before him, while his wife had even complained for months when they first moved in that she could, in this room on a warm day, detect the smell of urine, the truth is that Tyler liked the room very much. He liked the view; he'd even come to feel some affinity to the old man himself. And now Tyler thought he wouldn't go for his morning walk; he'd sit right here where another fellow had struggled apparently with righteousness, and probably loneliness, too.

There was a sermon to prepare. There always was; and the one for this Sunday the minister was going to call "On the Perils of Personal Vanity." A tricky topic, requiring discretion—what specifics would he use?—particularly as he was hoping with its teaching to head off a crisis that loomed on the ecclesiastical horizon here in West Annett regarding the purchase of a new organ. You can be sure that in a small town where there is only one church, the decision as to whether or not that church needs a new organ can take on some significance; the organist, Doris Austin, was ready to view any opposition to the purchase as an assault upon her character—a stance irritating to those who had a natural hesitancy toward any change. So with not much else to occupy itself at the time, the town was on the verge of being occupied by this. Reverend Caskey was opposed to the organ, but said nothing publicly, only tried through his preaching to make people think.

Last week had been World Communion Sunday, and the minister had emphasized this point to his congregation right before the special offering. They were Christians in communion with the *world*. As was tradition, on the Friday before World Communion Sunday, a noontime service of the Ladies' Aid Benevolent Society had been held, and that's when the minister had been hoping to speak on the Perils of Personal Vanity, guiding this group of women—responsible for raising much of the church's money— away from any frivolous expenditures. (Jane Watson wanted a new set of linen tablecloths for coffee hour.) But he'd not been able to gather his thoughts, and for Tyler, who used to like to picture himself, metaphorically speaking, as taking his listeners gently by the scruff of their white New England necks—*Listen while I tell you*—his Friday performance had been disappointing; he'd provided only general words of praise, for hard work, money raised.

Ora Kendall, whose droll voice always struck Tyler as being at odds with her small face and wild black hair, had called an hour after the service to give him a report, as she was apt to do. "Two things, Tyler. Alison doesn't like you quoting Catholic saints."

"Well," Tyler said easily, "I guess I won't worry about that."

"Second thing," said Ora. "Doris wants that new organ even more than she wants to divorce Charlie and marry you."

"The organ business, Ora—that's the board's decision."

Ora made a ruminative sound. "Don't be a nitwit, Tyler. If you showed any enthusiasm for it, the board would say yes in a second. She thinks you ought to do that because she's special."

"Everyone is special."

"Yuh. That's why you're a minister and I'm not."

This morning Tyler Caskey was trying again to compose some lines about vanity. He had jotted down notes from 12 Ecclesiastes on the apparent meaninglessness of life when viewed from the human perspective "under the sun." "Under the sun, all is vanity and vexation of spirit," he had written. He tapped the pen, and did not write down the business of viewing from "above the sun," which would show life to be a gift from the hand of God. No, he just sat, staring out the window of the room.

His eyes, wide and gazing, did not take in the birdbath, or the stone wall, or anything at all; he was just staring into space with his blue eyes. Little wispy thises and thats were floating by the edge of his memory—the poster that had hung in his childhood bedroom with the words A GOOD BOY NEVER TALKS BACK, picnic tables in the Applebys' field, where the bean-hole suppers used to be held, the maroon drapes in the living room of the house where his mother still lived, now with the baby, Jeannie—and here his mind hovered: the proprietary nature of his mother's large hands as she guided the child's little shoulders through the living room.

The minister looked down at the pen he was holding. "The best in a difficult situation" is how he had phrased it at first, but it didn't have to be phrased anymore. Everyone knew where the baby was, and no one, to his knowledge, frowned on the arrangement. And in fact, no one really did. Fathers were not, at that time, expected to raise small babies alone, particularly where there was so little money, and while the Ladies' Aid had supplied him with the light housekeeping duties of Mrs. Connie Hatch (she was paid pennies), his congregation understood the baby was better off for the time being with her Grandmother Caskey—who had never, by the way, offered to take in little Katherine, too.

No, Katherine was his.

*Cross to bear*—words that shot through his mind now, and made him grimace, for she was not his cross to bear. She was his gift from God.

He sat up straight and tried to picture himself talking with the young teacher, how he would listen earnestly, hands clasping his knees. But his cuffs were frayed. How could he not have noticed? Examining the cuffs more closely, he realized the shirt was simply old, had reached the point where his wife would have taken it for herself, cutting the sleeves off midway and wearing it with her bright pink ballet tights that had no feet.

"It frees me up," she would say. But she had sometimes answered the door that way, and when he had said jokingly that perhaps this put his job at risk, having Marilyn Dunlop drive up to the house and find the minister's wife running around in men's cut-off shirts and dancing tights, that Marilyn might even *elaborate* in her report back to the others, his wife had answered, "Say, Tyler, are there any things I can decide on my own?" Because it had bothered her dreadfully how the walls of the old farmhouse did not belong to her, belonged to the church instead, that she could not paint a wall without the church's permission, although permission was granted, of course, when the minister said he would buy the paint himself. "I want it all *pink,*" his wife had said excitedly, throwing her arms wide with exuberance, and he had not repeated to her later, of course, how his sister, Belle, on a visit had said, "For God's sake, Tyler, you're living inside a piece of bubble gum." (And right now the living room shone a candy-box pink, its walls in this bright sunshine glowing with a pinky haze that seemed to spill over into the hallway, see through the door of his study.)

Tyler stood up and walked down the hall, through the pink living room. "Mrs. Hatch?" he called.

Connie Hatch was finishing up the breakfast dishes, and, wiping her hands on a towel, she turned. A tall woman, she came almost eye-to-eye with him. It was rumored that far back an Agawam Indian had stealthily made his way into Connie's family line, and, studying the woman's face, you could easily wonder if this might not be true, for her cheekbones were high and wide, and her eyebrows dark, though not her hair: a soft brown, pinned back so loosely that parts often fell across her face, hiding at times the birthmark on the side of her nose, red as raspberry jam. She had green eyes that were really very pretty.

"What do you think I should do?" He held up his wrists. It was a serious question the minister asked, and his eyes searched his housekeeper's face. It might have been this quality, as much as any other, that continued to make the minister so popular with his congregation: these moments of sudden bafflement, deep uncertainty. Surfacing from a man who appeared always in control of himself, who shouldered his misfortunes with the gentle air of an abstracted acceptance, these instances of open-faced bewilderment allowed people, particularly women but by no means only women, to view him as surprisingly and suddenly vulnerable, and caused him to seem even more stoic in between these glimpses. Heroic, almost.

"About what?" his housekeeper asked. She held the dish towel with two hands and peered at the man's cuffs. "Shirt's worn, I guess." Connie's dark eyebrows, with the few gray hairs, rose in a kind of tired sympathy. "That happens," she said, and finished drying her hands.

"Do you think I should buy a new one?"

"Yes, I do." With her wrist, she pushed at a lock of hair that had slipped from behind her ear, then reached into her sweater pocket and found a bobby pin. "Goodness. Buy two."

The minister, relieved by this assignment of something specific to do, decided he would drive to Hollywell and do his shopping there rather than risk being seen by one of his congregants closer to West Annett, who might—after Sunday—wonder whether he himself had not fallen prey to the Perils of Personal Vanity. He found his wallet, his car keys, his hat, and, humming softly the hymn that had come into his head, "I would be true for there are those who trust me," the man walked down the tilting porch steps.

A SQUIRREL PATTERED across the porch, and a breeze knocked a branch against a window shutter. Inside, things were silent except for the opening and shutting of a closet door as Connie Hatch put away the bath towels, then took a mop to the living-room floor. Think, for a moment, about Connie. The woman was forty-six years old. She had expected to have children, and it had not happened. This, as well as certain incidents that *had* occurred (secrets that troubled her sleep, often with the horrible presence of two gazing eyes)—all this kept her beneath a private and growing carapace of confusion, and if someone had stepped into the minister's living room and said, "Connie, how has your life been?" she might not have known what to say. Well, nobody was going to ask her, anyway.

But she had trouble keeping a thought in her head. Her mind was like the skitter-skatter of a bad channel on the television set her husband had brought home last winter. She had forgotten to ask the minister if he would be back in time for lunch, though he probably would not be if he had gone all the way to Hollywell, but the uncertainty of this, of what was *expected of her,* occupied her mind. (Even though the minister was the easiest person she'd ever worked for; the same had not been true about his wife.) Years ago, Connie had done poorly in school, and no birthmark marked her as that had, the red horror of a *D* on the top of her test papers, red notes scrawled in the margins, one teacher who had written in block letters CONNIE MARDEN, USE YOUR HEAD. Connie whacked the mop against the squat wooden leg of the couch. If the minister came back in time for lunch, she would make him tomato soup from the can and set out a plate of buttered saltines; he always enjoyed that. She stopped to pin her hair up once again.

Did Connie know—she probably did—that she was one of those women you pass in the grocery store and see without seeing? But there was a softness in her face, a touching hesitancy, as though she had spent many years trying to be cheerful and no longer was, but the remnants of an earlier, eager kindness still remained. Her features had not hardened, in other words, and there were many women in that region whose features *had* hardened, women who had faces that could, by middle age, be the face of a man, but this was not the case for Connie Hatch.

People still said sometimes, "Doesn't that Connie Hatch have pretty eyes," although chances are the conversation stopped at that, because what else was there to say at this point about Connie? She had been married to Adrian Hatch for years, working for a while in the kitchen at the Academy, and then at the county farm—

what they called the county nursing home—but she'd quit two years ago to help take care of her mother-in-law, a fairly saintly thing to do, people agreed, since Evelyn Hatch got neither better nor worse, but stayed right on in the large old Hatch home, while Connie and Adrian remained in the trailer next door.

Later, people would try to recall what they could about Connie. Only a few would mention how attached she had been to her brother, Jerry, how she was never the same after he was killed in the Korean War. Connie didn't go to church anymore. Some women in the Ladies' Aid were bothered by this; Connie didn't care. What she cared about, as she stepped out the minister's back door to shake the mop, was how last night Adrian had not defended her when Evelyn said, "You can't even control your goddamn dog, Connie. Just imagine if you'd had kids." Adrian stood in the doorway of the trailer and didn't say a thing.

Connie shook the mop with a spasm of ferociousness, so the mop head fell off and she had to walk down the back steps to retrieve it from the leaves and gravel, all the while the bright sun slapping up against the barn.

THE MINISTER DROVE the back road to Hollywell, looking for God and hoping to avoid his parishioners. He drove with the window down, his elbow resting on the window edge, ducking his head to peer at the hills in the distance, or at a cloud, white as a huge dollop of frosting, and at the side of a barn, fresh with red paint, lit by this autumn sun; and he thought: I would have noticed this once. Even as he noticed it now. This feeling of incongruity was something he had come to fear, and he drove slowly because of it, and because he had sometimes been visited with the awful thought that he might run over a child—although there was not a person in sight— or that he might, without meaning to, drive straight into a tree.

Keep moving, he thought.

And keep an eye out for God. Who was, if you cared for the Psalms, as Tyler did, looking right now from heaven, beholding all the sons of men, considering all their works. But what Tyler longed for was to have The Feeling arrive; when every flicker of light that touched the dipping branches of a weeping willow, every breath of breeze that bent the grass toward the row of apple trees, every shower of yellow ginkgo leaves dropping to the ground with such direct and tender sweetness, would fill the minister with profound and irreducible knowledge that God was right there.

But Tyler was wary of shortcuts, and he was really afraid of cheap grace. He often thought of Pasteur's remarks that chance only helped those minds well prepared, and he hoped these days to have a moment of exalted understanding come to him as the "chance" result of his disciplined prayer. There was a fear the man lived with, a dark cave inside him: that he might not feel The Feeling again. That the exhilarating moments of transcendence had merely been the product of a youthful—and perhaps not even manly—form of hysteria, the kind that, taken to an extreme, could arguably produce the Catholic Saint Thérèse of Lisieux, who had died while still a young girl, and whose innocence surpassed him by the length and width of heaven. No, Tyler was earthly bound at the moment, and he accepted this. Sun bounced off the red hood of the old Rambler as the tires rumbled over the road. He passed a field of cows, pumpkins at a farm stand. On the way home he should buy a pumpkin for Katherine.

Hollywell's Main Street opened before him, with the ivy-covered post office and, not far from the men's clothing store, a parking space. In all things give thanks, and Tyler pulled the car in, checked for his wallet, stepped out into the sunshine.

But, oh.

Oh, boy.

Across the street, waiting for the traffic light to change—and there, it had changed now—Doris Austin, with the dark braid twisted tightly and neatly like a small basket on her head, was giving one more look to the right, to the left, cautious, holding a package in one hand, a brown pocketbook in the other, beginning to cross the street, and would, in just another moment, look up and see Reverend Caskey, and, oh, boy, he did not want to see her. He stepped into a pharmacy, walking over the threshold of its rubber mat while a little bell tinkled.

You never step in the same river twice, Heraclitus had said, and Tyler thought of this as he stood in the pharmacy, for he did feel frequently a sense of water rushing around him, and Doris Austin a twig that got caught in a little whirlpool by his ankles, because the woman—who played the church organ and directed the choir—seemed to show up everywhere, and would say in the church parking lot, or by the meat counter in the grocery store, "How *are* you, Tyler? Are you holding up?" in a quiet, confidential way. It put the man right on edge.

Nevertheless, last Sunday, in the vestibule after the service, as Doris was pulling on her sweater, Tyler had said, "You're pretty important to this community, Doris. I bet no one takes our fine music for granted." Of course people probably did. In fact, there were probably days people made fun of Doris once they got home and sat down for their Sunday meal, because the woman was compelled on communion Sundays to sing a solo, and every single time it was embarrassing—to see, as well as hear. A choir member would play a few notes on the organ while Doris draped herself over the balcony, swaying to and fro. Tyler, in his robe, seated in his chair on the chancel, would hold a hand to his face, eyes closed as though in pious meditation, when in truth he was avoiding the sight of his restless congregation, the adolescent girls giggling furiously in the back row.

But last week, hearing the operatic wails coming from Doris, it occurred to him he was listening to the manifestation of some inner desperate scream. This was a screeching plea from the woman's soul, begging not to be inconsequential: *Hear, O Lord, when I cry with my voice . . . have mercy . . . and answer me.* And so, coming across her in the vestibule, he had said, "I bet no one takes our fine music for granted." But the watery look of gratitude that came over her face as she tugged on her sweater alarmed him, and he thought it probably best to keep moving when he complimented her. He liked to compliment people—he always had. Who, after all, wasn't afraid, deep down, as Pascal had been, of those "spaces of nothing . . . which know nothing of me"? Who, in God's world, he thought, wasn't glad to hear that his presence really mattered?

But something else was at work here. Every night of Tyler's childhood, his father had said, "Always be considerate, Tyler. Always think of the other man first." (Who can estimate the effect of such a thing?) And if this had somehow mixed itself up with his own struggle to still believe *he* mattered, the connection was not one he pondered. What he knew were the simple facts: While his need to give praise had increased, his desire to avoid people had increased as well. He stood now glancing furtively at toothpaste.

"Something I can help you with?" A woman leaned across a counter of cosmetics.

"Well, let's see," Reverend Caskey said. "Let me think for a moment why I came in here."

"That happens to me," the woman said. Her fingernails were painted like pale shells. "I'll have some thought in mind and then it's gone." She snapped her fingers, a soft sound.

"I know just what you mean," said Tyler, shaking his head. "My mind is like a sieve. Pepto-Bismol. There we go." He placed the bottle on the counter.

"Say, do you know what I did the other day?" The woman

touched her hair with an open palm, bent unapologetically to glance in a mirror beside the cosmetics. "I looked in the refrigerator, thinking, What am I looking for? Stood there and stood there. And then it came to me."

The minister turned around just as Doris Austin stepped through the door, the tinkle of the bell announcing her entrance. Tyler said, "Why, hello, Doris," as the woman behind the counter said, "I was looking for an iron. May I help you?"

"An iron." In Tyler's confusion he felt he could see in Doris's eyes a sense of shame—she had followed him. "How are you?" he asked. "On this beautiful day." He put his large hand around the Pepto-Bismol. "She was just telling me," he said, nodding to the woman behind the counter, "how she spent hours looking for an iron in her refrigerator."

"I didn't say hours. Will that be all?"

"That's it." The minister reached for his wallet. "Not hours. Of course."

"Are you sick?" asked Doris. "Did you get that nasty intestinal bug going around?"

"Oh, no. No, Doris. I'm fine. Katherine had a little tummy ache the other night. Nothing serious."

"I don't know if you should be giving that stuff to a child," said Doris, and he realized she was trying to be helpful—an important member of the community.

"How old is she?" asked the woman behind the counter. Her fingernails touched his palm, handing him his change.

"Katherine's five," the minister said.

"Arnold, do you give Pepto-Bismol to a five-year-old?" called out the woman.

The pharmacist at the back of the store looked up. "Symptoms are—?"

"Little stomachache. Now and then." Tyler had grown warm.

"I bet she's not eating enough," offered Doris. "She is a tiny thing."

"How much does she weigh?" the pharmacist asked.

"I don't know exactly," said Tyler. His mother's dog weighed sixty-eight pounds. They were all looking at him.

"You can give her a small amount," said the pharmacist. "But if she's having stomachaches, she needs to see a doctor."

"Of course. Thank you." Reverend Caskey picked up the white paper bag and headed for the door.

Doris followed him out, which meant, since she bought nothing, she had followed him in. He had a fleeting image of her going into the men's clothing store with him, giving her opinion on shirts. On the sunny sidewalk she said, "You've lost some weight yourself, Tyler."

"Oh, I'm all right." He raised the white paper bag in a gesture of good-bye. "You enjoy this wonderful weather." And he walked in the opposite direction, up toward the clothing store.

He bought two white shirts from a man he suspected was homosexual. "Thank you very *much*," said Tyler, smiling at him quickly, looking him right in the eye as he took the package, and then that was that, back out onto the street, back into the car, where the sun seemed to follow him like a glaring spotlight as he drove carefully the twisting roads back home.

CONNIE'S HEAD WAS buzzing with that skitter-skatter feeling as she went about making the minister's lunch—he had not eaten in Hollywell, after all. When she rang the little bell to let him know lunch was ready, he walked into the kitchen and said, "Mrs. Hatch, let me ask you something. Do you think Katherine ought to be playing more with other children? Should I be inviting some kids here?" He pulled out a chair at the kitchen table, sitting down heavily, his long legs crossed out to the side. "I wanted to ask you before she got home." The child was picked up in the mornings and brought home from kindergarten after lunch by the mother of a boy who lived farther down the road.

Connie turned and washed out the soup pan. "I suppose it couldn't hurt," she said. But this embarrassed her, because didn't he know? Kids didn't *want* to play with the girl. Connie had heard people say this, and she could see it would be true. "She's quiet," Connie said. "I don't know what's to be done about that." Connie was glad it wasn't her job to make the girl more likable. She was sorry for the child—who wouldn't be?—but the girl, sullen and silent, was very hard to like.

"Her teacher called this morning and wants me to stop by after school for a chat. I'd better go change my shirt." But the minister sat. He added, "I expect she'll be okay. Kids are resilient, you know."

Connie opened the refrigerator, put the butter dish away. She wiped her hands on the dish towel. "Oh," she said, charitably, "Katherine will be all right. She'll pull out of things in time."

STILL. IT HAD BEEN A YEAR, and the girl collecting acorns in the afternoon sun, scuffing her new red shoes through the gravel (shoes bought last week by Aunt Belle, who, on a visit, had discovered the girl was pitifully dressed for her vast new world of kindergarten)—it had already been a year, and the child had barely spoken.

It was sad. Oh, absolutely. But the child exasperated people. She exasperated Connie Hatch, who couldn't help but remember how the little girl used to call her "Hatchet Foghorn," back when the little thing was still talking, prattling away to everyone, but especially to the resplendent, well-formed woman who had been her mother.

A woman who had probably come up with the name Hatchet Foghorn herself, and it was foolish—Connie being so quiet.

Well, now the child was quiet, too. And strange. "Maybe she isn't his," Jane Watson had said recently. "You take a careful look. There's no resemblance to Tyler there."

Actually, the child did not resemble either one of her parents. Not yet. Not now, as she scuffed through the gravel of the driveway, clutching acorns in her hand. There was no indication of her father's height or her mother's fullness. And while in time the minister's brow and mouth would appear with startling exactness on the face of his daughter, right now the girl looked almost part animal, like she came from nowhere, or was raising herself, living outdoors on roots and nuts: skinny little limbs, and hair so fine that in the back it stayed matted in a big snarl, hung in wisps down the front.

At school the teacher would move the hair from Katherine's face. "Doesn't it bother you, Katie, to have that hair hanging down over your eyes?" Katherine would gaze at her, oblivious. Which is how she was gazing now, as she watched the spit she'd been gathering in her mouth land on the toe of her scuffed shoe.

But here was her father's shoe, huge and dark in the crunching of the gravel, and then his face right in front of hers. "How was school today?" He had squatted down, parting the bangs that fell over her eyes.

She turned her face away.

"Did anything happen at school today?"

Katherine looked at her father quickly, and then away, past his bent leg to where the swallows were darting around the door of the barn. Because the most amazing thing *had* happened at school. One of the girls in the class had worn a pink dress and blue shoes, and another girl in the class had worn a blue dress and pink shoes. All day Katherine had followed them, thrilled at this coincidence of mismatched color.

"Mrs. Ingersoll," said one, "Katie's giving me the creeps. Make her get out of here."

"Be nice," said Mrs. Ingersoll. She put her hand on Katherine's shoulder and steered her away, Katherine craning her neck to keep watching.

Katherine ran over to the girls, wanting to say if they traded shoes it would be just right. But they told her to move, flicked their long hair. They called her a crybaby even though she wasn't crying. She went back to Mrs. Ingersoll—and screamed.

"Katie," said Mrs. Ingersoll tiredly, bending to wipe a boy's nose, "don't start. Please."

And now her father was squatted down in front of her asking if something important had happened at school, and the important thing—the amazement of those beautiful mismatched dresses and shoes—rose as big as a mountain and her words were little ants that couldn't make the climb; not even a scream could make the climb. She leaned against her father's arm.

"Mrs. Ingersoll called and told me you don't play with other children." He said this nicely, putting his big hand around her elbow.

Katherine moved her mouth, collecting spit in a warm pool next to her tongue.

"Do you have a favorite friend in class?" her father asked.

Katherine didn't answer.

"Would you like to go to Martha Watson's house after school someday? Have her come here? I can call her mother and ask."

Katherine shook her head, hard.

A sudden gust of wind sent dried leaves fluttering around them. The minister looked up, gazed at the maple next to the barn. "Gosh," he said. "Already the top is bare."

But Katherine was watching her father's shoe; the gob of spit landing slowly on the side of a shoe that was so big and dark it could have belonged to a giant.

"I'm going to be gone for a little while," her father said, standing up. "Mrs. Hatch will be watching you."

ALWAYS THINK of the other man first.

If Tyler, once again in his red Rambler, on the narrow, tree-lined road, wasn't exactly thinking of Mrs. Ingersoll first, he was, by habit, imagining what it must feel like to be her right now. Did she dread this conference? Possibly she did. She and her husband, after all, were C-and-E'rs, members who came to church only on Christmas and Easter, although this was the least of Tyler's worries. He had a lower rate of C-and-E'rs than many parishes, and he had never (good Lord) castigated such members, as he knew other ministers sometimes did. In any case, Tyler thought, as he got out of the car and walked across the school parking lot, he would do what he could to make this young woman feel comfortable.

Mrs. Ingersoll was seated at her desk. "Come in," she said, standing up. She wore a red knit dress with lint on it.

Tyler extended his hand. "Good afternoon." Her hand was so small it surprised him—as though instead of her own, she had slipped him the hand of a schoolchild. "Nice to see you, Mrs. Ingersoll."

"Thank you for coming in," she said.

They sat in little wooden chairs, and right away there was something in the woman's manner, a closed-off confidence, that Tyler found unsettling. When she said in her high, clear voice, "Why don't you tell me what Katherine is like at home," she looked at Tyler with such a steady gaze, he had to look away. The room, with its brightly colored letters pinned to a corkboard, its smell of children's paint, held a tension that took him by surprise, as though, without any memory of this at all, he had been miserable as a child that age.

"Does she sleep well? Cry a lot? Does she tell you what her day is like?"

"Well," the minister said, "let's see." Mrs. Ingersoll glanced at her sleeve, picked off a piece of gray lint, and turned her eyes back to Tyler, who said, "You know, she doesn't talk about what her day was like, I'm afraid. But I ask." He thought she might nod at that, but she didn't, so he added, "I try not to be aggressive about asking—you know, just encourage her to tell me on her own."

"Can you give me an example?" said Mrs. Ingersoll. "Of the kind of conversation you two might have?"

He thought there was, in her confidence, something hard, impermeable. He said, "I ask what she did at school. Who she played with at recess. Who her best friend in the class might be."

"And what does she say?"

"Not much, I'm afraid."

"We have a problem, Mr. Caskey."

The stinging pain arrived below his collarbone. "Well, then," he answered agreeably, "let's solve it."

"If we only could, just like that," the woman said. "But children aren't math problems to be solved with one right answer."

With a meditative motion, he rubbed the spot below his collarbone.

"Katherine wants my attention every minute, and when she doesn't get it, she has a screaming fit until she's tuckered out." Mrs. Ingersoll rearranged her hips, smoothed a hand over her lap. "She doesn't play with anyone; no one plays with her. And it's startling how she doesn't know one letter of the alphabet." Mrs. Ingersoll nodded toward the corkboard. "Doesn't seem the least bit interested in learning them, either. Last week she took a black crayon and scribbled over the pages in a picture book."

"Screaming fits?"

"You sound surprised."

"I am surprised," Tyler said.

"Are you saying she doesn't scream at home?"

"She doesn't scream at home. I am saying that, yes."

Mrs. Ingersoll tilted her head in what seemed to him an exaggerated pose of puzzlement. "Well, that's interesting. She screams here. And you have to understand—I have a room of other children to look after."

Tyler squinted. The stinging pain seemed to be affecting his vision.

"So, Reverend Caskey, you can see we need to do something."

The minister straightened his shoulders, crossed his arms.

"Who gives Katherine her baths?" Mrs. Ingersoll said.

"What's that?"

"Her baths," the woman said. "Who is it that bathes Katherine?"

The minister's eyebrows drew together. "The housekeeper, usually," he said.

"Does she like her?" Mrs. Ingersoll pulled a tiny chain out from beneath the neckline of her red dress, running it back and forth with a finger.

He said, "Oh, well. With Katherine it's sometimes hard to tell."

"I meant, does the housekeeper like Katherine?"

He saw that the chain held a small silver cross. "Oh. Of course. Connie Hatch is a fine woman. Solid. Solid citizen."

"Reverend Caskey, I'm asking the question because Katherine sometimes has the appearance of not being—well, not entirely groomed."

For a long time the minister said nothing. He placed his thumb beneath his chin and sat back. "I'll give it my attention," he finally said. The back of his head had grown warm.

Mrs. Ingersoll said: "I've talked to the principal a few times, and if Katie doesn't improve, we think it might be a good idea to have her tested. I'm not sure you're aware, but Rhonda Skillings—you know her, right?"

Tyler nodded.

"Rhonda's getting her doctorate at the university in psychology, on the effect of trauma on children. It's awfully interesting—now the studies are out on children who were displaced during the war. Rhonda's writing her dissertation, and she works with us as a counselor. Volunteer. She's got an office downstairs and when a child's having a—well, you know—a disruptive time in the classroom, it works out for everybody to have that pupil spend some time with her."

"I'm afraid I don't understand," Tyler said. "I'm afraid you've lost me here."

"I'm saying there's a problem, Mr. Caskey."

"Yes. That much I understand."

"And that having her scream in my classroom prevents me from getting my job done."

"Yes."

"And that we're lucky to have Rhonda Skillings, who can work with her on the days Katherine isn't doing well."

The minister looked at the blackboard, he looked at the little tables and chairs, looked at the small sink in the corner of the room. When he looked back at Mrs. Ingersoll, it was as though she had gone behind a pane of glass, the red shoulders of her dress, the brown hair that curled at her collarbone. He said, "Why didn't you let me know sooner?"

The woman stopped playing with her small neck chain. "We

were hoping the problem would straighten itself out. But it's gotten worse."

The minister uncrossed his long legs, rearranged himself in the ridiculous chair, crossed his legs the other way. "Katherine's not a refugee child displaced during the war," he said. "And she's not a guinea pig."

"But she is a problem in the classroom." The woman's voice took on a strident tone. "You asked why we didn't notify you sooner, and quite frankly, Mr. Caskey, we've been surprised you've never inquired about her. We have parents asking all the time how their child is making the adjustment to kindergarten. And of course Katherine's situation is—"

Tyler had lost the logic of the conversation; he knew only that something had gone wrong and he was being chastised. But he couldn't trace it back. He looked at the bright colors of the alphabet pinned to the corkboard, the basket of crayons on a table nearby, the red dress of Mrs. Ingersoll that had on its sleeve one long brown hair.

"Please," the woman was saying. "We have lots of sympathy for your loss. We really do. But I guess I'm surprised to hear that *you're* surprised to hear there's a problem."

He almost said, I'm a little rattled these days, but then he thought: It's nobody's business if I'm rattled these days. So he just gazed about the room, wondering if Rhonda Skillings had already been told about this.

"We understand you may not want to recognize there's a problem. That's not unusual." Mrs. Ingersoll was enunciating slowly, as though he might be a five-year-old with a crayon in his hand. "I'm sure it's been easier to believe Katherine's all right. But she's not. She's troubled."

Again, he squinted. Glancing at the young woman, he saw her watching him with her eyebrows raised, as though expecting something from him. He stood up and walked over toward the window. He saw how evening was on its way; in a few more weeks, it would be dark by this time in the day. The red glow of the sun sat above the horizon, right above the trees that were out past the playground, where the swing set stood gray and still.

"She hasn't been sent out of the classroom yet," Mrs. Ingersoll was saying. "We just wanted to keep you abreast. She painted a very nice picture the other day." He heard her chair scrape over the floor, the officious sound of her low-heeled pumps as she walked across the room. He turned to watch while she unscrolled a large sheet of paper. "But"—Mrs. Ingersoll held it out toward him— "you can see she covered it all with black."

Tyler said quietly, "You're not going to do that."

"Do what?"

"Send Katherine off to a room to be psychoanalyzed three days a week. No one's going to write a case study on my child."

Outside in the hallway, a janitor's pail clunked against the floor.

Mrs. Ingersoll rolled the picture back up, touching the masking tape that kept it in place. She said quietly, dropping her eyelids, "No one is going to psychoanalyze Katherine. But whether we decide to remove her from the classroom a few hours a week is not really your decision to make. This is a public school, Mr. Caskey. If the school decides she needs special help, then we do what we can to help her."

He had no idea if what she said was true.

"We'll keep you posted, Mr. Caskey."

"Thank you," he said. He walked across the room and shook her small hand.


THE BLUE OF the sky was deepening as the sun lowered over the towns along the river. Straight above, if you put your head back, was a blue so deep and rich that a person might have stopped and gazed at its wondrousness, except it was not the time of day people tended to look up. Leaving office buildings or grocery stores, walking across parking lots, people tended to tuck their chins down this time of day, to clutch at their coats, as though the darkening brought with it some inner shrinking.

And this was too bad, for it was quite a display spread out there, changing even from the time it took to open a car door, settle in, and close the door. By the time the key had turned, the engine started, the heavens had become a deeper, deeper, darker blue. And what a shame for Tyler Caskey, who, in different circumstances, taking a moment to glance at the sky, might have thought, *Yes, the heavens declare the glory of God; and the firmament sheweth his handywork.*

Instead, the man drove slowly, a hand raised against the final glaring sun that seemed only a thing to blind him as it hung brilliantly and massively above the horizon. He drove slowly past the fields and farms and pumpkin stands. As he pulled onto Stepping Stone Road, then turned in to the gravel of his driveway, he thought of his wife's final words, more than a year before. "Tyler," she had said, "you're such a coward, you know."

The farmhouse stood, white and plain, with its set of red shutters at each window. In the gathering dusk, its simple lines seemed to Tyler to contain some quietness of apology, to express a weariness from maintaining the understated dignity that had been its burden for a hundred years. But it was just a house. Only sticks and stones, and the porch railing was broken. As he parked near the barn, he felt the persistent pain beneath his collarbone, which over the months he had come to think of as the presence of a small rodent who lived inside him, clinging with tiny-needled claws. Tyler picked up his felt hat from the seat beside him and left the car slowly.

When he stepped through the back door, he heard nothing, and moved through the empty kitchen to the living room. Connie Hatch hurried down the stairs. "She's fallen asleep," Connie said. "I didn't know if I should let her, if you wanted—"

"It's fine, Mrs. Hatch." The minister stood in his long coat, his big shoulders slightly hunched. He dropped the car keys on the coffee table.

"How did it go?"

The minister didn't answer. But when he met the eyes of his housekeeper, he had one of those surprising moments that occur sometimes, when there's a fleeting sense of recognition, when, in less than half a second, there's the sense of having glimpsed the other's soul, some shred of real agreement being shared. This is what happened to the minister on that autumn evening, the walls of the living room now a dull, flat pink. *It's a sad world,* the house-keeper's eyes seemed to say. *And I'm sorry.*

The minister's eyes said, *It* is *a sad world, isn't it. I'm sorry, too.*

# TWO

Mary Ingersoll had worn the red knit dress because of the way it showed off her figure, and, washing it the night before, she'd been annoyed to discover her husband had not removed the Kleenex from his shirt pocket, as she'd told him many times to do, so that in the washing machine all those gunky little pieces of wet tissue were stuck, and then on her red dress, too. In the past, Mary had found Tyler Caskey attractive, and while she told people she'd been dreading the conference, she had, in fact, looked forward to it, rehearsing in front of the mirror, trying on expressions of kind-hearted, authoritative patience. She'd remembered to wear the little silver cross around her neck, so the man could see she was religious; she'd even thought she could apologize for not getting to church more often. "I'm simply *wrung out* from working all week," she would say, and he'd say he understood—working so hard to take care of problems like his little girl.

What a painful disappointment! The minister, in some odd way, didn't seem to notice her. Half the time he didn't even seem to be listening. He was tired—she could see this in his eyes—but his sudden coldness at the end had stung her. She went to the principal, Mr. Waterbury, in tears. "It wasn't called for," she told him, as he listened with his dark eyebrows drawn together.

"No, certainly not," he agreed.

That night Mary exaggerated in telling her husband—"The man sneered at me. He had a childish stare-down with me!"—and before she got ready for bed, she'd telephoned Rhonda Skillings and two friends, telling each of them the story, exaggerating a bit more, and when she fell asleep, she slept peacefully. The point is, she had the benefit of sympathetic listeners.

Tyler did not have this benefit, and he lay awake most of the night on his couch in the study. He was aware of something hard and dark inside him, like a small stone, and he had a sense *This is mine,* though he couldn't have said what; no words formed around it, just a quiet, growing fierceness of pleasant possession—and then it was gone—and the image of Katherine standing alone on the playground became the only thing in his mind. He sat up, looked around the darkened study, opened his hands, closed them. He thought of the teacher's high-pitched voice—"No one plays with her"—and was assaulted by a memory: his sister, Belle, standing on the playground in Shirley Falls, alone. He, two years younger, would see her and turn away, back to the group of boys who went on to remain his friends through high school. Belle, with an expression that feigned indifference, would watch a game of hopscotch, then wander away. It hurt Tyler to recall this. "You're a horse of a different color," his mother had said to him when he became president of his class, captain of the football team.

Slowly, he lay back down, and all sorts of nighttime worries bloomed. He hadn't finished his sermon; in a few weeks it would be Stewardship Sunday, then pledges came in, the annual budget would be shaped and presented for a vote in January; and Doris Austin (friendly with Rhonda) ought to be stopped sooner, rather than later, from manipulating the board members over the huge expense of a new organ. Only by recalling the kindness of Connie Hatch's green eyes was he able finally to doze. Even then, he woke and watched the windowpanes grow white. *It is a sin to rise up early, and eat the bread of sorrows.*

When he woke again, Katherine was standing near his face, watching him. "Pumpkin pie," he said. "Hello." He reached to put an arm around her. She had wet the bed, her pajama top soaked halfway up the back. Tyler sat up awkwardly. "Bath time for Katherine Estelle," he said. "But first." He rubbed his face. "This screaming at school," he finally said, leaning forward, his elbows on his knees. "It has to stop." The child turned away. "You can't do it anymore, Katherine. It's rude, and it drives the teacher nuts. Look at me."

She turned back, her face darkened with a blush. "That's all," he said. "Let's go."

The wet pajamas were tossed into a corner, the child lifted into the bathtub that was old and deep, and had those lion-clawed feet. It was so deep that when Katherine sat in it, she could barely see over the top. A saucepan for rinsing floated in front of her, rocking from the faucet water. Her father turned the faucet off when the water only covered her legs. When Hatchet Foghorn gave her a bath, the water was so deep it came up to Katherine's armpits, and she'd get a dizzy feeling. "Katherine?" her father said. "Did you hear me?"

She nodded, shivering.

"You just ask in a friendly voice, 'Hi there—can I play, too?'"

She squeezed her eyes shut and nodded again. "All right," he said. "Two rinses and we'll be done." She kept her eyes shut for both rinses, and he lifted her from the tub. Wrapped in a towel, she stood shivering. "Say, Kitty-Kat, do you *like* Mrs. Ingersoll?" Her father had different faraway voices, but this one she loved—it was so tired it included her in the big people's world. She shrugged. For a moment he knelt and looked into her eyes.

"Well," he said with a sigh. He looked around, picked up her wet pajamas. "I didn't think she was any prize."

THE MORNING LIGHT's radiance showed in the sharp, clear blue of the sky, in the twinkling of a fender of a car that passed by, in the open-handed beauty of the leaves moving in the tall maples along this section of the town's Main Street. It seemed impossible that man could, or would, choose to destroy this world. Nuclear arms must be gone within four years, Khrushchev had said, and yet he would not accept inspections of disarmament. What did any of this mean? Tyler, wearing one of his new white shirts and walking toward the church with a folded blanket tucked beneath his arm, might have prayed for the Russian leader, as well as Mrs. Ingersoll—*All we like sheep have gone astray.* Or he might have simply given thanks for the beauty of the world. But Tyler was thinking of Connie Hatch. He didn't want to dwell on the glance they'd exchanged, but he'd been surprised by the effect on him; it seemed as though he had not met the eyes of anyone for a very long time. He walked with long strides toward the church, a gusty wind whirling around him, everything crisp as an apple here in West Annett, leaves scattered on the ground.

The church was set back just slightly from the road, where Main Street veered in to Pottle's Lane. Built in 1796, it seemed to have settled itself comfortably against the small hillock and sloping lawn; you could even imagine it had its own spread of roots beneath the ground as large and lacily sturdy as those of the pines and cedars nearby. An addition had been built a few years back, off to the side, sinking slightly into the hollow of ground, so that the activities room and Sunday school could be housed in a building that barely showed from the road. The original study for the minister, though, remained in the basement of the church itself, and this was where Tyler was headed.

But first he stopped in to the sanctuary; the quietness and simplicity of the white painted pews, the slight chill to the air, pleasing him as it always did—that tiny prick of awe. He tucked the blanket beneath a back pew. It used to be that the church was locked at night. This started during the Depression, when a hobo had sometimes been found sleeping in the church. But Tyler, whose tendency was to stay away as much as he could from aspects of church management, had nevertheless said when he first arrived that the church must always be open. "Sanctuary," he had explained to his congregation. "From the Latin *sanctuarium*—a sacred place, sanctified, made holy. In fact," Tyler had said, with his particular brand of enthusiasm, "it used to be that a criminal, pursued, could find safety from arrest in the sanctuary of a church, because of the contagion of holiness." In any event, the West Annett church stayed open. Any hobo found sleeping in the church was to be fed and cared for, Tyler said, until he chose to move on. "If someone is caught stealing a candlestick, then the other candlestick must be given to him. This is the essence of Christian love."

No one fought him on this. And no one bothered to tell him that shortly after this pronouncement, the Ladies' Aid replaced the silver candlesticks with silver-coated ones, putting the originals in Jane Watson's care and bringing them quietly back for Christmas and Easter. If Tyler had known about the candlesticks, he wouldn't have said anything. He was more concerned with the fact that

Walter Wilcox, after the death of his wife, had been found sleeping in the church some nights, confused when woken, sometimes crying like a small child. Tyler invited the old man to sleep at the farmhouse on nights when he couldn't bear his own home. (Tyler's wife had said, "Is this going to be a *boardinghouse*, Tyler? Because I don't think I could stand that.") As it was, Walter had turned down the invitation, but Tyler thought of it sometimes, and he had thought of it last night, as he lay awake. The nights were cold now. And so he stopped in to the sanctuary this morning and put the folded blanket beneath the back pew. It was to stay in the church, though no one, as far as he knew, had been sleeping in the church since Walter.

Down into the basement he went, then, with the Perils of Personal Vanity. Tyler was hoping to write the sermon and commit it to memory, which is what the marvelous Dietrich Bonhoeffer had believed should be done, and what Reverend Caskey, before this year, had always done himself. He settled himself at his desk, tugged on his stiff white cuffs. Vanity impeded spiritual enlargement. A place of worship required no "outward pomp." Decency, but no magnificence. A place to worship God, not themselves— Tyler Caskey pursed his lips, squinted. He might, or might not, mention the organ business directly.

He folded his arms, dropped his head down. He imagined, in a deep and sudden drowsiness, a pleased look on Mrs. Ingersoll's face when she saw the difference their talk had made; there would be no need for any trip to Rhonda Skillings's office. Personal vanity was not to be confused with personal cleanliness. He might have to point that out in the sermon; always speak to the lowest common denominator in your audience—that would be Irma Rand, nice woman, dull-witted as a doorknob, but the testimony of the Lord is sure, making wise the simple, and the Hebrew word for wisdom, he was thinking in the delicious rocking wave of his sleepiness, meant "skill for living." Those Jews, practical people—

Tyler raised his head. The outer door upstairs had opened; he heard the squeaking of its hinge, and he got up, stuck his head out into the narrow hallway. Doris Austin was on the stairway, holding her pocketbook with both hands against her long gray coat, her head bent slightly, so that the small basket of her coiled braid seemed tilted forward as she came to the bottom of the stairs.

"Hello, Doris," said the minister. "Did you want to see me?"

She didn't answer.

Tyler said, "Please, come in." But a strange thing happened: He experienced, as he stepped back, a very brief and unexpected image—it really did amaze him—of giving a light smack to her obsequious face.

She sat down, and while he could have chosen to sit in the chair across from her, he sat instead behind his desk. She said, "I was hoping when I saw you in Hollywell to talk about what's bothering me."

"I'm sorry, Doris," he said. "My mind was on a number of things."

Doris said, "When something's wrong with your child, of course you're distracted."

"Wrong?" he asked. Was the whole town talking about his child?

"Those tummy aches," Doris said. "Almost easier if it *had* been a belly bug. Least you'd know."

Tyler nodded, remembering the Pepto-Bismol. "Tell me what it is that's bothering you." He tried to say this kindly, but he was very tired.

"I'm sad."

"Oh, I'm sorry, Doris." After a moment he asked, "What is it that makes you sad—do you know?"

"Everything," she answered.

"I see. Oh, boy," said Tyler, tapping his fingers against his mouth. "I am sorry."

"In the whole world," she added. And without any more warning than a slight reddening of her eyes, she began to weep.

He looked away. "Doris. You know . . ." He thought, *Bear ye one another's burdens, and so fulfill the law of Christ.* He could not think what to say. He felt debilitated by weariness, and thought how in the past months he had driven by the car dealership in Hollywell and felt jealous of the salesmen, whose responsibility for the souls of others would not, arguably, be so immediate or direct. ("Where's the calling there?" he could imagine his mother saying.)

"Charles makes me sad," Doris said.

"Yes, I see," Tyler said. "Well." This complicated things. Charlie Austin was head deacon of the church, a man reserved to the point of having, in Tyler's view, bad manners; and Tyler, as much as he could, had left him alone.

"He's irritated with me all the time."

Tyler put his hands in his lap and held them tightly. "Doris," he said, "marriages go through rough patches. Most of them do."

She didn't answer him.

"You might want to read the autobiography of Saint Thérèse of Lisieux," he said. "I read that at night sometimes, and it may seem at first blush rather hysterical in tone—of course it's very Catholic—but she writes about a nun who irritates her by clicking her rosary beads—"

"He hits me." The woman's chin was trembling.

"He hits you?"

The small puckers of her chin made him suddenly think of mashed potatoes.

"Oh," said Tyler. He shifted in his chair. "He does?"

"I'm not making it up," Doris said, umbrage in her voice.

"Of course not." He had so recently felt the startling impulse himself, he supposed he couldn't doubt her. You never knew what went on inside people's houses. His professor George Atwood had told him this in seminary: You never, ever knew.

"Often?" Tyler asked.

The tip of Doris's nose had become red. "Does it matter?"

"But are you in danger? Or the children?"

"Do you think I'm a mother who would let her children be in danger?"

Tyler reached for a tissue from the box on his desk and leaned forward with it. "Not for a second, Doris. But I think it's a serious situation. Would Charlie agree to counseling?"

"Charlie would kill me if he knew I'd come in here."

Tyler looked over at his sagging bookshelf, at the mess of papers on his desk, back at Doris. Two spots of pink had spread on her cheeks.

"Oh, not literally." She said this with such disgust that Tyler sat back. "He gets so angry. Out of nowhere. Yesterday the wind made the door slam shut, and he began to yell."

Tyler tapped his mouth with his fingers. He thought of Bonhoeffer writing that it was not love that sustained a marriage but the marriage that would sustain the love. Tyler wanted to mention this, but Doris's weeping had become very noisy. Tyler could not recall any parishioner making the noise Doris was making, sobs climbing on top of one another. He moved farther back in his chair.

"It's horrible," Doris cried, "living the way I do."

"Yes, of course it would be," Tyler said. "Listen, now." He held up a hand, and gradually her weeping slowed, but there was still a gasp or two. "I know a pastor from Brockmorton," Tyler said, "who works with married couples, and I'll give him a call if you think Charlie would agree to counseling. I'd be glad to provide counseling myself," he added, which was not true, "but it might be better to use someone outside. You'll need to ask Charlie," Tyler said. "You'll need to find that out."

"Well, I think it's hopeless."

"Doris," he said, "let's think. Let's think about what Reinhold Niebuhr has said: 'The intimacy of marriage can be endlessly transfigured by grace.' "

"Intimacy." Doris leaned forward. Her coat had fallen open and her white blouse was straining at the buttons down its front. "In our intimate life, he makes me feel very bad. In our private life. He makes me feel very inadequate."

Tyler looked at her seriously, so she wouldn't guess how much he didn't want to hear this.

"He gave me these pamphlets to read. Directions, sort of. When he went off to that conference in Boston."

Tyler waited. She blew her nose.

And then the black telephone began to ring. They both looked at it. Tyler let it ring twice before he said, "Excuse me for just one moment." He held up a finger, and saw Doris's mouth tighten as she yanked on her gloves. "No, no, Doris, don't go. Tyler Caskey speaking."

Doris would have to leave, though. And he would have to leave. Katherine had thrown up at school.


BUT THE LITTLE Jeannie Caskey was a love. There she was on Saturday morning, a blond, curly-haired little love, who toddled around with a hand in her mouth, making happy noises, and then reaching with her small wet hand for whatever leg or dog or person's face happened to be nearby. If her grandmother was forever pulling out a hanky to wipe the little hand dry, the child seemed not to care; she would wait, smiling, looking around, and as soon as the hand was released, back it would go, either into her mouth or to touch whatever suited her fancy. She was standing on the couch now, next to her father, patting his head with increasing vigor, until Tyler, in the midst of a conversation with his mother about the lack of cleanliness of his house, had to say to his younger child, "Easy. Easy, now."

"Be nice, Jeanne," said the grandmother, with tired but affectionate authority. Margaret Caskey's speech was apt to be slow, drawled out with a New England deliberateness. "Tyler," she said, "does she wash the windows? What is it she gets paid to do?"

It was all this bright sun. Tyler Caskey felt exposed, sitting on his couch in his living room while his mother criticized the work of the woman from whom he had received a moment's comfort. He nodded toward the window his mother had just pointed to. Earlier, she had taken a tissue from her bag, stood on one of the dining-room chairs, and swiped at a cobweb she found up there. "Mother," he had said, "be careful." She was not young. Her ankle could snap like kindling.

"It depresses me, Tyler. The way you live." Her lowered voice, the particular tilt of her head, the way her long fingers picked at her navy-blue dress with its big white dots—all this caused some flicker of ancient anxiety in Tyler. Perhaps Mrs. Caskey's old black Lab, Minnie, felt it as well; she had been sleeping next to Tyler on the couch, but now opened her eyes, moaned, stepped down. Her nails clicked across the hardwood floor, as Tyler said, "Don't worry about me, Mother."

Jeannie patted the dog's rump and plopped down on her father's lap. Tyler felt a wet diaper seeping through his trousers. "Katherine," he called, "come help me change your sister," and Katherine came over and didn't yell or pull away when Jeannie tugged on her bangs hard.

"I'll do it, Tyler," said his mother, reaching for the child. "You have a sermon to prepare."

Tyler nodded, and stood up, although in fact the sermon was "prepared" already. It was Tyler's habit to get his sermon title to the church secretary on Friday so she could get the programs mimeographed; he didn't like to have her work on a Saturday morning. The title was not, after all, On the Perils of Personal Vanity. Katherine's upset stomach, Doris's visit to his office, the conference with Mrs. Ingersoll—all this had taken a toll on Tyler's ability to concentrate; the sermon on vanity was left undone. Instead, Tyler would preach an old sermon on the Prophecies of Isaiah, left over from his seminary days, even though, he acknowledged to himself, patting Minnie on her head as he stepped by, nothing he'd written then seemed related to anything now.

Tyler sat at his desk, looking around the room. His eye fell upon Bonhoeffer's *Letters and Papers from Prison* on the table nearby. He could recite whole portions from memory—he had looked at it that often. He gazed out the window at the birdbath, the ivy, and imagined a house in Berlin where people talked excitedly about theological issues that Tyler knew reached beyond his own capacity to understand; he imagined the sound of a German radio broadcast, Bonhoeffer's clear voice declaring that man's responsibility against evil lay in *action,* and then the radio cut off in midsentence by the government authorities; oh, the intensity of the discussions that would have followed! He pictured Bonhoeffer, the young blond-haired pastor, walking through the narrow streets of Chichester, England, speaking earnestly with his friend Bishop Bell; the trip to New York, then boarding one of the last ships back to Germany; he imagined the green lawns of Finkenwalde (Tyler had no idea if there were lawns in Finkenwalde), where a community of Christians listened to Bonhoeffer say that man's sin was flight from responsibility. Tyler imagined the military prison, Tegel; the clanking of gated doors, the echo of booted steps . . . The vastness of such activity, the innumerable scenes of that man's courage and suffering, gave Tyler a heightened sense of how twisted—as a nail would be, banged through a plank of knotty pine—was his own despair. Whatever anguish Dietrich Bonhoeffer had endured seemed to glow with purity.

Tyler's love for this martyred man felt so personal that it sometimes surprised him to think they'd never met, that Bonhoeffer had never even known of Tyler's existence. We would have been friends, Tyler thought. But Dietrich Bonhoeffer had been born in Breslau, Germany, in 1906, twenty-one years before Tyler Caskey had come prematurely, scrunched-up and red, into the world of Shirley Falls, Maine. And while Tyler, whose digestion from the very beginning had caused Margaret Caskey sleepless nights, was being fed from the tip of a basting wand, Dietrich Bonhoeffer had already completed his first Ph.D. from Berlin University, producing a thesis entitled *The Communion of Saints*.

"Oooh, a smarty pants," the future Lauren Caskey said laughingly, on her second date with Tyler, having to listen to these intensely relayed facts.

Yes, Bonhoeffer was smart. And from a prominent family. Tyler, who had an American abhorrence of that term, had nevertheless used it as evidence—explaining this to Lauren—that the man had much to lose. And he dared to lose it. Not only did Bonhoeffer rise up against his church's implicit acceptance of Nazism and help found a seminary for the opposing Confessing Church—a place ultimately closed by the Nazis—the man chose (this was the part of the story that caused Tyler Caskey's voice to drop, so heavy was it with feeling, as he leaned across the table to deliver it), he chose, after spending a year in the United States in 1939, *to return to Germany,* and he must have known he would die. Others knew. Karl Barth, Paul Tillich. They did not return to the hands of Hitler's murderers, and they had begged him not to, either.

"So why did he?" the future Mrs. Caskey asked.

"He thought he'd have no credibility in Germany after the war if he hadn't been there at the time of its troubles."

"Well, that was noble of him," the future Mrs. Caskey said, sitting back, and if Tyler had detected any cynicism in this remark, he thought later, he would not have married her. But he had not detected cynicism, and even now, remembering this as he sat in his study, he did not believe there had been any in Lauren's remark. *Well, that was noble of him.* She had gazed at the saltshaker she was touching with the fingers of both hands, and lifted her dark, round eyes to look at him.

She said, in the childlike way she had of speaking sometimes, "I don't know as I'd have gone back," and he'd been touched by the honesty.

"It was his job, though—his calling." He told her how Bonhoeffer's fiancée, Maria von Wedemeyer, had gone to visit him in prison. She was only nineteen, and had visited him in the prison in Tegel; it must have been frightening for her. Bonhoeffer began to write poetry, and sent it to her, and to his closest friend, Eberhard Bethge, too. *Life, what have you done to me? Why did you come? Why do you pass away?*

Lauren leaned forward. "Do you write poetry?" she asked.

Oh, no, no. No. He'd been quick to reassure her, and thought he saw a tiny relaxing that took place around her eyes. It was one thing, he said, for a great martyr, imprisoned by the Nazis, to write poetry, but he, Tyler Caskey, just an ordinary fellow from Shirley Falls, Maine, he did not write poetry. Hopefully strong and meaningful sermons someday, but poetry, no.

And now Reverend Caskey, sitting in his study, put his fingers to his mouth and thought: What if, just what *if* he had been able to sit with Bonhoeffer in this very room, a year ago? What if Tyler, clasping the man's hands in his own, had said, "Please, listen to me. I—"

But he would not have said it.

Tyler turned his head slowly, looked out past the birdbath. Briefly he pictured the bedroom he had shared with his wife those last weeks—the sharp beauty to the August light as it had slanted through the room, the cardinal's call heard through the open window. He thought how Bonhoeffer had written from prison, "There is a wholeness about the fully grown man which enables him to face an existing situation squarely."

Tyler turned back to his desk. Bonhoeffer had taken part in a plot to kill Hitler. He had faced prison, his own death, and he had faced it all squarely; no one would argue he wasn't a fully grown man. "Isn't it a characteristic of a grown man, in contrast to an immature person, that his center of gravity is always where he actually is?" Bonhoeffer had written from his cell. Tyler tapped his fingers to his mouth; fragments of images jumped through his mind.

"Girls, leave your father alone!" The sound of tumbles and giggles, and dog's toenails clicking on the wooden floor, passed by his door.

For the sake of God, he would do his job. (What else could he do?) He would pray that his center of gravity would be where he was. And he was in West Annett. His job was to stand in church with his shoulders back and his chin up, and make his congregation understand that being a Christian was not a hobby. Being a Christian was serious stuff. Being a Christian meant asking yourself every step of the way: How can love best be served? His job was to be their leader, their teacher, their example. A small parish, perhaps. Not a small job.

Tyler pulled his chair in closer to his desk, looked through the notes he had. This was World Refugee Year. A million Arabs in the Middle East were close to starving to death, and thousands of people in Eastern Europe were still living in temporary camps. The Church World Service wasn't receiving any more powdered milk from the United States because the Department of Agriculture decided the stuff was no longer in surplus. This, in particular, bothered Tyler. More than ever now, help was needed for the Share Our Surplus program. *S.O.S.*, Tyler wrote on a piece of paper, hearing his mother in the next room directing Katherine to get the hair out of her face.

PEOPLE IN WEST ANNETT had been intrigued by Tyler Caskey right from the start. They had grown so used to the old Reverend Smith, whose watery eyes had looked out at his congregation with such indifference, whose wrinkled face had not, for years, broken into a smile, that Tyler Caskey's arrival was as surprising as it would have been if a big, vigorous bear had swum up the river and climbed onto the banks. He was a large man, tall and big-boned, and to shake his hand *was* kind of like taking the hand of a bear in your own. His voice, in keeping with the rest of him, was deep and resonant, and what saved him from being "too much" was a gentleness of expression that passed frequently over his features, and the way his pale Puritan eyes would twinkle as he thrust his head forward and down slightly, to look the person he was talking to straight in the eye. In other words, for someone who could, with that build and presence, walk into a room and throw his weight around, that he did just the opposite, that he tried to be accommodating, tried, as he moved through the activities room at coffee hour, greeting people and shaking hands, or as he stood in a hospital waiting room with a family whose child had fallen from a tractor, to speak quietly, gently, to otherwise harness the depths of power he displayed from the pulpit: There was something touching about this.

Although not everybody liked the man. Charlie Austin, without saying so, thought he was "too familiar"—that the soft eagerness beneath his bulk was not altogether genuine. A few others might have felt this, too, but the women of the church, and most of the men, had found him to be uniquely watchable, compelling in a way quite different from his wife, although she was a woman of some pulchritude. Lauren Caskey, it's true, had ended up becoming a town legend, but she'd certainly been talked about from the very beginning, when she had first shown up to have dinner with the deacons and their wives.

People not familiar with towns like West Annett may not realize as they drive through the gully of trees leading to the sparseness of its Main Street that a social hierarchy exists there, exactly as it does in prisons, sixth grades, and Beacon Hill apartment buildings. In West Annett, a great deal of weight was given to ancestry, and it was not ancestry of the tired, the hungry, the downtrodden masses—those people ostensibly welcomed in the vast doorway of New York. No, in West Annett it would not do to align oneself with the tired masses. You arrived on this shore for many reasons, but weariness would not be one of them. You may have arrived with the Puritans, or been an English tea merchant wanting land and a different life. You may have been a poor Scotsman, indentured for seven years of labor. Or you may have arrived on the *Mayflower*, as was the case with the forefathers of Bertha Babcock, who had in her living room a model of this marvelous ship measuring two feet in length.

When it was decided by the Pulpit Committee that Tyler Caskey should be asked to come preach—to audition, so to speak, although that was not the term used—he and his young wife were invited to be guests of the board, the deacons, and all of their wives at a potluck dinner the evening before. Seldom in West Annett did this many people gather in one home, and the house of Auggie and Sylvia Dean had been chosen for the event.

Auggie Dean "had money," which simply meant he had, through

his family, more money than most people in West Annett, but then most people didn't have much, nor was money, by any means, a requirement for respectability. Not long before the Caskeys arrived in town, the Deans' kitchen had been ripped out and redone, the first dishwasher in town placed next to a lovely Frigidaire with the swing-out shelves that were, that spring evening, getting swung out and back with some steadiness, as the women tucked away the food they had brought, commenting to Sylvia on how authentic-looking her fake marble countertop was.

"Oh, it's sweet," Lauren Caskey had been saying, as she peered through the window of their car. It was late April, and a fresh spring snow had fallen the night before, so by late afternoon, as Tyler and his wife drove into town, there was still the white covering on the dark branches, and on some rooftops, and some snow left around the steps of the little white church. "It's sweet," Lauren said again, turning her head to look as they passed through the center of town. "Your first church, Tyler."

"If they want me." He pulled the car to the side of the road in order to glance at the directions he'd been given.

"They'll want you. I'm the one who has to pass." Lauren turned the rearview mirror toward her, spread lipstick around her full mouth. "Honey," she said, snapping her blue pocketbook shut, "let's just get there. I need to pee."

The Main Street of West Annett had along it a small grocery store, a doctor's office, the Congregational church, the parsonage, a tiny white post office, and an old grange hall across from the cemetery. Farther along, the road split in two, and along Upper Main Street were the three white buildings of Annett Academy, which served the town and received students as well from nearby towns too small for high schools of their own. Upper Main Street continued on, winding its way through a gully, following along beside a stone wall, until you came to Ringrose Pond, and there, not far from the road, was the big white house of Auggie and Sylvia Dean, white curtains caught back from every window.

Tension had been building as the women uncovered their casserole dishes, laid out the paper napkins, fanned out the forks and spoons on the Samsonite portable table that had been covered with a white cloth and placed next to the table in the dining room, everything set up beneath the bowed window. "They're here, they're here" was heard throughout the house as Tyler and Lauren were spotted heading up the walkway, their car parked, presumably, back on the edge of the road, the driveway being already full of cars.

Lauren Caskey was different from what had been expected. Whatever people expected—she wasn't it. Shorter than her husband (just about everybody was), there was still something "big" about her, as she stood there in the doorway; her eyes were big, her mouth was big, her cheeks were big and round. And while her shoes—perfectly lovely things, but with a *strap* over the heel, and still snow on the ground!—were not as big as the rest of her seemed to require, her calves were magnificent and shapely, seen in their nylon stockings as she stepped through the door, holding a potted plant in both hands, a blue leather pocketbook hanging off one wrist. The expression on her face was hard to read, people agreed later. Those staring brown eyes, and her full face framed by the strawberry-red hair.

The plant was taken by Sylvia Dean—she would put it right by the living-room window; it was unnecessary, but very nice. Mrs. Caskey was helped out of her coat by Auggie, and then the fact that she was in the early stages of pregnancy became obvious. When she leaned forward and said, "Gosh, could I run straight to the bathroom? It's been a long drive," a number of women's voices assured her, Of course, right there off the kitchen, no, no, let her go upstairs, yes, here, I'll show you, we remember, don't we, how it is . . .

The attention, for those minutes of her absence, was turned to Tyler, who was remarkably at ease. His open face and big-pawed handshake (not too firm, but certainly not flabby—as prescribed in *The Pastor's Wife,* a book given to Lauren by his mother) was pleasing. "Hello, Charles," he said, nodding. "Hello there, Auggie. Nice to see you all again. Nice to meet you." And on he went, bending his head down to look people in the eye with his blue-eyed twinkling gaze. "Say, what a spread you've got here. This is *swell.*" His smile took in the cluster of women still moving about from the kitchen to the living room.

"Ginger ale, if you've got it," he answered Irma Rand. "Hey, that's great. Oh, I think she'd probably like some, but what do you say we wait and ask her."

This was discussed as well, that the minister let his wife speak for herself—and she did, asking for cranberry juice, wearing enough lipstick so as to immediately leave an imprint on the glass. But by the end of the evening, Mrs. Caskey's lipstick had worn off and her face appeared pale over there, where she had been seated by Sylvia Dean in the big easy chair. "Oh, no—you rest," the woman directed, as Lauren tried to hoist herself up from the chair.

"But I can't have you all waiting on me and not help with the dishes," the young woman cried, and it was Alison Chase who said, "Here, you come stand by the sink and dry." So Lauren Caskey stood in the kitchen drying forks, asking women about their children, or in certain cases, about their jobs, for Marilyn Dunlop taught art at the Academy and Doris Austin played the church organ and, with one hand and a nodding head, directed the choir.

"I can't sing," said Lauren.

"Wouldn't make you the only one in town," said Ora Kendall, pausing to gaze at Lauren through her huge black-framed glasses—her dark curly hair shooting in all directions—before she moved past, having found in a closet a dustpan and broom. A glass had been broken in the living room. Old Mr. Wilcox had backed up to the table and knocked it to the floor, and not even known it at first.

"A lot of people think they can't sing," said Doris, "but they can learn."

Droplets of sweat had appeared on the edge of Lauren's hairline.

"We have our own historical society," said Bertha Babcock. "You might want to join. We have people here going back twelve generations. The early settlers were a hardy lot."

"We have square dances in the grange hall," Rhonda Skillings said. "Alvin's a wonderful caller. The Couples Club's lucky to have him."

"What sorts of things do you like to do, Lauren?" asked Alison Chase.

"I like to shop," said Lauren. "I love the way department stores smell."

Alison glanced at Sylvia Dean, and handed Lauren a plate to dry. She nodded at Lauren's middle. "Well, I guess you'll have your hands full pretty soon. Do you have any hobbies? Irma and I have gotten very interested in painting birds."

"Gosh, I think I'm going to have to sit down," Lauren said.

"Come on," said Ora Kendall, and she led the woman back to the easy chair in the living room until it was time to say good-bye.

The Caskeys had declined an offer to spend the night at the house of Auggie and Sylvia Dean, saying they had plans to stay with friends in Bangor before returning in the morning for Tyler to preach. In fact, the Caskeys were staying in a roadside motel, and as they drove in the old Packard, given to them by Lauren's father, they left behind plenty of talk in the Deans' household. "A hail-fellow-well-met," someone said of Tyler, and others agreed, while Charlie Austin remained silent. About Lauren, the talk was guardedly positive. There was something the women had not liked about her, but no one wanted to be the person to say so. It was more than her remark about shopping and department stores. It had to do with her looks. (Ora Kendall murmured to Alison, "What happens when the sex wears off?") Lauren Caskey had seemed too aware of her looks, in a manner unbecoming to a minister's wife, and it could be that, had Tyler not delivered such a magnificent sermon the next morning, he would not have been offered the job. In any case, a great deal was made of Lauren Caskey's shoes that night. The strapped back was simply out of season. They were nice-looking, with the tiny braids across the toe, but wasn't it strange for a woman in her condition to be wearing heels? She could easily fall down and—well, that was her business, hers and Tyler's, and he did seem like an awfully nice man.

"THAT WASN'T SO BAD," said Tyler, as they drove the back roads. "Nice people." It had only recently got dark. They had been asked to arrive at four-thirty, as people in West Annett tended to eat their evening meal early, even on a Saturday night. Dinner had started at five-thirty, and by eight o'clock the Caskeys were on their way.

"It was strange," Lauren said.

Tyler wanted to make sure he didn't get lost on these back roads, and was looking to see if there was a turn he missed. "Weren't they friendly to you?" He reached for her hand.

Lauren yawned loudly. "Who was the one with that awful orange lipstick? She likes to paint birds. What does that mean she likes to paint birds?"

"I didn't notice the lipstick," Tyler said.

"The men were nice," Lauren said. "Quiet, though. But they'll love your sermon. And the women like you. They'll tell their husbands to vote for you."

"The whole congregation votes."

"Who was that redheaded fellow with the pink face? His wife is the organist, I think."

"Charles Austin."

"I feel sorry for him, Tyler. Deep down, he's a wolf."

"A wolf." He supposed she was using the term the way it was in the service, a man who went after women. He didn't think Charles Austin appeared to be a man who went after women.

"He's a wolf in pink skin. Trust me, Tyler. I'll tell you something else," Lauren had said in the car that night. "That Jane Watson woman. Watch out for her." Lauren snuggled close to him, put her head on his shoulder. "I'm going to take a nap."

But in the motel room, she sat on the edge of the bed and cried. Tyler sat next to her and put his big arms around her. "Gosh, Lauren," he said, "that was jumping off the high dive, and you did it beautifully." Streaks of what seemed like black paint were streaming down her round cheeks. He pulled out his handkerchief and blotted her face.

"You were good at talking to everyone," Lauren said. "You're good at that kind of thing."

"What I want to be good at is being your husband."

Oh, they were happy that night. Waking early, they were happy again, their breath mingling, the slipperiness beneath his arms as they loved each other.

LATER THAT MORNING, every church pew filled and sunlight pouring through the side windows, the congregation stood and sang all five verses of the opening hymn.

*Heaven's morning breaks, and earth's vain shadows flee;*
*In life, in death, O Lord, abide with me.*

The organ music stopped, people returned their hymnals to the wooden holders in front of them, arranging themselves with just the smallest tug on a sweater, a smoothing of a skirt or trouser leg as they sat down. In the silence that followed was an expectant, hopeful air. Tyler, stepping to the middle of the chancel, felt within him the irrepressible unfolding of great joy. "God is merciful," he told the people of West Annett, his voice deep with confidence. "God owes us nothing. We owe Him everything."

# THREE

If there were lingering doubts about Lauren Caskey—and there were—there were very few doubts about her husband, who, while the organ finished the prelude, would take his seat on the chancel, his large, black-robed self appearing at great ease, radiating something strong and open. What the congregation felt, during those first years as they settled into the pews, was that they were entering into the presence of warmth; and warmth up there in West Annett was not something found growing on trees. Understand—the inland reaches of northern New England, with its quick, hot summers, and long, dark winters, had bred for generations a way of life that had at its center the need to endure. A child slipping on an icy driveway, banging his chin against the car door, would most likely be told, "Grit your teeth and bear it," even when one of the teeth had, as in the case of Toby Dunlop, gone straight through the lower lip, poking out the other side. No trip to the doctor was needed. "You'll live," he was told, and he did—bearing a small white scar that he never showed anyone except his first girlfriend. If the men were not especially talkative, their fathers had not been, either. If the women cooked meals that might seem, to someone from other parts, flavorless and straightforward, it is because they cooked what was available to them: chicken, potatoes, canned corn. And if their children were not allowed Novocain when having their cavities drilled, it was not cold-heartedness but a belief that life was a struggle, character honed every step of the way.

And life *was* a struggle. There was, up in West Annett, thick ice that needed to be chipped away all winter long from doorsteps and windshields, chains to be put on tires so the cars could crawl slowly over snow-packed roads just to get to the grocery store. Often families heated only one or two rooms during the winter months; furnaces broke, wood-burning stoves needed logs brought in from the barn, or up through a cellar door. Most homes were not within easy walking distance of one another, and the isolation was hard on the old folks, mothers with small children—hard on everyone, really. People went to church not so much because they believed they should but because it gave them a chance to get out of the house, dress nicely, pick up a bit of local news. Sitting through the sermon during the long tenure of Reverend Smith had been something you had to grit your teeth and bear, and a lot of the men wouldn't do it. It was not uncommon during that time for men to stay home on Sunday mornings after dropping off their wife and kids.

But Tyler Caskey had been something altogether different. That he didn't read his sermons, or even appear to be using notes, allowed his parishioners to watch his open face as he spoke to them; a light seemed to flicker across his features. "Let us adore God," he said—and you could see that he meant this—"let us adore our mothers and fathers and children. Let us adore the snow-covered trees on the hills, the stone walls built by strong men, the chickadees who brave the winters, and the robins who return in spring. Let us give thanks. Let us adore him, Christ our Lord."

The idea that he was putting himself at risk by creating strong feelings of attachment in members of his parish—that attendance rose sharply as people came to sit in the presence of his earnest warmth—the idea there was danger in any of this, was something Tyler didn't recognize. When he went one weekday to visit George Atwood at Brockmorton Theological Seminary, and spoke of the thrill he felt at his new job, his old professor had listened and said only, "Reminds me of the remark Hirohito made to an aide: 'The fruits of victory are tumbling into our mouths too quickly.' " Tyler, driving home, thought perhaps the man held a tiny bitterness within him, because he was old and his enthusiasms gone.

HE REMEMBERED THIS NOW, buttoning his new shirt on Sunday morning. A storm front had moved in overnight, and the clear-skied October days with all their glittering sunlight had given way to a pouring rain. Tyler could see through his study window rain hitting the bricks in the garden with such force it splashed up again, watery bullets exploding.

He slipped his sermon into a folder and walked down the hall to the kitchen.

Margaret Caskey, scrubbing a potato, said she would forgo church this morning, stay with the baby, and get dinner ready, but Katherine Estelle should put on her boots and go to kinderkirk. "You don't want to ruin those new shoes your Aunt Belle bought you, although you've scuffed them up plenty already, I'd say, by the look of things."

The child knew her grandmother didn't like her. She wondered, sitting next to her father in the front seat with the windshield wipers going *flip-flip*, and her feet in the red boots sticking out in front of her, if her father knew this, too. She turned her head and gazed at him.

"What, honey?" he said. "You need to toss your cookies again?" He had picked the child up on Thursday at the nurse's office—not seeing Mrs. Ingersoll—and the child had seemed fine since. He'd let her stay at home on Friday, coloring silently in his study as he read. Later, they had gone for a drive, not returning until it was dark, the child asleep, her little neck bent to the side.

Now she kicked her red boots once. Her face got warm remembering Martha Watson yelling, "Katie Caskey threw up and it smells!" The children holding their noses.

"Katherine?" Her father put his huge hand over her knee, and gave a little squeeze. It made her laugh, that delicious squiggle of a golden magic wand inside her knee. And when, in a few moments, he took his big, warm hand away, the loss felt as awful as her knee had felt happy.

"There won't be many people, with the rain today," her father said to the watery windshield in front of him.

But there were as many people as usual. Alison Chase, in her kinderkirk room, had her hands full. Kids hopped all over, brightly dressed little birds. Mrs. Chase said, "Good morning, Katherine," her orange lipstick spreading in a smile, but then Mrs. Chase said nothing else to her and so Katherine kept her boots on all morning, her feet inside feeling moist and too warm.

The orange color of Mrs. Chase's lipstick was so icky that Katherine didn't like to even look at her, and when Mrs. Chase led the children into the activities room, Katherine dawdled off to the side while everyone sang "What a Friend We Have in Jesus" and Mrs. Chase played the piano. They had to say the Lord's Prayer with their heads bowed and their eyes closed, but Katherine didn't close her eyes. She looked at her red rubber boots and, in the middle of the prayer, Katherine said calmly and quietly, "I hate God."

DOWN THE HALL IN THE SANCTUARY, women shook the raindrops from their clear plastic bonnets and opened their coats, shifting the shoulders a bit, but keeping them on, for women were expected to keep their coats on in church; the men were not. The men, either in the vestibule or in the aisle before entering the pew, slipped off their overcoats and folded them today into damp squares, which they set beside them on the crimson-colored cushions or slipped beneath the pews. When the organ prelude stopped, there was the occasional stomach heard to be growling, a set of keys fell to the floor, and people arranged themselves, looking with expectant faces toward Reverend Caskey as he stepped up to the pulpit. But even now, a full year later, no one dared yet sit in the third-row pew.

The woman *had* been lovely.

She had been lovely, her bright hair visible above the fur collar of her beige woolen coat, lovely as she stood beside her husband on the church steps, her cheeks glowing in the winter sunlight. Even if some of this loveliness was the result of carefully applied makeup and expensive, well-fitting clothes. Lauren Caskey, it was said, must have been spending a great deal of time in front of the mirror, because she certainly didn't seem to be spending a great deal of time anywhere else. It's true—there was a curious absence from functions at which you might reasonably expect to find a minister's wife. The Ladies' Aid, the Sunshine Committee, the Missionary Committee—she wasn't there. But she did have a baby to attend to, as well as (an eyebrow going up) her hair. Whose color of ripe apples in the sunshine came directly from a bottle, and whose roots would require, it was decided by people who knew, monthly attention and special care.

But if Lauren Caskey was aware of the ambivalence she inspired, you never would have known it to see her seated in the third-row pew every Sunday, beaming pleasantly at those around her. Eventually, the tiny, tow-headed Katherine Estelle would sit there, too, playing with a rag doll and a ratty little blanket. Occasionally the child would cluck her tongue, or sing her baby to sleep, and the churchgoers sitting behind them would see Mrs. Caskey tap the little girl on her shoulder, putting a finger to her lips, and the little girl and her mother would raise their shoulders and squinch their faces in a smile to each other, as though they had some secret between them, and the girl would be quiet again. There was something—you couldn't put your finger on it exactly, but they had continued to provoke a reaction, this mother and her little girl. The mother wasn't friendly enough, was part of it. As much as Lauren Caskey would beam and smile and shake hands in the vestibule after the service, she had a certain carelessness about her, as though she had no interest in coming to your house, no real interest in how other people lived, here in their small town.

But then Mrs. Caskey became pregnant again, and her husband ushered her about town with a hand beneath her elbow. She could often be found in the children's room of the Academy's library with Katherine. The librarian, Mrs. White, reported how the mother was good to the girl, reading to her on the big window seat, how the girl would press her ear to her mother's bulbous stomach. One day, however, Mrs. White observed the mother whispering to the child while drawing on a piece of paper, and the child whispered back, loudly, "In the *beegina?*"

Mrs. White, recalling all this as she shifted her weight against the side of the pew on this rainy October Sunday, let herself wonder for a moment if even before the tragedy, the minister might have felt—at times, anyway—that he'd gotten more than he had bargained for.

TYLER, UP THERE in his black robe—was he feeling the presence of God? No, he was feeling the presence of Rhonda Skillings, seated where she always sat, toward the back, with her husband. Tyler was sure she would have been told about Katherine, that she was waiting—with her pearl earrings and white ruffled blouse—like a well-combed cat to pounce on the child. He recalled Rhonda telling him once she had been Phi Beta Kappa in college.

But as he walked to the pulpit, there was a momentary comfort in the familiar creak of the floorboard beneath the carpet, and in the familiar words he read. *They that wait upon the Lord shall renew their strength . . . they shall run, and not be weary; and they shall walk, and not faint.* There was the familiar smell of the heat that rose from the radiators, the sounds of the bumped knee against the back of a pew, the quiet, apologetic fit of coughing. He was oddly pleased to hear the tiny click, snap, click, as someone in a side pew cut his fingernails. As he placed one hand on the Bible (*And a highway shall be there . . . and it shall be called the way of holiness*), he had a strong memory of how in the past he had enjoyed—oh, tremendously!—all of this. He, the Reverend Tyler Caskey, was leading these people to a life filled with the bountifulness of God.

Very, very far away—so far away it lived in a tiny hut on a distant horizon—was the word failure. So far away it couldn't be seen, and there was no need to see it: Mrs. White was smiling up at him, her head cocked in a position of attentiveness. " 'Peace between countries,' " Tyler said slowly, " 'must rest on the solid foundation of love between individuals.' " He added, "The teaching of Mahatma Gandhi." He stepped back from the pulpit, almost tripping over a pot of beet-colored chrysanthemums. As he sat during the offering, he jotted down the letters *OK* on the edge of his sermon. The Ladies' Aid took turns with the flowers, and this month Ora Kendall had supplied an abundance of chrysanthemums. Last Sunday he wrote *OK* to remind himself to speak to Ora Kendall, but then had forgotten to do so.

While he sat in his chair on the chancel—what they had jokingly called in seminary "The Throne"—and watched as the ushers went from pew to pew with the collection plate, it seemed to him Charlie Austin's face was pinker than usual, as the man stood in the aisle, tapping the side of his trousers while he waited for the plate to be passed back to him. *DA,* Tyler wrote under *OK,* although he hardly had to remind himself to call Doris—her earlier visit to his office hung over his shoulders like a cape dampened with rain. He had tried calling her on Friday, when he knew Charlie and the kids would be at school, but she had not answered the phone. He would try her again in the morning. He stood for the doxology, dimly aware of the rain against the windows, the dark gray of the visible sky. *Praise Father, Son, and Holy Ghost.*

"The sermon today," Tyler said, "is on the faithfulness of God." He cleared his throat. "As taught by Isaiah through the Prophecies of Condemnation and Comfort." He was glad his mother had chosen to stay home. He didn't like to read a sermon, but he read this one with expression, he felt. Still, early into it, he sensed he was losing them; even when he spoke of Isaiah being sawed in half during the reign of Manasseh, he did not detect one flicker of interest. When Tyler raised his head to take a beat, he saw Charlie Austin sitting in a position of the most appalling disrespect—half turned away, practically facing the aisle, his elbow on the back of the pew and gazing with such abstracted intensity at the window across from him that it could leave no doubt in anyone's mind that he was not thinking of Isaiah or Manasseh or Tyler

Caskey, but perhaps wondering if he should call someone to get the gutters fixed.

Tyler kept reading, stumbled, read on, and when he glanced up again, he saw Carol Meadows, perhaps one of the kindest women in his parish, looking discreetly at her watch.

*O God, give unto thy servants that peace which the world cannot give . . .*

In the vestibule, as organ music spilled down the aisle, he shook hands with extra firmness. He looked Rhonda Skillings right in the eye and smiled warmly. "Good morning, Rhonda." And here was Charlie Austin, whose face seemed a mask of pink-skinned contempt, who only nodded when Tyler said, "Good morning there, Charlie." Ora Kendall was next, and Tyler said, taking her hand, "Ora. You've supplied beautiful flowers. Thank you very much. They've been absolutely beautiful. Thank you very much."

THE RAIN DASHED against the window of the parked car with such force it seemed to contain nails, but inside the car, where Charlie Austin sat smoking a Lucky Strike, it made a different sound, the small, steady *plink-plink* as the drops of water landed on the seat, the armrest, rolling toward his trousers, dampening them. The tip of his cigarette, held toward the inch of open window, became damp, too. He tossed it through the crack, rolled the window up, and looked at the mess of newspapers on the seat beside him. After sitting inside that white, maroon-lined coffin of a church, enduring the uneasiness of watching Caskey slip around up there like an overgrown, splay-legged foal, a kind of heavy depression folded down over Charlie, and beneath it he found relief; he welcomed the flatness, a reprieve.

He had with him the newspapers of last week, thinking to glance through them as he sometimes did, waiting out coffee hour here in the car. He eyed them now cautiously, for the state of the world worried him. There was Eisenhower, a smart man, fud-duddling around these days, not able, even, to get the steelworkers back to work, while Khrushchev came over bellowing at the U.N., and America, too young to know the difference, was driving its new big cars straight to hell; this is how it seemed to Charlie—the country was naïve; there were spies everywhere. Not that he knew what should be done. He didn't have a clue and couldn't seem to form an opinion, just felt the increasing vise-pinch of danger and he thought it was funny—odd—that even if you didn't care if you died, which is how he felt most of the time, you could still be scared to death.

He lit another cigarette, opened the window, raised his arm in greeting to Alvin Merrick, who was ducking through the rain to his own car—they exchanged, through the rainy, grainy blur of window and smoke, a grin, the acknowledgment of their own private coffee hours spent in their cars. But it was enough to disturb the sense of dullness; inside Charlie now the blocks of desire rose and arranged themselves. The woman in Boston, who in Charlie's mind appeared not so much by her name, but by her head of dark, glossy hair, seemed to bring her entire presence into the car, and with a suddenness so keen that he felt a nauseating ache, as though the inside of his chest were being scraped by a serrated grapefruit spoon, his hand began to tremble and he sucked hard on his cigarette and pulled a newspaper onto his lap.

"Oh, God have mercy," he murmured, although he didn't believe in God—didn't *not* believe in Him—just wanted this all to stop, cease and desist as they had said in the army, and he closed his eyes, thought of her bottom, like a pear, the beautiful split of it revealed as she thrust it toward them in the hotel room, her finger lowering the panties, the elastic ribbing. They had been playing poker, he and another fellow and her; he could not believe they would go through with it, but they did. He might have hated her for the way she enjoyed that power, were it not for the fact that she had clearly wanted them—wanted him, especially, it seemed—so that in her final sounds he had understood the phrase *possessed her.* He had possessed her, and now, God knew, she possessed him.

A loud metallic creak, as the back door of the car opened, and the quick, scrambling commotion of someone entering—Charlie jerked with such fear he shouted, "*Jesus!*"

"Sorry, Dad." The kid, his older son, was now in the seat behind him. "Were you sleeping? Sorry, Dad."

Charlie didn't answer. Sometimes the boy did this, sat in the car with him during coffee hour, cracking his knuckles, moving his feet across the gritty floor mat, his presence behind Charlie like a cobweb spreading down over Charlie's head.

"Sorry," the boy said again softly.

"I wasn't asleep. You want some of the paper?" Charlie gathered up the newspapers left on the seat beside him, and the boy must have taken this as an invitation, because he was sliding head-first over the back of the seat, his long, skinny body stuck now—he was too big to do this, and his dark pant leg was practically in Charlie's face, the long black shoe ready to make contact with his cheek. "Oh, for God's sake," said Charlie, taking the tangle of gawky legs and helping to pull him over. The boy laughed nervously, as though he were still a young child, instead of the terrible in-between mess of pitiful self-consciousness that made up his thirteen-year-old self.

Finally he was there, his Sunday-school coat too short in the sleeves, twisted around him as he arranged himself, his bright red hair darkened in streaks from the rain, a few drops still making their way down in front of his big, pale ears. He did not yet have the pimples of his older sister, but Charlie thought the boy was, in a way, one of the homeliest kids he had ever seen, his nose large and then suddenly round at the end, his chin—there was no way around it—would be the chin of a "weak-chinned man," and if the kid's face got any longer, you might not find the chin at all. Charlie didn't know for sure, but he thought the boy had few friends. Maybe he didn't have any friends at all.

"Dad, what d'ya think about that Dodger Stadium in Los Angeles, huh?"

"What about it?"

"Pretty swell, huh? Fifty-five thousand people in there. It's going to cost twelve million bucks, Dad."

Charlie nodded, looked at the paper he was holding. Fathers talked to their sons about sports. He read the words in front of him. Six hundred and fifty million dollars for urban renewal. What would that do to the Combat Zone in Boston? Renew what? This country wasn't old enough to *renew*.

"Hey, Dad. What d'ya think about the NHL letting the goalies wear a face mask? They're thinking about it, you know. Look—" The kid thrust before Charlie a picture of Jacques Plante with a basketlike thing across his face during a scrimmage game. Charlie looked hard at the picture. You couldn't blame the guy, he supposed, for not wanting to get any more teeth knocked out by a puck sailing a hundred miles an hour. But he didn't even look like a man anymore with all that stuff on and the face hidden by that basket. The guy looked crazy, to Charlie. We're all going crazy, he thought. Even in sports. Everyone scared and vicious. He felt an unaccountable surge of fear; he thought of all the juvenile delinquency in the country now; there it was on the third page—in Brooklyn a principal had committed suicide because he had so much delinquency in his school. People thought it was just in the cities, but it was making its way up the river. Charlie had seen some hoods loitering in the bus station in Hollywell last week, not much older than his own kid, whose eager, homely face was watching his father, waiting for an answer—kids wanted fathers to have answers.

"A good idea," Charlie said. "It'll change the nature of the game, but what the hell."

The boy nodded, looked back down at the paper, the side folded just the way the newspaper on Charlie's lap was. That he had reproduced any part of himself seemed to Charlie a mistake of almost biblical proportions. That this reproduction should present itself in such big-eared, pale-skinned innocence brought a searing pain to Charlie's troubled stomach. For years he had taught at the Academy, and he viewed the variety of his students' awkwardness from behind a safe shield of indifference; they had the benefit, after all, of not being *his*. He closed his eyes, and an image came to mind: walking up behind his boy, wrapping an arm around his skinny body, pressing his own cheek against the boy's, saying quietly, "You are good, and you are loved. And for your own sad sake I wish you hadn't been born."

ON THE STOVE TOP sat three baked potatoes, their skins indented and dark. "Thank you, Mother," Tyler said.

"I like to help," his mother answered. "When there's no one left for me to help, I will just be a worthless old woman."

At the dining-room table, while the rain tapped against the porch roof outside, Jeannie reached for the butter dish while Tyler said grace. Her grandmother, opening one eye, pushed the butter dish farther toward the center of the table. Katherine ate some potato and left her chicken alone. Her grandmother said, "Children in some areas of the world right now are crying. They are so hungry they can only cry, and then they get too tired to cry. Some children are so hungry they have eaten dirt."

"Mother, it's all right," Tyler said. "Her stomach's been a little upset."

Sitting in the living room after the meal, watching the girls down the hall tie a doll's bonnet around the patient head of Minnie, Tyler said nothing to his mother about the conference with Mrs. Ingersoll or the church organ or the visit from Doris. He simply listened as his mother recalled, "I made mackerel that night. And roasted potatoes. He said, 'Thank you, Megs,' and sat down in his chair. His last words, Tyler. 'Thank you.' "

Tyler watched the girls and wondered why it was people told the same story over and over again, wondered fleetingly if he did this, too. He didn't think he did.

"Your father was a good man."

"Yes, he certainly was," said Tyler.

" 'Always be considerate,' he used to say. 'Always think of the other man first.' Do you remember how he told you that?"

"Every night." Tyler nodded. "And then you'd climb the stairs and hear my prayers." His father, due to a sledding accident years before, had been too lame to climb stairs—had in fact, referred to himself as a cripple.

"Say," said his mother, "do you remember Saul Feiffer's wife?"

"Sure," said Tyler. "Ilse. Saul met her when he was over there liberating the camps. She was practically a kid at the time."

"That's right. Seventeen years old when she met him. They were active in that small synagogue outside of Arrington."

"Yes, sure."

"Well, the woman killed herself."

"Who did?"

"Ilse."

Tyler closed his eyes.

"Horrible thing to do," his mother said. "Imagine surviving the camps just to commit suicide one day. They lived in a nice house. Saul had it built for them. And they were so pleased when they had that little boy. Evidently there'd been some question if that could happen because of Ilse's health, the earlier malnutrition. She *hated* dogs. I remember that. Hated them."

Tyler opened his eyes. "Mother—"

"Oh, they can't hear me. They're in the other room. But an awful story, isn't it."

"Yes," said Tyler.

"Maybe Jews don't find that a sin."

Tyler stood up. "What are the girls doing?"

"Do you know, Tyler? If the Jews find that a sin?"

"My understanding," said Tyler, "is they believe as we do. Our souls are not ours to extinguish."

"All the more galling when you think of her little boy, and Saul, I think, is a decent man. I wish your sister had married a better man. Not a Jew, of course. That would hardly work out."

"Tom's a nice fellow," Tyler said. He heard the girls laughing down the hall, and seated himself once more on the couch. He did not look at his mother.

"He drives a bus, Tyler."

"Well, that's an honest living."

"Your sister's unhappy, and there's nothing I can do."

"I think Belle is fine."

"You do, do you. Ay-yuh. I'm going to gather my things." She called down the hall, "Katherine, kiss your sister good-bye."

Katherine loved her sister. Anyone paying attention could see how this was true. While Katherine seldom reached out to pull Jeannie toward her, she would stand close to the toddler and wait for the small hands to pat her. Katherine would smile, pat her back, and once, when Jeannie fell, running across the dining-room floor, banging her head hard enough to make her cry, Katherine tried, with her own small arms, to hold her sister, whispering, "Hush, hush." But how much did anyone notice?

Margaret Caskey noticed that her son's study, when she peered in while he was at church, had the fetid smell of a schoolboy; she suspected that he slept on the couch there, rather than in his bedroom, and she found the thought distasteful. Facing Tyler now, she said, "The good Lord willing, then, we will see you next week."

"The rain's letting up." Tyler looked out the window. "That's good. I hate to think of you driving in the rain."

"Tyler, listen to me. There's a girl Sara Appleby knows. She left school to care for her mother, who I guess recently passed away, and the girl—it's very convenient, Tyler. She lives in Hollywell. Sara says she's a lovely person and you should give her a call."

"Jeannie," said Tyler, as the girls chased the dog down the hallway into the living room. "Be easy with the doggie."

"Minnie loves the attention," said the child's grandmother, her gaze on Katherine. "Any improvement in that particular department, Tyler? Because there doesn't seem to be."

"Coming along, I think." He waved his fingers at Katherine, who looked over as though she knew she was being talked about, her eyes shining out from behind her hair.

Tyler said, "What's the name of this girl Sara knows?"

"Susan Bradford. Give it a chance, Tyler." His mother looked around the living room. "It becomes unhealthy. You can't go on like this."

He hugged the wiggling Jeannie good-bye, stood by the door, resting a hand on Katherine's head, and watched as his mother pulled out of the driveway. The rain had stopped, but a darkness and a wetness remained, and inside the house it was quiet.


THAT EVENING ORA KENDALL CALLED, and he was glad to hear her droll, unexcited voice. "Ora," he said, "how nice to hear your voice."

"Fred Chase thinks you're starting to look Catholic."

"Oh, well," said Tyler, "that's rubbish."

"Of course it's rubbish. He doesn't like the way you raise your arms when you pray, and truthfully, Tyler, I don't give a damn what you do with your arms, but I haven't seen a minister pray that way. When did you start that? Fred says it looks like a Catholic priest. Skogie says it looks like you're about to start a Southern revival and have us all hold hands."

"Well, Ora. I can't say I've been to many Southern revivals lately."

"You make people touch each other, Tyler, and you'll be out of here in no time."

"No touching, Ora. Promise." He glanced down at Katherine, coloring on the floor nearby. "I've been meaning to tell you—the chrysanthemums have been beautiful this month."

"You told me already," Ora said. "Good night."


CHARLIE AUSTIN WAS the only person in town who knew that Connie Hatch was being investigated by the state police. Charlie was privy to this information because his cousin, who was not on the force but worked in their office in Augusta, often told Charlie things on the side. Last night he had mentioned this to Charlie. It seemed some money and valuables had disappeared from the county farm at the time Connie last worked there, now more than two years ago. Connie was one of three women being investigated, and Charlie was not supposed to tell anyone.

Charlie, as he watched Doris this morning, making orange juice from a frozen can, was nevertheless tempted to say, "Hey, Doris, do you think Connie Hatch might be stealing from Tyler?" But he didn't much care if that was the case, nor did he think Tyler had an extra nickel to steal, and so he just sat at the table, running his hand down his face, still smelling the Dial soap from his morning shower, and realizing slowly that Doris was in a particularly foul mood, banging away at the frozen orange juice with the back of a wooden spoon.

Doris stopped to tug on her bathrobe. "I hate winter," she said. "I hate the dark and I hate to think about months of snow."

Charlie loved snow. But he said nothing.

"It makes getting around just hellish," his wife said. "This isn't going to thaw in time." She glanced at the clock.

"It's okay," Charlie told her. "We can live one morning without orange juice—can't we, kids?"

"Sure," said his younger son, with a kind of buoyant hopefulness.

"Mother," said Lisa, "forget it. Sit down. Your toast is cold."

"Oh, don't worry about me," said Doris, working intently, pressing the frozen stuff with the back of a spoon.

Charlie watched her, then looked away, because he did not want to watch her. She could have been a stranger, yet her physical presence was as familiar to him as the sight of his own hand, which he now spread out on the table and stared at. The woman in Boston had said you could tell the size of a man's cock by the size of his hands, but in his case, she said, it wasn't true. She had told him his hands were medium, but he was huge. He did not think he was huge, but he knew, from locker rooms in college, and his time in the army, that he was bigger than most. Doris did not know this. She had never seen any other man.

"Charlie, hold on," said Doris, looking over at him. "I think you can drink this in a minute. I know you like your orange juice."

"It's all right," he said. "I just told you it was all right."

He did not want to dominate her. He did not want her to be frightened of him. He did not want anything at all, except to have his children healthy and to be in a hotel bed in Boston, where the woman had spoken to him in such appallingly frank and dirty terms, had become, herself, so excited by his excitement that she made sounds he never knew a woman could make.

"Dad?"

He turned to look at Lisa.

"I just asked you a question."

"I didn't catch it," he said.

"I asked have you heard of Operation Blue Skies?" Lisa said this with a kind of arrogant self-consciousness; she was showing off.

Doris said, "What's Operation Blue Skies?"

"I was talking to Dad," Lisa said.

He should say, "Lisa, be polite to your mother." But he didn't like the smell of the kitchen. The boys were eating oatmeal, their heads too close to the bowls. Oatmeal must have burned in the pan. He looked over at the stove, frowned. He said, "No, I haven't. Or maybe I have. Is that the government project on biological warfare?"

"I'm tying you up," the woman had said. "Because you are a bad, bad man." She had used his necktie first—dark blue with red stripes, a birthday present from his sons, picked out by Doris; he had seen in their eyes when he opened it and thanked them that they hadn't looked at it before—but the woman had other ties in her bag.

"Have you heard about the vigil?" Lisa asked.

"No," Charlie said. "What vigil is that?" But he was pushing back his chair, standing up. "Let's go, kids," he said. "Finish up."

"There's time, Charlie. Lisa is talking to you."

And so he forced himself to look at his daughter, but she seemed uncharacteristically vehement, self-righteous. He felt frightened.

She was telling him how every day a group of people stood outside the gates of Fort Detrick in Maryland. They wanted to stop the research on germ warfare. What did he think?

"Who?" Charlie asked.

"You," Lisa said.

"Think of what?"

Lisa began to cry. Her pink face, with its series of tiny red pimples across the top of her forehead, got splotchy. "Dad," she said, "you're not *listening*."

"Why aren't you listening?" asked Doris.

Charlie sat down again. "You're such a bad boy," the woman had said. "You need to be tortured." Running her hand down over him. "I need to hear you beg."

He felt sick. "I'm listening," he said. "You were talking about people holding a vigil every day to ask the government to stop research on germ warfare. See? I heard every word."

Lisa's mouth trembled. "I just wondered what you think," she said.

He looked around the kitchen. Doris was pouring orange juice into glasses. The boys sat with their heads down.

"I don't know," Charlie said.

"Well, I just *thought*," Lisa said, rolling her wet eyes, "since you've been in the war, you know, you might have an opinion."

He could think of nothing to say. He could not remember any of his children mentioning to him, before this, that he had been in the war.

"I'll tell you what I think," Doris said, setting down the orange juice. "I think we better know how to defend ourselves, and if we know about germ warfare maybe the Russians won't start an atomic war."

"Why don't we build a bomb shelter?" asked the younger boy

in earnest. "The Clarks are. And the Meadowses have one. They have two cots and cans of food—"

"We don't need a bomb shelter," Charlie said, putting his hand out to stop the boy's words. He would rather melt in an atomic blast than be stuck in an underground shelter with his wife. If he couldn't be stuck in a room with the woman in Boston, he almost didn't care if the world came to an end.

"I think your mother is right," he told Lisa. "You can be damn sure the Russians are doing their own experiments on biological warfare. I think your mother is right."

"I don't," Lisa said. "People shouldn't be making bomb shelters, either, you little idiot," she said to her brother. "That makes Russia and us think it's okay to use bombs. *Stupid*."

"Get your coats," Charlie said. "We have to go to school."

CONNIE RODE ALONGSIDE Adrian in his new red truck, its shiny hood spread before them through the windshield. Where the road narrowed, tips of branches touched the window next to Connie. The skies this morning were pale, and the leaves that remained seemed richer, serious, not so screechingly proud of their beauty as on those sunny, blue-skied days.

"I've got to plant those tulip bulbs for your mother," Connie said, "before the ground gets frozen." There was no answer, and she had not expected one. Adrian reached to switch gears at the corner, and the gearshift, long and skinny as a golf club, moved under his big hand. She glanced at his immobile profile, his strong chin, the ruddy cheeks, the slight puffiness under his eyes that had increased over time. She looked out the window again. The overcast sky was not low; it stretched above the fields and trees and stone walls in the distance. Connie had the sense of a big cake cover—a glass dome—placed down over the world of West Annett; but inside was no cake, just hollowness. Her body swayed slightly as the truck turned onto Stepping Stone Road.

FROM HIS STUDY, Tyler sat watching as a nuthatch hopped along the birdbath's edge, bathed one wing in a quick flurry. A fat chickadee joined the splashing, then sat still as a stone. It seemed to Tyler he had not noticed birds in quite some time, that in a peculiar way he was not noticing them now, only remembering them. *Was there not a time when cheerfully and without a care you were glad with the glad?* A book of Kierkegaard lay open on his lap. He closed it slowly, saw how, beyond the birdbath, the hills with their remaining leaves held patches of yellow amid deep red; and closer, were the dried stalks of parchmenty corn in the Langleys' field. Tyler turned back to his desk.

It was the minister's habit, once Katherine went off to school, to devote the first hour of his day to prayer and meditation: *My voice shalt thou hear in the morning, O Lord,* and this included intercessionary prayer for his congregation. *Deliver the needy . . . they walk on in darkness.* But this morning he was troubled by a memory: When he first arrived in town, he had told his parish that anyone caring to expand his life of prayer should come to speak with him. Rhonda Skillings had taken him up on this offer, arriving in his office wearing a plaid sweater vest and sitting forward on the chair. They had discussed the fourth-century practice of contemplative reading, *lectio divina,* and he had spoken of Augustine and Tillich and Niebuhr—and Bonhoeffer, of course. He asked if she would like to start a prayer group, and she had smiled and said she didn't think so. She mentioned she'd been Phi Beta Kappa in college. She had not come back.

Tyler's eyebrows drew together as he thought of this now, looking to his desk, straightening some papers. He needed to call Doris Austin this morning, while Charlie was at work. But he heard the heavy tires of a truck in the gravelly driveway, and he rose to greet his housekeeper.

He found her hanging her long sweater in the back hall closet. He said, "Good morning, Mrs. Hatch." Unexpectedly, a real shyness overtook him.

But she was what she had been, a tall, not-young woman, whose green eyes looked at him with tired pleasantness. "Good morning," she said. "Nice day out there. Overcast. But nice."

It seemed a calmly played middle C hung in the air between them. "Yes, a nice day after that rain." He stood back to let her by. *In whose spirit there is no guile*, he thought.

"I'll put some laundry in," Connie said. "Then go get started on the bathroom upstairs."

"Thank you," Tyler said.

Sitting in his study, he could hear the bathtub faucet running, the occasional knocking of the plastic bucket, her footsteps overhead as she walked back and forth between the linen closet and the bathroom. In the mudroom, the washing machine stopped chugging and, with a noisy whine, began its whirring spin. He worked again on his sermon, On the Perils of Personal Vanity, quoting from Tolstoy's *Gospel in Brief:* "The house of God is not the church building, but the whole of God's people." He could not think of a next line. Anxiety—familiar and tiresome—pressed at his eyes. He touched his fingers to his mouth. *Let not the heart in sorrow sin.* He dialed the phone of the Austin home; nobody answered.

When he heard Connie descending the stairs, he went into the kitchen. "Mrs. Hatch," he said, "join me for a cup of coffee."

"I'll just run these through the wringer first."

He leaned against the doorway of the mudroom while she fed the clothes into the old beige rollers fixed above the tub of the machine. Katherine's pajama top came out flat. Connie tossed it in the laundry basket.

"Say—Mrs. Hatch," Tyler said, jiggling change in his trouser pocket, "how did you learn the alphabet?"

"I've no idea." Her hands were back in the washing machine. "No memory at all."

"No—me, either." He watched while his new white shirt went through the wringer, and added idly, "Bonhoeffer said our ability to forget is a gift."

"Then I'm gifted." She turned with a brightness of a smile that changed her face into a youthful one; but the smile seemed to exacerbate some sadness in her eyes, and he was surprised, once more, by her effect on him; he had to look away.

"It's only that Katherine's teacher's irritated because she doesn't know the alphabet," he said.

"Oh, she'll learn it," Connie said. She unscrewed the hose from the faucet. "I expect the child won't grow up illiterate."

Tyler stepped back to let her by. "I expect you're right," he said, following her into the kitchen, where he seated himself at the kitchen table, his long legs out to the side. He watched while she poured the coffee, brought out a box of doughnuts. "Mrs. Hatch," he said, "tell me about yourself. Do you come from around here? Perhaps you've said—I'm sorry."

"A little town called Edding, farther up the river." Connie sat down and drank her coffee with a deliberate sip.

"Oh, yes. I've seen signs along the turnpike."

Connie couldn't recall anybody ever saying, "Tell me about yourself." She didn't know what to tell. In her mind, she was a faint pencil line on a piece of paper; everyone else was drawn in ink, some—like the minister—with a firm Magic Marker.

"Do you have brothers and sisters?"

"An older sister, Becky. She lives way up north."

"Do you see her often?"

"No. Becky had some problems."

Tyler nodded. The morning sun, breaking through its white overcast, showed for a moment on the chrome edge of the table.

"And I had a younger brother, Jerry. Twelve years younger, so he was like my little boy." She looked at Tyler, her green eyes wide, as though something painful had surprised her.

"Nice for him," the minister said. "Big age difference like that can be nice, I think."

"Well, I did love him. He had that. My mother was sick of life by then, sick of kids and dogs, she said. 'No more kids and dogs,' she'd say. She'd lose her temper over anything. We had to stay out of her way. And I took care of Jerry."

"Then he was lucky to have you."

"He died in Korea. Nine years ago, next week."

"Oh, Connie."

To say her name like that! She bent her head and drank her coffee.

"Oh, I am sorry, Connie." Tyler shook his head. After a moment he said, "Boy, MacArthur made a mess of all that. Such arrogance, sending in those kids not trained." Tyler turned his coffee mug around slowly in his hand.

"Well, he was trained. He joined up before, you know. He wanted to fight the Germans overseas. But he got a desk job stateside, and never saw any action." Connie had to wait a moment; she felt a moistness in her eyes. "He said that made him feel like a sissy. So when the next damned war came along—" She shook her head, and saw that the minister was watching her kindly. "That's the part that gets to me," she said. "He didn't have to go to Korea. Just did it so people wouldn't think he was a sissy."

"Oh, that is sad." The minister grimaced.

"I was packing him a box," Connie said. "I'd knit some red mittens, and made some fudge, and I was packing the box for him, when Adrian drove up in the middle of the day—and then I knew. I just knew."

Tyler nodded.

"I had Adrian take the box away, couldn't stand to look at it."

"Oh, of course," Tyler said.

Connie wiped her mouth with a napkin. "It still doesn't feel real," she told Tyler, looking at him with puzzlement.

Tyler watched her. After a moment he put his chin in his hand. "Funny feeling, isn't it," he finally said.

"It was *cold* over there, you know," Connie said. "Thirty degrees below zero. They had to piss on their rifles to get them to work."

"Awful," said Tyler, startled at the word "piss." He shook his head meditatively. "Just an awful mess. I am sorry."

"A few years back I went to visit a man at Togas hospital—he was Jerry's officer. I thought if I could talk to him, you know, see what it had been like, it would feel more real to me." Connie shook her head, pushed back her coffee cup. "But, sheesh—"

"What's that, Connie?"

"Oh, the fellow just sat in a wheelchair all day, trembling, smoking cigarettes. They had to put his wheelchair against the wall, 'cause he was so scared someone would come up behind him. Just sat there, trembling." Connie drummed her fingers on the tabletop. "Hard to think he was an officer. At least Jerry didn't end up like that."

"No," Tyler said. "At least he's not suffering."

"That's right." Connie's voice got louder as she said with sudden urgency, "And that's the *point*, isn't it? That's exactly the point."

"Point? Point of what, Connie?" A sudden, vague uneasiness moved through him.

Connie's eyes had moistened. She looked at Tyler. "That this man's life is no life, is it? No life at all. Worse than death, if you ask me. He can't even talk. They'd wrapped him in freezing sheets once, the nurse said. Try and shock him out of it. But it didn't work. I say that's no life. Don't you think it's better to be dead?"

"Seems that way sometimes, I guess. Maybe they'll be able to help the fellow."

"They can't help him," Connie said. "Were you in the war?"

"Just the tail end. It was over, really."

"I see." Connie nodded. Her voice had returned to its normal pitch. "Were you sent off overseas somewhere?"

Tyler leaned back in his chair and talked about his year in the navy in Guam, doing cleanup operations; the war had just ended. He told how his father had died while he was on the train coming back from San Francisco. "What I didn't know about death," Tyler said, squinting at his fingernails, "was that it was not just the death of my father, but the death of my childhood, the death of the family as I'd known it. It reminds me of Glenn Miller's plane disappearing above the channel. Not just the death of a bandleader, you see, but the death of a band." He looked out the window. "That's what death does. If that makes any sense."

"Well," Connie said, tapping her spoon loudly against the table, "truthfully, none of it makes sense. Not to me. Let me ask you a question." The minister turned and raised his eyebrows. "Does it make it better to—you know, have these deaths happen— if you're a minister?"

He gazed at her for a moment. "I don't think so," he said.

She nodded, looking down at her spoon, and he thought he saw a spasm of bewilderment and fear pass over her face—a moment of nakedness.

"What is it, Connie?"

She said, "I just thought of something. Alpha-Bits cereal. I've seen it in the grocery store and it might get Katherine interested. Spell out her name in the cereal bowl."

"Say," said the minister, "that's a swell idea."

"I have to go back to the grocery store soon for Evelyn. I'll pick it up. I was to go this weekend but there was trouble with the car."

"Oh, cars can be a nuisance," Tyler said. "Dad had a car that hated rain. Every time it rained, that car wouldn't start." As he remembered this, a faint sweetness of feeling arose in him.

"Car's a nuisance all right," Connie said. "Say, look. I found this in the back of the linen closet upstairs. It must belong to Katherine." From her sweater pocket she brought out a small gold ring, and held it between her fingers. A tiny red stone was set in it.

Tyler looked at it carefully. "Doesn't look familiar. Are you sure it's not yours?"

"Oh, heavens no. Why would I have a child's ring? Maybe it's been here a hundred years. Anyway, give it to Katherine."

"Well, thank you, then." He took the ring, turning it in his fingers. "Say, Mrs. Hatch, I just wondered—I wondered if you might want to babysit full-time. If I brought Jeannie here to live. I'd like to have the girls together."

To his surprise, the woman blushed.

"Just a thought," he said easily. "It's going to take me some time to get the details worked out."

"Oh, I'd like that a lot. I would."

"Well, let's keep it in mind." He slipped the ring into his pocket. "Thanks for suggesting the cereal and picking it up for me. I'd forget it, I'm sure. My mind is like a sieve."

"Mine, too." Connie nodded, and gave him a smile so warm and sudden that Tyler had a momentary sense of seeing a younger version of herself come forward in her older face. She stood up, put the coffee mugs in the sink, stepped into the mudroom.

Tyler heard the plastic laundry basket move across the floor.

HE HAD MARRIED a summer girl. Almost never—plenty of people would have told you this—was that a good idea. He had married a summer girl from Massachusetts, and that alone brought complications. Had Lauren been from New Hampshire, better still, Vermont, it probably would not have mattered. But to come from Massachusetts meant a certain kind of crassness, most likely money, probably cocktails, and Massachusetts people were the rudest drivers in the world.

But what's a man to do when Love appears before him?

Tyler, sent out into "the field" as a seminary student, had initially been dismayed at the paucity of the congregations in some of the outlying, isolated towns. On his first day of student preaching, there had been six people sitting before him—one of whom, he realized very soon, was what was referred to (easily, in those days, without apology) as the town idiot. But Tyler grew used to this, adjusted even to the fact that such a person would often get up and leave during the service. He understood the inability to sit still, for there was inside himself a restiveness.

That's where he had learned to preach, in those small white churches sometimes as far as one hundred miles from the Brockmorton Theological Seminary. Free from homiletics class, free from the self-consciousness of standing before the grim professor, free from the lack of charity he sensed in some of his classmates, Tyler found his voice, speaking to the small congregations, sometimes stepping back from the pulpit to move more directly in front of them, to quote the simple verse from Daniel: *Do not be afraid, for you are deeply loved by God. Be at peace; take heart and be strong.*

And because reports of approbation came back to the field director at Brockmorton, Tyler had been sent to preach in a coastal town too small to support a full-time minister year-round, but whose congregation rose like an ocean swell during the month of July because of the summer people from out of town. Out of state.

Picture: A day in early July, warm enough that the door to the church is left open, and the windows in the sanctuary are open, too, so the sweet, warm air of the morning is there inside the small village church built two centuries earlier. Beside the church is a rose garden, where a few tea roses are still in bloom, and on this Sunday the gloriosa lilies are draping over the trellis, and there are white Madonna lilies, too, which send their smell into the church in the warm, clear air. Every pew is filled—mostly with people who have come over from the Auburn Colony, or up from Massachusetts or Connecticut to spend part of their summer here. In church today, wearing a blue dress and a blue hat, is the beautiful Lauren Slatin, a summer girl, seated next to her father, who is broad-shouldered and serious. But the beautiful Lauren has none of her father's soberness—she is all color, all light, a light shines from her face, from her eyes, as she stares at the young Reverend Caskey—and what a sermon he delivers! He has never felt so powerful, his eyes intense, his cheeks flushed. They are in love by the benediction.

Was this God's will? It was. They were lifted up into the wondrous arms of God, for God is love, and love filled Tyler to the point of dizziness when he visited the Slatin cottage a few days later, Lauren standing on the grass in a blue gingham dress. And when autumn arrived and the letters showed up in his mail slot outside the common room at Brockmorton, he would open them right there, his heart thick with love as he read the large, uneven handwriting, whose surprising untidiness touched him deeply. There had been those rare and splendid long-distance phone calls made from George Atwood's home in the evening (Tyler always careful to ask George about the bill so that George never had to raise it himself), waiting, waiting in the quiet of the study for that sparkle to flash through the phone. "Hello?" Oh, it was God's work. Love is always God's work.

"A local boy?" Mrs. Slatin had said, her pretty brown eyes smiling at him.

"A country club?" Margaret Caskey had said. "They belong to a country club? Tyler," she said quietly, "rich people are like Negroes. They're fine. There is nothing wrong with them. But I say, and I have always said, let them live their lives, and I will live mine."

He understood—as he stared out his kitchen window now—that on both sides of the aisle on the day of their wedding was the unspoken understanding that each was marrying down.

A FEW WOMEN from the Ladies' Aid were gathered for coffee in the living room of Jane Watson's clean house. This kind of thing gave the women something to look forward to, especially now that the days were shorter and darker, and the boredom of changing sheets or cleaning a bathroom could sometimes mushroom into a private despair before noontime even arrived. Having coffee allowed the women to show off a new sweater, a clean house, exchange recipes, and swap the latest news, which now included the misbehavior of Katherine Caskey. Bertha Babcock—the bossy, old retired schoolteacher who could be a disapproving presence when gossip began—was, thankfully, not at Jane's today, so the details of Katherine could be gone over with some relish. The fact that Tyler had sent Mary Ingersoll home in tears seemed quite remarkable, although Doris Austin, reaching for a blueberry muffin, said, "What makes that remarkable?" The fact the child had said, "I hate God," during the Lord's Prayer was remarkable as well, and

Jane Watson, tapping her cigarette into a plaid bean-bag ashtray, said Tyler should be told.

Nobody wanted to tell him.

But Katherine had shown no remorse—coffee spoons clinking against saucers—and when children didn't show remorse, it could indicate a social pathology. There was an article in a recent *Newsweek* and that's what it said. Wasn't it just insane, by the way, how people were spending fortunes to lie on a couch five days a week and talk about anything that came to mind? In New York, especially, where the Jewish psychoanalysts were having a heyday.

"I would love it," Alison Chase said. "Put my feet up every day and talk about my problems."

"No, you wouldn't," Jane said. "They don't care about your real problems, just any old thing you can think up from your childhood. Eventually the psychoanalyst tries to convince you that you wanted to sleep with your mother when you were a child."

"My mother?"

"Father, in a woman's case. I suppose. But it's all about sex, sex, sex."

Say, wasn't it rude, Irma Rand suggested—her cheeks having colored at Jane's remarks—of Mrs. Khrushchev to say no when she was offered hotel soaps to take home? But then, they did write awful things about her in the newspaper out there in California, saying her suit looked like a slipcover for an old couch. "True, though," someone said. And, it was agreed, both those Khrushchevs were homely as hedgehogs. She'd been just a peasant, you know. Working in the fields before the Bolshevik revolution, before she wandered out and married him. Maybe a matter of principle that she's supposed to look plain.

Jane Watson, irritated now because no one had complimented her blueberry muffins, said they should decide whether or not to tell Tyler what had happened in Sunday school, because she had to get going. "Have Ora tell him," someone suggested, since it was known that Ora would say anything. No, Ora wasn't here—she didn't know the details; Alison should tell him, since it happened in her kinderkirk class.

"Someone ought to tell him," said Doris, eating a second blueberry muffin. "I'd want to know if my child said such a thing, but I'm not telling him. I'm a little tired of Tyler, frankly. I went to speak to him about the new organ and he told me to read the works of some Catholic, Saint Thérèse from Lisieux."

Jane Watson touched her red button earring, and looked at Alison Chase.

But why, exactly, had Mary Ingersoll been in tears? This was gone over once again, and it was agreed: Rhonda Skillings, who had been the one to report this to Jane, was not a woman who lied (insufferable as she might be—you'd think she was the first person to ever get a doctorate). And Rhonda had said that Mary Ingersoll said Tyler had been awfully rude.

Tyler was never rude.

Well, *something* had happened. And the little girl was certainly rude. Sad. Saying something like that in Sunday school. Alison Chase tugged her sweater close. "Hold on, hold on." She pointed to each woman sitting around the table. "Eeny, meeny, miney, moe," she said. "Catch a nigger by the toe. If he hollers let him go. Out goes Y-O-U."

Jane would make the call.

# FOUR

The fact is: What had happened to the minister's beautiful wife was the kind of tragedy that holds a small town in a certain thrall. No sooner had the Caskeys' new baby been born—and she was an adorable thing, pink-cheeked and chubby; she could have fallen off the ceiling of the Sistine Chapel, said Marilyn Dunlop, who taught art at the Academy, and had taken a trip to Italy, becoming tiresome about things Italian—no sooner had the sweet Jeanne Caskey been born than rumors began that Lauren Caskey was having a nervous breakdown. Something very odd occurred: Lauren Caskey, with both children in the car, had driven to Hollywell one day and suddenly not known where she was. From a pay phone in the bus station, she called her husband, who was in his office in the basement of the church, and because Skogie Gowen, who was retired from his law practice and used to go talk to the minister about fishing, was in Tyler's office at the time, word made its way around town that the panicked minister had to ask his wife to read the names of the signs nearby, the name on any bus she saw, to determine that she was, in fact, in the bus station in Hollywell. And then, after begging her to stay exactly where she was, he drove with Skogie to get her.

She was standing out on the sidewalk looking pale and baffled, but, more than that, she looked "gone." This was the only way Skogie could think to describe it to people. Skogie said the minister was beside himself, getting the woman into the car, making sure the kids were all right. When Skogie called later that night, the minister thanked him, sounding subdued, and said Lauren was overtired.

"I think we forget how hard it can be," Skogie assured him. "Chemical changes and things when you have a baby." He was embarrassed, and he thought Tyler Caskey, who only said, "Yes, it's true, and thanks again," was, too.

Stories were recalled of postpartum breakdowns. Sharon Merrimen, after her fourth child, got into bed in November and didn't climb out until March. Betsy Bumpus had tears streaming down her cheeks the entire first year of her twins' lives; she'd actually become dehydrated. This sort of thing was hard on the husbands, but what could you do? At least no one had drowned their kids in the bathtub, like you heard about once in a while.

Lauren Caskey wasn't drowning her kids, or bathing them, either. What was happening didn't have anything to do with her kids. She was in Boston having surgery. The words "gone to Hanover for treatments" were repeated quietly that spring, on the telephone, in the grocery store, in backyards as women shook their heads over hyacinth blooms. "Wig" was sometimes heard.

The word "cancer" was not. This was a time, remember, when you immediately and shudderingly would equate that word with doom. Even though *Life* magazine—right around the time that Lauren got sick—had its lead article on this disease, claiming new hope for unfortunate victims, the full-page pictures of a woman ready to be rolled beneath a radiation machine had caused some to turn the pages quickly; for the woman in the photographs appeared to be in the prime of her life, and it was compelling and horrible, more frightening for some than a nuclear war, because its source was nature, and its victims chosen at random.

Soon, women in West Annett who had not wept in years stood in their kitchens weeping. That Lauren Caskey was a person who had held herself apart was forgotten or forgiven. Her fate seemed to provide a luxury of emotion that had been held in check for some time. Poor, poor thing, people said—how terrible. Was there family arriving to help out? Nobody knew. Jane Watson, being a member of the Sunshine Committee, had driven out to the farmhouse one day and offered, in the long and sure-to-be-difficult days that lay ahead, to read to the woman when she needed distraction. Reverend Caskey seemed surprised by this, and said it wouldn't be necessary—Lauren was going to be fine.

Connie Hatch, who had been working at that point two mornings a week for the Caskeys, began receiving phone calls at her home. But she was not forthcoming, saying only that Mrs. Caskey's family and the minister's mother and sister had all arrived to help. The biggest piece of news slipped through the cracks when Jane Watson called the Hatch place one night and an inebriated Adrian answered the phone, and said, "Oh, yeah, the lady's real sick. She's dying, for sure—pissed as hell about it, too."

There was other stuff as well. Even Connie—because the minister had said she could take time off, now that the family was here—did not know that Lauren's parents and sister wanted to take the young woman back to Massachusetts, where they could give her proper care. *"Where at least there's running water!"* the sister had hissed out in the hall one night, causing Belle to turn on the faucet in the kitchen and say loudly, "Oh, look! Water coming through the spout! Soon we can get rid of the outhouse!"

But the minister said no, Lauren would stay right there; this farmhouse was her home. He delivered this with infinite politeness, but it spelled the end, essentially, to the minister's relationship with his in-laws. He had taken this stand because he could not bear—or even understand—their certainty that she would die ("Only a miracle will save her now," his father-in-law said), and because there was as well a bitterness between him and them that had silently escalated over the years regarding matters of money.

Every night and every morning Tyler prayed. Always he ended, "Thy will be done." He did not think a miracle was needed, nor did he believe in them—he saw all of life as a miracle. And if Tyler believed instead in the power of prayer, it's because his praying felt strong and right, like a swimmer who has trained for years and feels safe in the water that buoys him up. Tyler loved God very much, and God would naturally know that. Tyler loved Lauren, and God would know that, too.

But when the Massachusetts contingent had departed, offering to take Katherine with them for the summer—even that he refused—and it was left to him, and to his mother and Belle to handle things, his wife began to lash out at him. Terrible things were said.

"It's the disease talking," Tyler had murmured to his mother in the kitchen one morning, knowing she had overheard.

Margaret Caskey said nothing. She worked steadily, drying the dishes, changing the baby, going back upstairs to change the pillowcase beneath Lauren's head.

Jane Watson, appearing that day on the minister's porch, standing in her summer dress, holding a straw handbag, white-framed sunglasses pushed up on her head, had struck him as obscene in her healthiness. He had not invited her in. "I would invite you in," he said, "but Lauren is resting."

"Of course," said Jane. "I'm simply here to offer my help."

"That's very kind of you."

"We've all just been sick about this," the woman said. She was wearing a dress with big red flowers on it.

"Yes." The minister looked past her. It was a magnificent day. He thought he had never seen such a beautiful world. The birch trees lining the driveway were like newly whitewashed lampposts, only instead of lights they offered lovely green arms of leaves.

"Tyler, I wanted to say, when my sister's husband was dying, we found it helpful to read to him. It helped pass the time."

"Lauren isn't dying." He said this with a slight lilt, as though genuinely surprised to hear assumptions to the contrary.

"I thought—"

"She's ill," said Tyler. "But with the power of God's love, she'll recover."

"Well, say, then. The doctors indicate a chance?"

"Oh, sure. They've seen recovery in a case like this."

"That's marvelous, then," Jane said. "Hold on, Tyler. I have a casserole in the car."

He moved out onto the porch, closing the screen door behind him, and waited while she walked across the gravel in her pumps. The fullness of her haunches as she bent to reach into the backseat offended him with their display of vigor. She walked up the tilting steps holding a casserole dish covered with shiny aluminum foil, and he thought how she seemed to come here from a far-off country, that this farmhouse was now a ship in the middle of nowhere; he had been summoned to the deck, and the sunlight hurt his eyes. She would get back in her boat, the shiny blue Oldsmobile, and return to the continent of free, healthy people, reporting on this visit, perhaps disappointed there had been no "sighting."

He thanked her and went back inside. Noodles and creamy stuff were there when he removed the foil, and, scraping the mess into the garbage, he heard his mother say behind him, "You mustn't become bitter, Tyler."

"No one wants to eat this." But he had flinched—to be caught throwing food away.

For three days, then, Lauren lay with what appeared to be a peacefulness. Her brown eyes seemed lit from behind so they shone like dark cedar chips with sun on them. And there was sun, a sharp, beautiful August sunlight filling the room in the afternoons. Tyler bathed Lauren with a facecloth, starting at her hairline, back over her ears. Gently, he bathed his wife, gently he pushed the cloth between her toes. Once she said softly, "Oh, look at the balloons," and then fell into a nap.

A cardinal called from the fir tree by the window, swooping past in a flash of red. Tyler tucked the pillow behind his wife's head, then sat in a chair beside her, his big hands in his lap. Deep inside himself, he felt what might have been incipient sobs; he raised his chin and ignored them with deliberateness. God was in the room. The air was not merely air, it was the presence of God— you could feel it as distinctly as you would feel the water around you if you were swimming in a lake. It seemed to Tyler that each time during his life when he had experienced The Feeling, it had been leading to this. The Feeling was large and quiet and magnificent. Tyler, while his wife lay sleeping, and he sat inwardly denying his tears, gave silent prayers of thanksgiving and praise.

The next day Lauren sat up and spoke. "Goddamn your God!" Belle said it was time she took the children away.

Katherine's clothes were packed in a small suitcase belonging to Lauren. It had brown leather edging at its corners and a brass clasp beneath the leather handle. It was the sight of this suitcase, which in the past had held the delicate and dear clothes of his betrothed when she came to visit him, now standing in the kitchen with little Katherine next to it, the child holding tight to her sock-doll—it was the sight of this suitcase and child that Tyler suddenly thought would do him in.

"I have to go to the bathroom," Katherine said.

"Go on, then," said Belle. "We'll wait."

But Tyler followed the child into the bathroom off the kitchen, and he helped Katherine arrange herself, get the little corduroy pants pulled down, get her seated on the toilet.

"I already went a little." Katherine pointed to a wet spot on her red underpants stretched between her little knees.

"It will dry," Tyler said.

"Daddy," the child whispered, "Aunt Belle's house smells funny. I don't want to go there."

"It won't be for long. Help take care of the baby."

"Aunt Belle says don't touch the baby."

"Belle has a lot on her mind right now. Help sing the baby to sleep when she gets fussy. You can do that."

In the driveway he knelt beside her. "Daddy loves you."

"I want to see Mommy," Katherine said. Oh, she was trying not to cry, but her chin wobbled.

"Mommy's sick right now."

"But she'll wonder where I am," the child pleaded, crying now.

He took out his handkerchief. "Blow." She blew. "Katherine," he whispered, "you have to stop."

"I want to see Mommy."

"Katherine," he whispered.

The child pulled her head back to stare at him. Fear moved in little flickers across her face.

"Mommy wants you to go to Belle's now, and be a good girl."

"Tyler," said Belle, in a warning kind of voice, and Tyler stood up and looked at her hard.

"Belle," he said firmly.

He had to peel Katherine from his leg, had to pick her up—she would not on her own get into the car.

THERE HAD BEEN some fear, after his wife's death, that the minister would leave town. But he did not leave town. He took time off, then returned with Katherine, saying his mother would be caring for Jeannie for the time being, and she would bring the child up on weekends. He did become very busy, throwing himself into activities that took him around the state: the New England Chapter of Christian Young People, the Seacoast Charter of Ministries, the governor's task force on poverty. With all the running around, it was difficult for anyone to find time to talk with him. But people understood. And they understood, as well, that his sermons were now read, as he preached with his deep voice, standing tall and broad-shouldered, on the power of God's eternal love, the grace of Jesus Christ. He moved through the activities room during coffee hour, smiling and nodding and shaking hands, much as he had done in the past. The only sign that he had held the hand of tragedy was the slightly subdued level of his affability, and also the swift, deep look of bafflement that might suddenly pass over his face.

When November arrived that first year, people remembered: How that man could skate! He moved as though in the arms of God. Really, you would not know he had anything strapped onto his feet, you would not know he had feet at all. All you could see was the large shape of him moving about that frozen lake in his long coat. As he moved between children playing, or couples holding hands, his body leaned one way, then the other, his ankles effortlessly close, one foot crossing over the other so he looked as though he were merely out for a stroll, and yet he was fast as the wind; oh, he was a marvelous thing to see on ice.

The minister could often be seen skating late in the afternoon, or walking home near dusk with his skates hung over his shoulders. Sometimes he could be seen standing and gazing at the sky, as though overcome by the barren trees back-lit by the day's final yellow light. Old Bertha Babcock, who stopped her car one day to offer him a ride, was surprised when the minister said, "It seems as if right beyond the horizon, Bertha, right there, out of reach, past the gray rooftops and dark, leafless trees, is some richly viable presence of activity." And then, putting his hands to his face: "I wonder if we are all condemned forever to live outside the grace of God."

Perhaps she hadn't heard him right.

As that winter passed, giving way to a late spring, the minister appeared increasingly tired, so that his eyes began to have a slightly sunken, tubercular look, and he lost weight. As summer arrived, he sometimes did not go to coffee hour, and when he did, he threw out a compliment in a voice slightly too loud. "Say, Pete," he said, "great slide show the other night. The Missionary Committee is lucky to have you." But by summer he seemed like a big tractor being driven by a teenage kid, slipping in and out of gear. When Skogie Gowen reported that the minister had mentioned he would like to go down south someday to help the ministers with the colored people, some felt a sting of betrayal. But *we* are his people, was the thought. In any event, nothing more had been said about this as autumn rolled around once more, and Katherine, now decidedly ratty-looking, began her education. But there was a slight reticulation of unease. People wanted their minister back.

Doris Austin wanted him back; she loved him.

And she wanted a new organ. This was not unreasonable. The organ in the church had been there for twenty-four years, and every time she played a note, there was a small gap in time, so the congregation, singing their hymns, often seemed confusedly dis-

jointed, some singing a beat ahead, others waiting for the beat behind. Doris often went to the church during the week to play, hoping she would come across the minister there, as she sometimes
had. What joy it gave her to know this man was praying while she
provided, above him in the choir loft, the music of the divinely inspired Johann Bach.

Today, after leaving Jane Watson's house, where she had been
privately pleased to hear of Katherine Caskey saying, "I hate God"
(a terrible thing for a minister's child to say; and Tyler had humiliated her last week, just letting her sit there and bawl like a baby, and
had not even called her since!), Doris went off to the church. The
minister's car wasn't there, but then sometimes he walked into town.
Feeling like a criminal, she crept down the stairs to his office, and
found his door was closed. That he was not there felt deliberate.

In the sanctuary, she sat in a back pew, her hands folded on her
lap, ankles tucked beneath her. Sometimes when she prayed in here
alone, the silence opening out before her seemed a thrilling presence. This feeling could expand into a joyous thing, but then she'd
soon become anxious, excited, no longer serene, and it would col-
lapse within her, a bubble whose delicate skin, reflecting the shadows and lights of her thoughts, would simply disappear, and then
she felt peevish; once this happened, the large feeling would not
come back.

Today her face flushed to suddenly think how this was like sex
with Charlie. Praying was like sex? She was a failure at both, because even now she was glancing at this carpet thinking what a
good job Bruce Gilgore did vacuuming it each week, and keeping
these long windows clean, and why was she thinking that? But that
happened in bed with Charlie, too. She would think how she
hadn't checked one of the kids' homework, or if the washing machine had been properly fixed, while Charlie's head would move
over her breasts, and she would pat his back.

She picked up her pocketbook and left. On the steps of the church she thought again how she had wept in front of Tyler, told him of being struck by Charlie, and he had never called her back. Tears came again into her eyes. "Damn you right to hell," she said.

TYLER SAT WITH his Bible on his lap, staring out the window of his study. He was picturing the young fiancée of Dietrich Bonhoeffer, a girl with her dark hair pulled back from her earnest, intelligent face, walking boldly into the prison to visit him. Since Bonhoeffer's death, Maria von Wedemeyer had not made public their letters, and this moved Tyler—that she would hold their love privately to her heart. It was said that the last time she saw him in prison, when the guards indicated their time was up and began escorting her to the door, she suddenly turned, calling, "Dietrich!" and ran past the guards and threw her arms around him.

Tyler turned his attention back to his desk. A deep sorrow for the young woman swept through him, and he looked to his Bible and read Zophar's reply to Job: *If thou prepare thine heart, and stretch out thine hands toward him . . . thou shalt forget thy misery. . . . And thou shalt be secure, because there is hope—*

The telephone rang.

"Tyler, Jane here."

In the next room Connie turned on the vacuum cleaner. Tyler stood up. "Jane. Hello."

"Are you all right, Tyler?"

"Yes. I am."

"All right, then. Listen. Alison was here, and it seems a small incident occurred with Katherine. Alison was embarrassed to tell you, but yesterday during the Lord's Prayer, Katherine said, 'I hate God.' "

Tyler sat back down, put his elbows on his desk.

"Tyler?"

"Yes, Jane."

"We thought if this was our child, we'd want to know. So Alison asked me to give you a call."

"I'm sorry," said Tyler, "but I don't understand." The back of his head had grown warm. He heard Jane sighing, or exhaling after having lit a cigarette.

"I guess the way to understand it," said Jane, "is to know that Katherine's angry."

"During the Lord's Prayer?" Tyler asked. "Where during the Lord's Prayer?"

"Where? I don't know. You mean during what part of the prayer?" A pause. "We debated whether to tell you, and maybe it wasn't a good idea. But when Alison explained to the class that this hurt God's feelings, well—Katherine didn't seem to care."

"And why didn't Alison speak to me herself?"

"Because she was embarrassed, Tyler."

"I see."

"Personally, I was against it."

"Against what?"

"Telling you."

"But you are telling me."

"Gosh, you're not making this easy, Tyler. Alison and Irma and Doris all thought you should know, but nobody wanted to tell you—we know the child's had some trouble at school, and it's awkward, of course—so as a favor I took on the assignment. If *Martha* had said this kind of thing, *I'd* want to know. I'd wash her mouth right out with soap, but how you respond to Katherine is your business."

"What do you mean—the way to understand this is that Katherine's angry?"

"Well, Tyler—"

In the living room the vacuum cleaner went off; he heard the nozzle knock against the floor. He pictured the living room of Jane Watson—all those women sitting around discussing his child? A large, dark fist seemed to squeeze him.

"Tyler?"

"Yes."

"You're making me feel pretty bad here."

"The child lost her mother, Jane."

"Well, we know that. My goodness."

"If you think this through, the child's lost half her family, with Jeannie not being here."

"We merely thought you'd want to know, that's all. My goodness," Jane repeated.

"All right. I appreciate your concern. I'll take care of it. Thank you."

He rubbed his face with both hands, then went to the doorway of his study. Connie was tossing the couch pillows onto the easy chair.

"Say, I'm sorry about that," Tyler said. His mouth felt dry. "The dog makes a mess of the couch."

"Oh, it's all right," Connie told him. "I've got a dog myself. A big German shepherd. Dog hairs big as pine needles." She glanced at him, and in the midst of his anxiety, there was something in the innocent eagerness of her expression that touched him. *He will beautify the meek with salvation.*

"Say, Connie—I'm going to be gone for a little while. I wondered—would you be able to watch Katherine for just a little while if I'm not back in time?"

"Ay-yuh, sure."

He was already opening the closet door, getting out his coat.

"And thank you," he added, "for all this," sweeping a hand toward the living room.

"Just doing my job," Connie said.

THE UNPLEASANTNESS OF JANE and Tyler's phone call was hardly what you'd call a catastrophe, but it was not a happy note to get played in the little town of West Annett, and Tyler instinctively knew this. His impulse was to flee (keep moving) and Jane's impulse, of course, was to share this with as many women friends as she could before children and husbands came home and the much-needed element of feminine camaraderie was lost in the clutter and clatter of others' needs.

Connie Hatch, however, was as oblivious to these small-town tremors as she was to the problem of the church's old organ being one beat behind, and when the minister left the house, she was encased in an aura of sunshine, regardless of the pale skies outside the windows, the high cloud covering that wouldn't clear. No, as Connie stuck the vacuum nozzle into the crevices of the couch, she felt remarkably airy and light, in a way quite unusual for her, thinking how lovely it was the minister had apologized for the dog hairs, and how—most amazingly—he wanted her to babysit full-time. She liked how in the minister's eyes there was something bewildered; this was pleasing to Connie—she was bewildered herself. She sometimes felt life was a game of checkers, and a big hand from above had reached down and smashed Jerry, flipped Becky over on her back like a beetle, while she, Connie, was simply moved aside. And who knew why? Maybe the minister knew why. She'd spent time wondering why, and she thought probably there was no reason. But she had never forgotten the first time her mother-in-law had said to her years ago, "You know, Connie,

I've often thought when a woman can't have children, there's a reason why."

"What do you mean?" Connie had asked, water springing to her eyes.

"I heard on the radio," Evelyn had said, "when a woman miscarries, the fetus is deformed. Nature knows who to give children to."

"I guess I don't know what you mean."

"Oh, Connie, now. You're strung a little tight. You know that."

Connie'd had to sit down in a chair.

She bent now to unplug the vacuum cleaner, and hauled it back to the closet. It's true that she didn't like Katherine. But that could change. A picture ran through her mind: Katherine would come home from school and have a scraped knee. Shyly, she would show Connie. And Connie would say, "Oh, a little boo-boo. Let's put a Band-Aid on it and make it all better." Jeannie might want a Band-Aid, too, seeing that Katherine had one. Connie would say to Katherine, "Let's let Jeannie have one, too," and both girls would clap their hands. In her mind, Connie talked to Jerry as she hunted for the floor wax. I'm going to take care of the minister's kids, she said.

But thinking of Jerry made her so sad that, while she was down on her hands and knees to wax the floor, tears dropped, and she had to sit back on her heels and wipe at her eyes. *All the time it smells like shit, Con. People shit. Remember when Ma made us stay in the outhouse? And I was scared of the spiders. How come people shit smells worse than animal shit? This place is bad, Connie.*

Connie poured some wax onto the floor, rubbed it with the cloth. Every night after Jerry died, Connie had woken with a dark heaviness in her, more awful than anything she'd known. It's done now, she would think. He isn't scared anymore. But she was never the same. Slowly she had come to realize this. You go along in life—you're just Connie. And then you're not the same; inside a stem has snapped. After that, you're nothing. Nobody knows it, but you're a simple "nothing" in the whole wide world.

*Remember the toboggan rides we took, Connie? If you thought it was dangerous, you told me to sit behind you so you'd hit the tree first. It's cold here, Con. I'm scared.*

"Shit," Connie said. She had been waxing the same spot over and over, and it was thickly shiny. "Shit, hell, and piss," she said. But the minister would most likely not notice, and he certainly wouldn't care. She stood up and put the wax away, and started dusting the dining-room table. The image of Katherine ran back through her head, shyly showing her the scraped knee, Connie standing there with the baby on her hip. Connie thought how, when the Caskey girls were grown, they'd say, "We had a house-keeper when we were little. She just about saved our lives. Dad couldn't have managed without her. She really saved our lives. Her name was Connie Hatch, and she was the kindest woman you ever knew." They would say this to their college roommates, their boyfriends, their in-laws.

Connie dusted the dining-room chairs, and thought how—poking around one day—she'd discovered that every picture of Lauren Caskey had been put in the attic, in a cardboard box, along with the woman's watch and wedding ring. "Don't you think that's strange, Adrian, not to have any pictures of the woman around?" Connie had asked, not expecting an answer. But after a long silence, Adrian had said, "No." Connie pushed in the chair, dusted the one beside it. Lauren Caskey hadn't liked her, and Connie'd known it right away. Even though Lauren had been one of those messy, careless women—dropping a pink sweater right on the floor, tossing a high heel into the corner—and certainly in need of Connie's help, she'd never said a kind word to Connie, never really said a word at all.

But to get sick like that! Just horrible. Connie stopped dusting and sat down in the dining-room chair, the dust cloth loose in her hand. She couldn't for the life of her understand why things went that way, bodies becoming like prisons with the person stuck inside. Screaming, or not screaming, but staring at you like you should do something. Connie had been glad when Tyler's mother sent her away—who wanted to watch such a thing? She didn't. But she wondered if Tyler "believed" in suffering. People thought suffering made you stronger, but Connie thought that was baloney; stronger for what? Death? If there was some kind of afterlife, then was the suffering supposed to get you a faster train ride to heaven?

The idea that there might be an afterlife horrified Connie. She had a hard enough time with this one. What if death was a big garbage bag where the body went, but the mind was left to hang on forever, suspended with its thoughts? That was Connie's idea of hell. (Not that she wouldn't like to see Jerry, or have their minds wink to each other in some netherland. But she doubted she'd be that lucky—her mind would get stuck in a different room.) Except it was all foolishness; there weren't rooms in heaven or hell; there was no heaven or hell.

But there was this—the warmth of the minister's house.

Connie looked around at the pink walls while she drummed her fingers on the dining-room table. Up in the attic, she remembered now, were—along with all those other things—lots of women's new clothes with the price tags still on. Someday she'd offer to help Tyler with that; he shouldn't have to have them up there forever. He'd trust her to figure out the best way to do these things, just like the way he asked her about his frayed cuffs.

For lunch Connie ate a slice of cold meat loaf she had brought with her, banging her palm against the bottom of the ketchup bottle. She planned in her head the minister's meals. She got up to check in the freezer for peas. There were none; she wrote it on the grocery list. Peas. She was good at this. After she'd done the laundry, earlier this morning, the minister had said, "You're pretty important to this household, you know."

Connie, who, years before, had loved to square-dance in the grange hall, felt this morning the possibility of being once again, graceful and light-footed, as she rose to look through the minister's cupboards, as though her entire relationship to the world might turn into a happy *dos-à-dos* of partnering.

THE ACADEMY HAD recently put in a pay phone by the gym. Charlie Austin had a free period, and he stood now putting quarters into the slot. She answered on the second ring.

"It's me," he said, glancing around. A few girls had come out of the locker room way down on the other side, wearing their blue gym suits snapped up the front.

"Hi, me," she said, laughing.

"I have three minutes," Charlie said. "And then my quarters run out. I just wanted to say hi."

She laughed again. "Just hi? Nothing else?"

"I can't really talk. I'm on the phone by the gym, and the girls are about to have gym class." Already a basketball bounced.

"Are they sexy? The girls?"

"No," he said. To his horror, he saw that his daughter was one of them. He turned his back.

"We could get a girl, Charlie. Wouldn't you like to see me with a girl? Listen, if you can't talk, maybe I can."

"That would be good." His voice had gone hoarse.

"Know what I was thinking about this morning?"

"Tell me," he said.

"Doing it doggie-style. In front of a mirror. So I can watch what you look like. Should I tell you more?"

"More," he said. He closed his eyes.

"I'll keep my skirt on, and you just hike it up. I'll have my garter belt on, but no panties. Charlie," she said softly, "I love fucking you."

He could not believe a woman could speak this way. His cock was rising as he stood there. He heard the gym teacher's whistle. "I miss you," he whispered.

"I miss you, too."

"What are we going to do?" he asked.

"Screw whenever we can, I guess. Remember, you belong to me."

"Only to you," he said. He hung up and walked back to the teachers' room without glancing at the girls. He had no idea if Lisa had seen him or not. She probably had, he thought. You are a bad, bad man.

THE BROCKMORTON THEOLOGICAL Seminary sat on a hill, its old stone buildings and large elms dominating the town with a kind of quiet stateliness. Only the new library seemed out of place, built off to the side with a squat angularity, and the sight of it saddened Tyler, made him feel older than he was, for he would have preferred it match the old architecture instead. He understood this was "modern," and he disliked it. It seemed to have the shape of something alien invaders would construct.

But the familiar smell of Blake Hall gave him a deep, nostalgic pang, disorienting in its sense of not having changed at all, the large clock at the end of the hall, the pictures of past presidents looming on the wall; the faces of these men, white-haired, dignified, cheeks pinker than they might have been in real life, gazed at Tyler impassively.

George Atwood's door was open. Tyler, standing in the doorway, saw George reading by the window. The man's eyes were hidden for a moment by the light reflecting off his gold-rimmed glasses as he looked over at Tyler, but his voice, as he stood, held a genuine, if restrained, gladness. "Tyler Caskey. What an unexpected pleasure. What brings you up here? Sit down, sit down."

"I had some business not far off." Tyler waved a hand dismissively. "In Edding. I thought I'd stop in to see if you were around."

George Atwood nodded, his old eyes peering at Tyler through his glasses. There was a look of dry and absolute cleanliness about him, as if his shirts, or even his undershirts, would be as clean at the end of the day as they had been when he first put them on. He lowered himself into a deacon's chair that had on its black back the school insignia, and crossed one of his long, thin legs over the other.

The Brockmorton Seminary had been founded two centuries earlier, and it was different from other seminaries because it had been designed to train men—and sometimes a woman—who had previously held other jobs. A butcher, for example, or an electrician, who decided in midlife to become a minister, received his training here, and went on to one of the small parishes sprinkled throughout northern New England.

But Tyler had arrived straight from the university, and was the youngest man in his class. And, at first, the loneliest. The affability that had seemed his natural gift since early childhood—and that had only taken one swift, ferocious hit when he was in the navy— had deserted him when first on this campus. The older men tended to be taciturn as they juggled the responsibilities of books, children, and wives, and some were competitive with Tyler, as though they thought he was a show-off. George Atwood, professor of systemic theology, had taken him under his wing. "He's been like a father to me," Tyler would say, not realizing that he sometimes even got the men confused, that George Atwood, who had a limp (though not as pronounced as Tyler's father's had been) and wore gold-rimmed glasses similar to those that his father had worn, made Tyler's heart ache with a certain longing when he saw him across the leafy lawn, or watched him limp slowly down the church aisle to a pew. George had married Tyler and Lauren, and presided at Lauren's funeral.

"How's Katherine faring?" the man asked now.

"She's all right," Tyler said, tapping his fingers on the arm-chair. "Having a little trouble, I think. A little trouble adjusting to school. I happened to speak to her teacher the other day. Katherine cries a bit, apparently."

After a moment George said, "I guess some of that's to be expected."

Tyler nodded.

"You say her prayers with her?"

"Oh, sure. Every night."

"And you include her mother in the prayers?" George Atwood was examining one of the leather-covered buttons on the long cardigan he wore. When Tyler didn't answer, he looked up.

"No," said Tyler.

"Why is that?"

"I don't know." The stinging pain below his collarbone began. "I guess we've got a little routine that goes way back, and, well— I don't."

"It might be a good idea."

"Yes." Tyler nodded. He squinted out the window and realized he was looking at the corner of the church in which he got married. "I was thinking the other day," he said, feeling the need to take attention away from the—he saw now—appalling revelation that he had kept Lauren from her daughter's prayers, "how Saint Thérèse was Katherine's age exactly when her mother died."

"Godfrey, Tyler. You're not still reading the Catholic saints, are you?"

Tyler looked at him, smiled. "Now and then."

"Oh, I know. You're drawn to the passions. Be careful. That can get you booted out of a parish in a heck of a hurry. I've seen it happen."

Tyler smiled again, with half his mouth. "I don't intend to get booted anywhere."

"No. I expect you don't." George uncrossed his legs, pressed his knees together in their gray trousers, turned his body sideways in the chair. "So, you're managing then, Tyler?"

Tyler nodded, looked out the window again. "I can't memorize, though, and that irritates me. Cuts down on the joy of delivering. Boy, I loved that. Knowing I had them right there with me, that they'd go home and think over what I'd had to say, that, you know, it wasn't just abstract stuff I was—" Too late he remembered that George's homilies were unrelentingly dreary, read as though each word had the same weight, a deadening monotony. Did George know that about himself, he wondered. What *did* people know about themselves? Tyler leaned forward in the chair, resting his elbows on his knees. (What did people know about their children? When he thought of the quiet, obedient Katherine at home, and then pictured her screaming at school, saying, "I hate God," in kinderkirk, this discrepancy—his own knowledge of the child, and the way others might see her—frightened him, as though when Katherine left the house she fell through the ice into some dark water where he could barely see her.)

The sky above the church was very gray. Tyler rubbed his face, sat back, and saw George watching him. "You'll get your sea legs back," the man said to him. And then added thoughtfully, "You have always needed an audience, Tyler." George shifted in the black deacon's chair, raising himself just slightly by his arms before sinking his thin self back down. "Trouble is," George said, and cleared his throat, "for a man who needs an audience, the audience will never be enough. He'll even come to dislike the audience. It's a trap, you see."

Tyler nodded slowly, to give the impression of pondering this, but in fact, a pain was blossoming beneath his collarbone. "Well." Tyler let out a sigh. "Stewardship is coming up, and I'd like to do a good job. The organist wants a new organ, and if there's any controversy I'd just as soon stay out of it."

"Leave that to the board."

"Oh, I am."

"You've done all right with pledges in the past."

"Yes. There won't be any problem with that."

The two men were silent; a door closed down the hallway. George said, "Remember the Lamentations: 'It is good for a man that he bear the yoke in his youth.' "

"I'm not in my youth," Tyler said.

George simply held up a pale, bony hand. After a moment, he asked: "The baby is fine?"

"With Mother, still. Yes, she's fine."

" 'Dark though the night, joy cometh with the morrow,' Tyler." George lifted a bony haunch and took a white handkerchief from a back pocket. He blew his nose almost soundlessly. "Bereavement is a sacrament. You're taking care of yourself? Looks like you've lost a little weight."

"Plenty in the bank, I guess." Tyler patted his stomach. It seemed an odd thing for George to mention joy. When, he wondered, was the last time George Atwood had felt joy? But joy was what Tyler missed. Joy was what he had been full of, it seemed. Even when marriage had brought along its worries. And joy was what C. S. Lewis had used to describe his yearning for God. That's what The Feeling was, Tyler realized now. But how was joy to be available to him ever again? He felt that in one swift, exhausted decision on that final day of Lauren's life, he had allowed a barn door to fall on him, and in the darkness beneath he saw no way out. "Say, George—" Tyler leaned forward, his elbows on his knees.

But right then George looked over at the doorway, and said, "Philip, come in. Were you looking for me?" A young man stood there, his shoulders slumped deferentially.

Tyler, after he had shaken hands with Philip, turned and shook hands with George. "Well," he said, "it's time I get going."

"All right then, Tyler." The old man did not even walk him to the office door.

Outside in the chilly air, he tried to find an equilibrium within the enormousness of his disappointment over his visit with George. He sat in his car a few moments, looking at the campus, the massive gray trunks of the elms before him. *Abide with me; fast falls the eventide . . .* Odd to think that had been his favorite hymn for years, because what had he really known until this year about the sadness and pleading tone of that hymn? *The darkness deepens; Lord with me abide.* Tyler started the car, drove down the hill, past the church where he'd been married. *When other helpers fail and comforts flee . . . O Lord, abide with me.*

The trees along the river appeared caught in a state of half-undress. There were still some leaves, but enough were gone that you could look straight through to the trunks and sky; there was a sense of coming nakedness. Tyler unrolled the car window to have the air wash over him, and the sharp smell of autumn brought to mind a memory of himself as a youth standing on the football field right before the starting whistle. He had thought: I am a large man, and I will do large things.

———

KATHERINE, SITTING IN the backseat of Mrs. Carlson's car, looked out the window with a tiny smile on her face, and Mrs. Carlson, glancing briefly in the rearview mirror, thought perhaps the child had seen the pumpkin stand they passed and had been promised a pumpkin.

"Going to make a jack-o'-lantern for Halloween?" Mrs. Carlson asked, but Katherine didn't answer, just kept smiling out the window. She was picturing her house, the porch, the broken railing, the tilting steps, her climbing each one, and then inside, waiting with her arms wide, would be her mother. "Kitty-Kat, I've missed you!" her mother would cry, and then they would go bounce on the bed.

Katherine frequently pictured this. The fact that it had not happened yet did not discourage her. She thought of it whenever she was in a car that was taking her home. This picture kept her safe, so that when the strange Carlson boy said mockingly, "Thank you, Mrs. Carlson," as she silently stepped out of the car, and Mrs. Carlson said, "Stop that, Bob—good-bye now, Katherine," it all had nothing to do with her.

Up the steps she went, turned the handle of the door that was rattley and loose. And there was Hatchet Foghorn, her big red hands right by Katherine's head. "Hello, Pumpkin," she said.

Katherine dropped her red plastic lunch box on the floor, and ran up the stairs into her room. *Pumpkin?* It made Katherine feel sick to hear this woman call her that. She looked around frantically, then slid under her bed, where it was dark and private and a dusty sock lay by her face. She heard the woman coming up the stairs, heard her hesitate by the bedroom door. "Come on out now, Katherine," the woman said. Katherine closed her eyes tight and held her breath.

—

THE CLOUDS LOWERED and became the color of galvanized metal, then thickened and lowered some more, so that all the trees were gray and still, and the world along the river seemed compressed and made tense by an umbrageous sky. In her messy kitchen, the kinderkirk teacher, Alison Chase, baked an apple crisp for Tyler, and, after putting on her orange lipstick, she drove over to the farmhouse to drop it off with Connie Hatch.

"Tyler hates apples," Ora Kendall told her later on the telephone.

"Nobody hates apples."

"Tyler does. Said they make him sick, ever since Lauren died. She died just as apples were starting to come into season. Can't eat scrambled eggs, either, he said. After the powdered eggs in the navy."

Alison called Jane Watson, who was busy cutting up an onion with a piece of bread stuck in her mouth to keep her eyes from watering. "I tried calling you just a few minutes ago," Jane said from the side of her mouth. "I already called Rhonda and Marilyn about my awful conversation with Tyler. It was like speaking to a man, just barely polite, who didn't care if the phone lines were down. Why did you make him the apple crisp?"

"I felt sorry for him."

"Tyler hates apples. He'll give it to Connie Hatch."

"I'm bored to death with my life," Alison said. "I'm so bored I could just puke."

"It will pass," Jane assured her. "You've got the Historical Society meeting next week at Bertha's house. Bring an apple crisp to that."

"Don't you ever get bored to death?"

"You have to *do* things, Alison."

"I can't even clean my house."

"Make the beds," Jane told her, finally taking the bread from her mouth. "Just make the beds and you'll feel better. And buy a girdle. I've ordered a new girdle from Sears. The ad said, 'Why eat cottage cheese when you can lose five pounds in five seconds?'"

"Why make the beds when they just get right back in them? I've never understood that. Speaking of, I found a magazine yesterday under Raymond's bed. A girlie one."

"Oh. Well. He's the age, I guess. Get Fred to have a talk with him. Or talk to Rhonda Skillings. She knows everything these days—have you noticed? Freud this, Freud that. Anything sexual, she'll talk about it."

"The woman in the magazine looked like Lauren Caskey."

"Alison. That is a *horrible* thing to say."

"Thank you," said Alison. "Thank you very much."

THAT NIGHT TYLER watched his child run around her bedroom as though stung by a bee. She ran to the door, ran back to her bed, got up on it, jumped. She shook her head vehemently back and forth, then fell in a tiny heap, hiding her face in the pillow.

"Katherine. Right now. Stop this."

The child sat up.

"Somebody said it," Tyler told her. "It's a dreadful thing for anyone to say."

The girl shook her head again, starting to hit her head against the wall.

"*Stop* it." The sudden rise in his voice caused the child to stare at him, and then, fast as a squirrel, she curled herself against her pillow.

"Get under the covers, and let's say your prayers."

Tyler had driven back from Brockmorton that afternoon understanding that the seminary's campus belonged to other men, and yet it had seemed, when he was a student there, to be constructed wholly and utterly for him. "I am not in my youth," he had said to George, and it was true that when he walked back through the hallway of Blake Hall, the building seemed diminished, as though it had shriveled imperceptibly, taking with it the stateliness Tyler's younger self had imbued it with. On the way to his car, he thought the campus seemed no more than old gray buildings set on a hill. As he drove along the narrow road, the clouds lowering so it seemed he was driving into a hallway, he remembered the perfect *smack* of a football catch on that field out behind his old high school, and he felt he had been catapulted straight from his childhood to driving this car as a widower and father—and he was absolutely stunned.

When he arrived home, it was Connie Hatch once again (the knowing, quiet glow of her green eyes) who steadied him. She pointed out the apple crisp on the counter, dropped off by Alison Chase. "Take it with you," Tyler said. "I loathe the smell of apples."

"Smells can get you, can't they?" Connie nodded easily, as she slipped it into a brown grocery bag. "When I worked at the county farm, I had to take my clothes off right away when I got home, put them in another room. Even then, seemed like little pieces of that place got stuck right on my nose hairs."

"I should think so," Tyler said, remembering an old woman, the widow Dorothy, who had been packed off by her daughter to the county nursing home—called the county farm—a few months after Tyler had first come to town. "I don't know how you stood working there."

"I didn't stand it," Connie said. "Katherine's upstairs coloring."

"Thank you," Tyler said. Then: "Can you stay for a quick cup of tea?"

And so she had stayed, her strong, red-tipped fingers circling a steaming cup, tilting her head to the side as she listened as he spoke of Brockmorton, how it seemed a hundred years ago he had been a student there.

"Time," Connie said. "It's a funny thing. Haven't got that one figured out yet."

She left, taking with her the apple crisp and the barrier her presence provided between the voices of Jane Watson and Mary Ingersoll and him; for these voices returned to him with the sense of a rolled-up barbed wire inside him, as he sat now on Katherine's bed. The child spoke the Lord's Prayer with enunciated obedience.

For Katherine—if she shook her head enough times, it would be true: She had not said, "I hate God." Alongside the skinny fact she *had* said, "I hate God," sat the bigger fact that she had not said it. And the only thing that mattered was that her father look at her right now as though he saw her, that he rub his big paw of a hand over her head, that the frown marks between his eyebrows disappear. But they did not disappear—they stayed throughout the prayer, and there was no extra word after, as there sometimes was, when he would say to her conversationally, "Walter Wilcox fell asleep in church today and his own snoring woke him up."

No, tonight her father stood up, the lines still in that thick skin above his nose, and when he turned out the light, he hesitated in the doorway, saying, as he sometimes had before, "Remember, Katherine. Always be considerate. Always think of the other man first."

She lay wondering who the other man was. It must be Jesus. She was glad it wasn't Connie Hatch, who wasn't a man, and so didn't have to be thought of first. Katherine shut her eyes tight, to see if that would bring sleep. She didn't like Connie. Didn't like to even look at her.

—

"DORIS, GO TO BED," Charlie Austin said. He felt like they'd been sitting there forever, watching television. He'd had to watch that new show *Twilight Zone,* which he hated, about a "fifth dimension beyond that which is known to man." He'd sat there with his kids, his older son hunched beside him on the arm of the couch, eating potato chips, every munching mouthful making Charlie nuts.

"Isn't this great, Dad?" the kid said, poking his father's leg.

"Why don't you sit in a chair?" Charlie said.

"I like it here. It's a great show, huh, Dad? Look at that, Dad!" On the television a hand came up out of the ground; it gave Charlie the absolute willies.

The kids were finally sent off to bed, and now they were watching *The Untouchables,* and Charlie might have been able to enjoy it—he kind of liked the fellow who played Eliot Ness—if he'd been alone, and, glancing at his wife's profile, he thought she wasn't watching, really, just looking at the television set, her face immobile with an expression of anxious waiting. "Go," he said.

"I'm all right. I'll stay up with you." Still, she looked straight ahead.

"I'm not tired," he said. "I'm worked up. Just go to bed."

She looked at him. "Let me help you relax," she said, and she put a hand on his thigh.

He leaned his head back on the couch, closed his eyes.

"I'd like to try," she said. She moved her hand, and his cock, tucked inside his undershorts and trousers, stirred. Capricious thing—it had no shame, only its own foolish hunger. If he kept his eyes closed . . . thought of the woman in Boston, her garter belt, the tops of her stockings, her toes pointed as she lay back on the edge of the hotel bed . . . "Let's play doctor," she'd said. Her hands touching his ears.

He opened his eyes. "Doris," he said, taking her hand, moving it away, "please go to bed."

There were tears on her face as she stood up, folded the crocheted afghan, put it carefully over the edge of the couch. She plumped the pillows, tears dripping over her nose.

"Goddamn it," he said quietly. "Blow your nose and go to bed."

His cruelty caused her to burst into noisy sobs, and he said, "Shut *up*, for God's sake—you'll wake the kids," and something in his stomach curdled.

Exhibitionism, the woman in Boston had said, wanting to open a curtain in their hotel room, I've certainly been accused of that, turning to him, laughing.

He thought his wife was an exhibitionist of a different sort. He thought her tears said: Witness my unhappiness. And he wanted to shout: Why should I witness your unhappiness? Your unhappiness makes me sick!

She had walked partway up the stairs when he heard her turn and walk back down. She came and stood in front of where he sat on the couch. "You should know," she said, and her voice trembled, "that I went to Tyler Caskey and told him you hit me."

He gazed up at her. Quietly, he said, "Are you out of your mind?"

"You're asking if I'm out of my mind? That's a laugh, Charlie. You asking me."

He looked down, shook his head. "Well," he said, "I don't believe you. I know you're making it up."

"I'm not. He said we should go see some other minister to help us out. He didn't want to be bothered."

"Now I know you're making it up," Charlie said, waving a hand dismissively. "Tyler never would say he didn't want to be bothered. Although I'm sure if you had told him, he would feel that way."

"I did tell him, and he did feel that way, and he didn't use those words. He said we could go to him if you were comfortable with that. But he didn't think you would be."

He saw now she was telling the truth, and his windpipe felt tight, his voice breathy, as he said, "Doris. For God's sake. You hit me first! Did you *tell* him you hit me first? Of course not. Did you tell him about the faces you make? He'd want to hit you himself, if he could see you sticking your lower lip out, wagging your face in front of me." He stood up. "Go to bed." Adding, as she went up the stairs, "Perhaps your compassionate minister will deliver you a glorious new pipe organ as a prize for your suffering." Charlie turned the television off and sat in the dark. But he was afraid of the dark, and his heart pounded. He went to the window, but beyond just a few inches he could see only the dark night, and it frightened him. He turned the television back on.

# FIVE

It was still October when the first snow fell. It came in the afternoon, light as white dandelion thistles being dropped from high in the sky. They took their time reaching ground, so light and sparse they floated. But there was a quiet steadiness to the snow, and by late afternoon, a soft covering lay over places where the ground swelled. Right before it got dark, the skies cleared and the temperatures dropped, and a cold wind swept through the towns by the river, so the new snow swirled like it was being swept by a fast broom. In the morning it lay where the wind had taken it, curled in long, arcing sweeps across a field, or mingled with dried leaves against the base of a tree. There was not much, but the ground was frozen and the branches bare. The sky was a luminous gray; it was to warm up, and then more snow was expected.

"What do you do with Katherine in the case of a snow day?" asked Tyler's sister over the phone.

"Oh, she can stay here with me," Tyler answered. "Or Connie can watch her. Connie's a great help."

"I spoke to Mother," said Belle, "and she thinks your house is depressing. The second year after a death, you know, is always worse than the first. You've got to get yourself a wife. Mother is driving me bughouse. I swear to God, Tyler. If you don't call this Susan Bradford, I will."

"Well," said Tyler, shifting his legs, "I've been busy." Then, cautiously: "Belle, I've been thinking. I'd like to work out a way to have the girls together. If I hired a sitter full-time, Jeannie could live here."

"Tyler," said Belle, "have you forgotten? You have no money. And, frankly, neither do I. Besides, if you take that child away from Mother right now, you'll take away her whole reason for living."

"Oh, Belle, I don't think that's true."

"No? You're lucky she finds that farmhouse depressing, or she'd move right in with you. Call Susan Bradford. Get yourself to Hollywell and meet her for supper. *That* would make Mother happy, if such a thing is possible. Try marrying a woman she likes, who is nice to her, who will help care for her in her old age. I'm not going to be up for the task—I can tell you that right now."

"Now, Belle. Let's be considerate. Let's think of the other person first."

Silence. He thought she might have walked away from the phone. "Belle?"

"I heard you. Do you know why Dad said that crap about thinking of the other one first? Always be considerate?"

"Because he was kind and—"

"Because he was scared. He was scared to have an opinion. The only opinion that ever mattered in that house was Mother's. What he meant was, Always think of Margaret Caskey first, because if you don't, God help you."

"Belle, for—"

"It's true. And I'm sorry, Tyler, about what you've gone through, but you are—excuse me—an idiot. If you're always thinking of the other person first, you don't have to bother with what *you're* feeling. Or thinking."

Tyler turned in his chair and watched as a chickadee, landing on the birdbath, give one tiny shake of his wing. "What do you mean, the second year is worse?"

"Because the first one goes by in a blur. And then you start remembering things. Call this Susan Bradford creature, Tyler, before Mother drives us all nuts."

"Yes," said Tyler. "Regards to Tom and the kids."

He hung up and leaned back in his chair. The truth is, Tyler had less money than Belle—or anyone—knew. Tyler was in debt. The man's aversion to matters of money may have been a bit stronger than most, but it was not—if you understood his background— especially unusual. Many people, particularly Protestants whose ancestors had come from Puritan stock and had been living up in New England for many, many years, held an attitude toward money that had wrapped around it some cloak of unsavory secrecy. The less spent, the better. The less talked about—better still. It was a bit like food: there to sustain you but not, past a certain point, to be fully enjoyed. That was gluttony.

In any event, the dreary fact was that Lauren's intemperance had left Tyler in debt. Her shopping sprees had depleted their small savings at an alarming rate, and there were still doctors' bills not covered by insurance. But it was the dress shops outside of Hollywell that had allowed her to buy clothes on credit, apparently because she was the minister's wife, which had really racked up the bills. Her father had sent her money occasionally, and she had sometimes paid with that. But when she died, Tyler had discovered dresses hidden in the attic, shoes and bracelets and pocketbooks, many with the price tags still on. He would not have dreamed of trying to take them back—he could not even bear to think of them. But the bills still came in from the shops. He had taken out a bank loan, but it would be a year, at least, on his current small salary, before he was even returned to square one. He had hoped, with the new budget being planned, that the board would give him a raise, but he'd heard no talk of this, and he was certainly not a man to ask for one. At the same time, he did think he might inquire about more money for Connie, so he could have his kids together.

*My heart is unquiet 'til it rests with you.* Tyler stood up and rubbed the stinging pain beneath his collarbone. "Are you having a pity party?" his mother used to say to him when he was small and distressed over something. "Where's your dignity?" his mother would say. "Nobody likes a weak person."

Bonhoeffer, Tyler thought, beginning to walk back and forth, would have agreed with that. Bonhoeffer had been disgusted by those men in prison who messed their trousers when the bomb alert was heard, men who moaned and collapsed "under the slightest test of endurance. There are seventeen year olds here in much more dangerous places during the raids who behave splendidly, while these others go around whimpering," Bonhoeffer had written to his friend Bethge. "It really makes me sick."

Tyler rubbed his shoulder. If Bonhoeffer could spend a year in a prison cell, only to find himself taken naked out into the woods to be hanged, then he, Tyler Caskey, could pay his debts, care for his children, and do his job. He turned back to his desk and saw the words he had written for a new sermon: "God is on your side if "— he picked up a pencil and leaned over to finish—"you live your life as honestly as you can each day that goes by." Tyler looked at the words for a long time, then stood and walked out into the hallway.

It may not have been a German prison cell, but the quietness unnerved him, and he thought there might not be anything as empty as an empty house in autumn. Outside, branches of oaks moved, bits of snow stuck in their crevices. He could see across to patches of brown field, he heard a car go past on the road. He thought: *One day is with the Lord as a thousand years, and a thousand years as one day.* The rooms of the old farmhouse seemed scarred, as though a sword had been whipped through them, in spite of the fact that the furniture sat complacent and intact, the dining table and ladder-back chairs, the couch in the living room, the lamp in the corner. In this room he had once said to his wife that he liked that Kierkegaard's name meant "churchyard." Lauren had rolled her large eyes and said, "That's so like you, Tyler. The name means 'graveyard.'" Remembering this, he frowned. They'd had a real squabble about it. What *was* a churchyard, after all, he had argued. A graveyard, yes, but what was wrong with preferring the sound of the word "churchyard"? Why did she have to insist on "graveyard"? And what had she meant? "That's so like you, Tyler." It was like being pinched, he thought now. Little pinches unexpectedly in his marriage. "Reverend Don't Make Waves," she had called him once. He could not remember why.

The kitchen door slammed.

"Oh, my goodness," said Connie, when Tyler stepped into the hallway. "The wind just did that, just as I came in here. The wind's picked up out there."

"Well, Connie Hatch," said Tyler, "how awfully nice to see you."

IN THE CLASSROOM on the top floor of the Academy, Charlie Austin faced his senior Latin class. Toby Dunlop had not done his homework, and he bent his head over his desk after the confession had been forced by Charlie. The other students sat sprawled in their seats, only a few glancing at Charlie. But his silence, as it continued, made them uneasy, and they stopped rustling their papers, their notebooks, the girls stopped pulling at their kneesocks. They had been translating one of Horace's odes. "What shame or limit should there be to grief for a person so dear? Teach the songs of mourning—" and the fact that these students showed so little interest made Charlie want to go to the window and smash the glass with his fist. He had often felt sympathetically toward these kids, their youthful unknowingness, their polite, deferential desire to please. He had wanted—at times as much as he wanted anything—to give them the beauty of this language, the poetry from centuries before that could speak to their own nascent needs.

The fact that on this wintry autumn day they had not been able to attend to what he said, that in fact they had not (for it was not just Toby Dunlop) bothered to finish their assignment, filled Charlie with images of violence—a munitions dump exploding, glass flying through the air. "Class is dismissed," he said, and he was gratified in a tiny way by the quiet sense of amazement that followed this. "I mean it," he said, waving an arm. "Get out of here. I can't teach you if you don't do your part. So go away. Go home, go sit in your cars, go wherever you want. But this class is over." He picked up his books and left.

In the library, he went to the dictionary and looked up the words "nervous breakdown": "Any disabling mental disorder requiring treatment." Charlie looked at this for a long time, taking the dictionary with him to the window seat of the library. Mrs. White, behind the desk, smiled at him.

"Requiring treatment." That simplified things, since he would have no treatment. He knew a fellow veteran in Togas hospital who'd been shocked; they stuck a piece of rubber in his mouth, turned on the switch, the guy crapped all over the place, and now he just sat in a chair all day. Charlie long ago had stopped visiting him. No, there would be no treatment.

Charlie pondered the other words. "Mental disorder." The whole world had a mental disorder. It was the word "disabling" that was dangerous. He pictured a wheelchair, his head drooping down to his chest as he sat in it. Pretty goddamn spooky. Disabling. He flipped through the pages of the dictionary, looked "disable" up: "to make unable; cripple, incapacitate," or "2) to make legally incapable, disqualify." So a mental disorder that incapacitated him. Which meant, Charlie thought, closing the dictionary, taking it back to the book stand, that one just kept on going. He nodded toward Mrs. White.

The sun set quickly this time of year: it rested on the horizon a minute, then sank like a huge stone. Charlie got into his car and drove home. Seeing the lighted windows made him want to weep; he understood that were he ever to leave, this image before him, the small gray house with its white shutters, the juniper bushes to the side, the blue spruce by the porch—this image would haunt him forever.

"Doris," he called, walking through the door. "Doris?"

His older son was watching television. Charlie walked past, up the stairs. Doris was standing in the bedroom. "Do you think I don't know?" she said. Her lips had no color, and he had the sense that someone had suddenly poured water on him; he could barely stand up. Doris yanked back the quilt, the sheet, and pointed. "Do you think I don't hear you, awake at night? Do you think I don't know what you're lying there doing *right next to me*? At first I thought, Well it happened in his sleep, no one can help what they dream. But then I checked every morning, and a new stain, every morning, and I started lying awake pretending I was asleep, and I could hear you.

Last night I heard you, Charlie, and then even this morning early! Are you a pervert, for God's sake? Are you, Charlie?"

"Doris, keep your voice down."

"I know perfectly well you're not thinking of me when you do that. Who are you thinking of?"

"Doris." He stood there, his coat still on, still holding his briefcase.

She stepped toward him. "I can't slap you," she said fiercely, "because the kids are downstairs, but I would like to slap you until you fall over." She followed him as he tried to move away from her, and pushed him hard.

"Jesus," he murmured, hunching over. "Jesus, Doris. Please stop."


TYLER WAS NOT in the business of converting people, and the fact that Connie had not been to church for many years was not something he would have thought to ask her about. He was surprised when she said one morning, "Why did Jesus say to love our enemies?" She had just cut two squares from a pan of coffee cake that sat on the kitchen table between them. She licked the knife and looked at him.

A pattern of frost, like tiny snowflakes, spread above the corners of the kitchen window, and a wind blew, so that even with the storm window, a cold draft leaked through. Connie put the knife down and tugged on the cuffs of her woolen sweater.

"Because it's easy to love our friends."

Connie took a big bite of coffee cake, pressed the tip of her finger into the brown sugar left on the plate. "Not for me," she said. "It was hard for me to love my friends. And now I don't have too many anymore."

He watched her.

"I got jealous of them," she said, eating the brown sugar from her finger. "They have kids, they have houses. Some even have mother-in-laws they can stand."

Tyler nodded.

"When I was a kid," Connie continued, "I knew a really fat woman. One day she said to me, 'Inside me is a slim, beautiful girl.' " Connie took another bite of coffee cake. "And then she died," she added, wiping crumbs off her fingers.

Tyler set his coffee mug down quietly. "And inside you is a mother?"

"That's right," said Connie. "Just like the fat woman. And then I'll die." She shook her head. "I've dreamed about those kids so much, Mr. Caskey, I've practically thought they were real. Jane and Jerry are their names. Nice kids. Well behaved."

"I've always liked the name Jane," Tyler said.

"Yuh." Connie wiped at her nose with a tissue. "Well, I've lived in a dream world."

The minister looked out the window. "I think people often do."

"Sometimes I don't even know what's true and not true. What I've done, or haven't done. The mind's a funny thing, isn't it?"

"It is."

"It's like we have to make things up to keep on going. Pretending we did do this, or didn't do that."

He looked back at her; her wet eyes, as she smiled at him, seemed to be winking.

"What dreams keep you going?" she asked.

Tyler pushed back his plate of coffee cake, cleared his throat. "Oh, sometimes these days I dream of going down south to help the ministers with the Negroes there. They organize sit-ins at the counters in five-and-dime stores."

"I know. I've seen pictures. But sometimes those people get beaten. Sometimes the ministers go to jail. You'd want to do that? Godfrey. I'd rather die than go to jail."

"I'm not crazy about that part," Tyler admitted. "But it's an awfully good cause."

Connie nodded, stared at her coffee mug. "Well, I'd sure miss you," she said.

*Out of the abundance of the heart the mouth speaketh.* "Yes," Tyler said. "I don't think you need to worry. I'm not going anywhere. I've no one to watch the children, and—" He raised his eyebrows. "The truth is, Connie, I'm in debt. I'll be staying right here for some time to come, and when the church gives me a few more dollars, I can give *you* a full-time job. If you're still interested."

"Oh, I am."

Washing the bathroom floor, Connie felt as though Scotch tape had been removed from her eyes. Everything now had a vividness; each tile she wiped clean seemed to have its own loveliness. Later, with a small whisk broom, she swept the mopboards of the upstairs hallway. The light above the stair landing cast a friendly feeling over the worn carpet runner; the wallpaper, with its thin blue stripes, seemed the cozy color of butter. And yet it was odd. Because accompanying the sense of lightness Connie felt in the minister's house these days was a seeping upward of dark things, as though the warmth of the man's friendship was like the sun on a field of snow, beneath which things deep in the soil were affected. Long-ago terrors from childhood, disappointments from her years of marriage, more recent anxieties and confusions, were all tucked down inside her, and, changing the sheets on Katherine's bed, Connie wished she could weed out these deep shoots of darkness. She thought of the minister saying how that Bonhoeffer fellow had thought forgetting was a gift. Tossing the pillow on the bed, she nodded. She straightened the pillow, gave it a small punch.

Meanwhile, Tyler worked at his desk, and was glad to hear her footsteps on the stairs, the whisper of the whisk broom, the slight clumping of a pail, as he wrote a list of things to include in Sunday's intercessionary prayer.

- All those affected by the steelworkers' strike
- Negroes in the South who were visited daily by hatred, and found the courage to continue their quest for dignity
- The family of George Marshall, recently deceased, winner of the Nobel Peace Prize

Tyler tapped his pencil. Bertha Babcock had said on her way out of church last week, "I wish you'd say a prayer for Bob Hope, who just lost the sight in his left eye," and Tyler said, "Certainly." But he did not want to include Bob Hope, and he put his pencil down.

The telephone rang. "Reporting in, Tyler," said Ora Kendall. "The Ladies' Aid, that little coven of witches, is having a fight, a revolution to match Cuba's."

"Oh, dear," said Tyler.

"Irma Rand thinks it would be nice to have one of those little billboards out in front of the church. I think it would look like a movie theater. What do you think?"

"Well, Ora, I guess that's for others to decide."

"Have an opinion, for crying out loud. It's your church."

"Actually, Ora, the church belongs to the congregation."

"All right. Don't be surprised when you drive by and see a sign that says COME IN AND HAVE YOUR FAITH LIFTED. Doris is still mad at you because you haven't said anything about the organ."

When he hung up, he added Bob Hope to the list, and then, hearing the little bell ringing, he went into the kitchen for his lunch. He wanted to tell Connie that of course the steelworkers' strike couldn't be settled, when the congregation of one small town couldn't even agree on a billboard. He wanted to tell Connie that Doris Austin dreamed of a new organ as much as Connie dreamed of children. He wanted to tell Connie that the Ladies' Aid was gossiping about Katherine. He wanted to tell Connie everything! But a minister had to be careful. So Tyler said, "Will you be seeing your sister at Thanksgiving?" as he picked up his grilled-cheese sandwich.

"No." Connie shook her head. She told him, in between bites of her sandwich, how her sister had, during the war, gone to live with their Uncle Ardell on a potato farm up north. There were German prisoners working the farm and Becky got pregnant by one. She stole money from Ardell and followed the man back to Germany after the war, but it turned out he was married. Connie propped both elbows up on the table and looked at Tyler. "A terrible, terrible mess. Adrian won't have anything to do with her, I guess because of the German."

"What happened to the baby?" Tyler asked.

"She lost it." Connie drank some tomato soup from a mug in a big swallow. "Had it lost, is more the truth. Went to someone who did those things. And then she bled and bled and almost died. But she didn't die. She's still up there, living over the bar."

Tyler straightened the napkin on his lap. Connie looked at him carefully, leaning toward him slightly, over the table. "Don't you see?" she asked.

"See what?"

"I come from a family of sinners."

"Oh, Connie," the man said. "We all do."


ON THE PLAYGROUND, Mary Ingersoll watched to make sure no child ate snow, but she was thinking of her wedding day three years ago. A winter wedding in New Hampshire; there had been candles in the church, and she had a white fur muff to tuck her hands into on the way to the reception. She had never felt so pretty, she thought, glancing around the playground, and maybe she never would again.

With her galoshes and brown wool coat, a scarf tied around her head, she felt matronly. This was the word that went through her mind, and she didn't like it. It puzzled her, but she felt as though the long road of her life that lay ahead, that long, open-ended road where all sorts of wonderful things could happen (because she was young and wouldn't die for *ages*) had curved around, and so many things were now decided. That delicious question—who will I marry?—had been answered. That delicious desire—I will be a teacher!—had come to pass. She hadn't had her children yet—there was still that—but sometimes, like this morning, she had a momentary shiver of some irretrievable loss, and even as the principal, Mr. Waterbury, raised a cheerful hand and she waved back, she longed, in some deep part of her, to bury herself in a grown-up's lap.

Katherine Caskey took a nasty spill. A group of boys had been running, and one knocked into her—it was an accident, but Katherine, so little, had been pushed right off her feet. She fell and banged her head against the metal pole of the swing set. Mary saw this, and ran over. "Katie," she said, "are you all right?" She picked up the little girl, whose crying was genuine and full. "Let me see your head, honey," Mary said, smoothing back the girl's hair, but glad to hear the crying, because in these cases of a bang on the head, it was a good sign. "I think you're all right," Mary said. "But let's see if you're getting an egg." She set the girl down gently and felt for the spot. "That was scary, wasn't it?"

Katherine nodded, still crying. There was the blur of a blue jacket, Martha Watson's voice singing as though she owned the whole playground: "Teddy Bear, Teddy Bear, turn around! Teddy Bear, Teddy Bear, touch the ground!" Katherine stepped closer to her teacher.

And Mary Ingersoll experienced a fullness of feeling that included the sweet edge of relief: She was not a matron headed down a dead-end street. *This* was her job, to care for this child, and she could do it well. The child's earlier obstinacy made the victory greater; what Mary felt was love. "Blow your nose," she said, bringing a tissue from her pocket, and Katherine blew. "There's the bump," said Mary, feeling Katherine's scalp. "How many fingers am I holding up?"

Katherine looked. She held up three of her own.

"Good girl," said Mrs. Ingersoll, officious and teacherly. "Very scary to get knocked over like that." She started to hug the girl again.

But Katherine was suddenly remembering how her father had said, "I didn't think she was any prize." She stood stiffly, not crying anymore.

"Katie?"

The girl turned away.

"Katherine?" Mrs. Ingersoll touched the tiny shoulder, and was amazed when Katherine turned once again, sharply away. It hurt the woman's feelings. And when Katherine, running now, turned her head and stuck her tongue out at her teacher, Mrs. Ingersoll felt a swell of swift anger. "Katie Caskey, that's rude!" she yelled.

Katherine kept running.


TYLER DROVE HOME in silence, the child next to him. He kept hearing the voice of Mary Ingersoll, high-pitched, like shards of glass. He pictured her speaking to him in the hallway outside the nurse's room, her face closed off, lacking any vestige of warmth.

"But is Katherine all right?" he had asked.

"I doubt she has a concussion. But is she all right? I told you before she is not all right. There are agreed-upon rules of social behavior," the young woman had said, looking at him with cold eyes. "And sticking out your tongue at people isn't one of them."

"Did Katherine apologize to you?"

"She did not."

"Could you give us a moment, please?" And he had taken Katherine down the hall and whispered fiercely in her ear. "You apologize to Mrs. Ingersoll, or I will spank your bottom when we get home."

The child stared at him, her pale lips parting. Back they went to Mrs. Ingersoll. Looking down, Katherine said a barely audible "I'm sorry."

As he walked the child across the parking lot, he pictured telling Mary Ingersoll that, *by the way,* there was no point in her coming to church only on Christmas and Easter. The point in coming to church was to learn the Christian rules of behavior of love and understanding. The point of coming to church was to take into your heart the troubles of a little girl who had lost her mother. He suspected that Mary Ingersoll was on her way, right now, to tattle to Rhonda Skillings. It made him sick.

Through the bare trees, the horizon seemed to leak a pale, watery yellow that spread upward into the gray sky. A squirrel ran across the road. "Why did you stick your tongue out at Mrs. Ingersoll?"

The child didn't move or speak.

"Answer me."

Katherine whispered something.

"What was that?"

A tiny voice, not looking at him. "I don't know." She sat with her red boots stuck out in front of her, staring at her lap.

"Katherine. Do you feel like you might throw up?"

She shook her head.

"Do you feel sleepy?"

She shook her head.

He reached over and put a hand on her tiny knee; she turned her head toward the window. "Kitty-Kat," he said. But he said nothing more. As he turned in to the driveway, he saw the light was on in the living room, and in the kitchen, too. He followed the child inside, and saw that she had wet her pants. "Go upstairs, Pumpkin," he said. "You're going to need a bath."

Connie looked up from polishing the table. The room smelled like lemons. Tyler stood still, letting her gaze meet him straight on. Then he walked past her, unbuttoning his coat, and he thought of the line from Matthew: *I was in prison, and you visited me.*

ALL NIGHT IT SNOWED, slowly at times, then quickly. It didn't taper off until dawn, and in the morning everything was white, fields of white snow so brilliant in the sunshine you had to look away because you could go snow-blind. The evergreens had their branches weighed down by the stuff, and the back roads were narrow, only as wide as a snowplow. Mrs. Carlson's car drove slowly in to the driveway.

Katherine pushed back her bowl of Alpha-Bits and got down from her chair. "Wonderful out there," her father said, opening the door for her. He had not bent down to zip up her coat, and the winter cold blasted Katherine's front while the brightness of the new snow made her eyes twinkle and swirl—she felt she had become a pinwheel, and it scared her.

She reached for her father's hand, but felt the plastic handle of her lunch box instead, and her father's voice far above her saying, "It reminds me of snow days when I was a kid, and we'd build snow forts all day." He was calling this out to Mrs. Carlson, perhaps.

Her father a kid, building snow forts—all this belonged in a world outside her own, which carried in its tiny globe the smell of the Carlsons' car, which she would have to soon climb into, the gritty sand that waited on the floors in the backseat, the freckled, stunned face of the Carlson boy, who was peering right now through the car window, whose eyelashes always had crusty stuff in them.

Her father was not walking down the steps. She stayed with him, the cold air going straight through her dress, the hole in the knee of her tights. "Katherine. Are you?" He had asked if she was going to be a good girl today, and the question brought back the astonishing thing he had said to her in the car yesterday. Her father had said the word "bottom." That he would spank her bottom. Embarrassment so deep it had no equivalent to any earlier shame in Katherine's short life brought a color to her cheeks as she stood on the porch.

She nodded her head.

They walked down the steps together, and she climbed into the car.

TYLER WENT INTO his study for his morning prayer. It was Friday, and Connie would be here soon. He read from Winkworth's translation of the *Theologia Germanica: When a man truly findeth himself utterly vile and wicked and unworthy, he falleth into such a deep abasement that it seemeth to him reasonable that all creatures in heaven and earth should rise up against him.* Tyler glanced at his watch, thinking perhaps Connie had had trouble with her car in the snow. *And therefore he will not and dare not desire any consolation and release.* But it was unlike her not to telephone. He lifted the receiver and heard the dial tone. *And he who in this present time entereth into this hell, none may console him.*

When later he tried calling her, nobody answered.

She did not show up.

ON SATURDAY NIGHT, after the children were in bed, and while a light snow fell outside the darkened windows, Tyler sat in the living room with his mother. Margaret Caskey said nothing. Leaning her narrow shoulders forward, she put the cup of tea Tyler had made for her onto its saucer there on the coffee table. Then she took a hankie and touched it to her lips.

"Mother," Tyler finally said, "are you all right?"

"I guess," she said slowly, her eyebrows rising high, "I've never heard anything so ridiculous."

"How is it ridiculous?"

The woman stared off into the corner of the ceiling as though transfixed by a strange spiderweb that only she could see. She put her head back, studied the ceiling above her, before looking back at her son. "You amaze me, Tyler. We think we know someone, but we don't. I guess we never really know someone."

The stinging pain beneath his collarbone began. He rubbed it with his thumb. "Tell me," he said pleasantly, "why it's a ridiculous idea."

"Oh, the stars in heaven, Tyler. That woman has the education of a twelve-year-old. She has no children of her own, she's married to a man who drinks. I can only imagine what her home life is like. She's odd, Tyler. Where does she come from, anyway? And you're going to entrust your children to her?"

Now it was Tyler's turn to be silent. Disappointment seemed to pour through him like an astringent.

"Have you already broached this idea to her?"

Tyler nodded.

"My word, Tyler." Margaret Caskey's eyes were shiny. "Well, you'll simply have to tell her it's not going to happen."

"I think the children need to be together."

"And they'll be together as soon as you find yourself a proper wife."

The word "proper" was like a small stone hurled across the room at him; he leaned back in his rocking chair. His heart was beating quickly.

"You've been through a great deal," his mother conceded. "But the back strengthens to the burdens it has to bear, and I'd like to see a little more backbone in you."

"How," asked Tyler, "am I not showing backbone?"

"You've lost weight. You're a big man, and big men need the meat on them or they look ill, and you look tired all the time. It's very clear that, except for when I come here on weekends, you do not take care of yourself, sleeping in that study, for heaven's sake." The woman's voice was trembling, and she nodded with a sharp, vehement gesture toward the study door. "Not even living as a civilized man. And Katherine," she added, "so sulky and unpleasant now—"

"Her mother died."

"Tyler, you've grown vulgar. I'm aware that the child's mother passed away. And it's awful. It is awful. But this happens when God so chooses. What I'm trying to point out to you is that you can barely hang on these days with one child in the house, and now you're telling me you want two. Aren't you grateful that Jeannie is happy? And she is happy. I take very good care of her."

"I know you do."

"I don't know, actually, Tyler, if you do know. You say Connie could watch them during the day—but you have no idea, men don't, how much work a baby is twenty-four hours a day." The woman put her hankie to her mouth again, and Tyler saw her hand was shaking. She added, "You've given me quite a shock."

"Yes. I can see. And it's the last thing I intended to do." But it was difficult to speak these words. His mouth was very dry. "Let's leave it alone for now," he offered.

"I try," his mother said, "to help. I try to do my little bit."

"Yes," Tyler said. "And I'm grateful. We are all grateful."


*And seekest thou great things? Seek them not.*

Tyler had slept very little, and he stood before his congregation feeling as though his eyelids were coated with sand. His sermon, a permutation of the unfinished On the Perils of Personal Vanity, was called Is There Meaning in the Modern Age? Paul Tillich, Tyler said, clearing his throat, believed that anxiety was the phenomenon of modern man. And why shouldn't it be, Tyler asked, when modern culture has allowed us to worship ourselves? Why wouldn't we be suffering anxiety? The age of science, natural and social, has allowed us to believe the mystery of who we are can be explained, instead of *celebrating* these discoveries as a further example of the mysteriousness of God. Why shouldn't we be anxious when we are told that love is nothing more than a self-serving mechanism of nature? When we are told that the world's ills lie in suppressed memories of childhood? But the son of King David, Solomon, one of the wisest and richest kings in ancient times, a man who had never heard of Khrushchev or atom bombs or hydrogen bombs, never heard of Galileo (who kept his faith right to the end), had never known any physics or biology or psychology—this man, writing the books of Ecclesiastes, asked some of the very same questions being asked today. And concluded that, without the ability to view life as a gift from the hand of God, all is vanity and vexation of spirit.

Tyler, knowing his mother was sitting in the back, over toward the right, glanced up toward the left instead, and saw a new-comer—a woman seated in the back row, touching an open palm to the back of her head.

Tyler straightened his shoulders, read on. "When a doomsayer told Ralph Waldo Emerson that the world was coming to an end, Emerson replied, 'Very well, we'll get along without it.' " Bertha Babcock, bless her old schoolteacherly soul, let out one sound, like a faint honk, which he took to be a chuckle, but, glancing up, he saw only blank, unsmiling faces. On he went. He heard his voice grow louder. When he glanced up again, his jaw felt as though it had wire in it, and when he saw Charlie Austin watching him with cool disdain, saw Rhonda Skillings squinting toward the window, he paused for a rather long moment, before saying, "Christians are now wrangling with insufferable sentimentality. The ability to love appears to be a simple possibility. But who among us can argue that while we ought to love one another, *we do not?*"

He stepped away from the pulpit, and said, "Let us pray." Right before he bowed his head, he realized that the newcomer in the back row was the woman from the pharmacy in Hollywell.

"KATHERINE," SAID ALISON CHASE in the kinderkirk room, "it's your turn to wear the blindfold." The woman held a scarf in her hand and approached Katherine. Katherine stepped back. "Now, stop it," said Mrs. Chase.

Terrible, but a tiny ferociousness had taken hold of Alison this morning. When the minister brought Katherine to the kinderkirk room, holding a wriggling Jeannie on his hip (who would be taken in a moment to the room across the hall, where the Austin girl took care of the toddlers), he had said, "Alison. Hello. Say, thanks again for that apple crisp," then adding over his shoulder, "it was really *delicious.*" And it just made Alison mad. He could thank her, but he didn't have to lie.

Katherine Caskey may not have been Alison's favorite child, but the woman had felt some degree of pity for her. She did not feel that way today. Today she felt she didn't like the girl, who always, when she saw Alison looking at her, turned away. "Katherine, look at this sign the class just read," Alison said. Alison had worked on it the evening before. THIS IS LOVE OF GOD; TO KNOW HIS COMMANDMENTS. I JOHN. The exercise included leading the children around blindfolded so they could learn about faith and obedience.

"What's that of?" asked Martha Watson, pointing to a new picture on the wall.

"That," said Mrs. Chase, "is a picture of the Christians waiting to be thrown to the lions. Back then, if you were a Christian, the Romans wanted to kill you." The children in the room had become quiet. "They put you in a cage, and a guard would come and ask each person in the cage, 'Are you a Christian?' And people prayed for courage not to deny our Lord. When the brave person said, 'Yes, I am a Christian, I believe in Jesus Christ,' he, or she, for they did this even to old ladies, would be taken into a big arena, just like a football field, and the lions would eat them. While people cheered."

Some of the children sat down in the little chairs. One boy made a sound like a roaring lion. Martha Watson said, "Cut it out, Timmy."

"Come here, Katherine," said Mrs. Chase, walking toward Katherine, holding out the scarf. Katherine flailed her arms and started to cry.

CERTAINLY NO ONE knew what it cost Tyler to give a sermon. They were not ministers—how could they know? Many Sundays he felt ill, a peculiar kind of exhaustion washing through his bones. Other times he felt a manicky high, as though some inner furnace had its thermostat turned up, and he would take long, fast walks, or in summer months, ride his bicycle for miles. But often—and especially these days—he would feel undone. He felt this now as he walked across the lower parking lot, while his mother went to fetch the girls from Sunday school. His limbs seemed filled with wet sand, and he would not go to coffee hour.

Standing by his car was the woman from the pharmacy. She wore a navy-blue coat, and she smiled at him with a composure he found notable. Tyler extended his hand. "I believe we've met before."

Her face was plainer than he remembered, ordinary and pleasing. Her eyes were smaller than he remembered, too. "I'm Susan Bradford," she said. "Gosh, I hope you don't find me too forward, but we both know Sara Appleby, I think."

"Yes, we do, and no, I don't."

"I hope your little girl's feeling well," the woman said. "She was having stomachaches, but that was weeks ago, wasn't it?"

"Oh, she's fine. She's doing fine." The minister's eyes rested on her for a moment, then traveled slowly around the parking lot, the horizon, the trees, the blue sky. Far off in a parked car was a motion, and he saw that Charlie Austin was reading the paper. Tyler turned his tired eyes back to Susan Bradford. "What would you say to coming back and joining us for Sunday dinner?"

She followed in her car while Margaret Caskey turned her head and spoke to the girls in the back. "You are to be very, very good. We're having company for dinner. Katherine. Do you hear me?"

"Mother—"

"Tyler." She spoke firmly, looked at him severely. "I'm glad I cleaned up the house this morning. I slept so poorly. I'm glad we have that ham steak."

In the rearview mirror he saw Susan Bradford put her blinker on, following him down Stepping Stone Road; a careful driver, to put her blinker on—there were no other cars in sight. He always did the same, put his blinker on, even with no other cars in sight. How Lauren had hated that.

"Oh, for God's sake, just go," she would say.

"This isn't Massachusetts," he would answer.

The world, with its pale noonday light washing down through the mostly bare trees, seemed filled with invisible currents—strips of knowledge he seemed unable to get hold of. He glanced again in the rearview mirror. Katherine was staring down at her hands, then she looked out the window, and her eyes, even with her bangs falling over her face, shone with a deep, hard thoughtfulness. "You all right in the backseat there, Kitty-Kat?"

She nodded, still looking out the window.

AS HIS WIFE AND DAUGHTER set the table, Charlie stared at the wallpaper print above the wainscoting. A pale-blue print against a white background. He felt like he'd never seen it before. Vines? A trumpet wrapped in vines? He coughed.

"I've asked you twice now," said Doris. "Are you coming down with a cold?"

"I'm not coming down with a cold," he said.

"If you're coming down with a cold, you shouldn't go to Boston next week. I still don't understand what kind of meeting this is. Who cares what the Massachusetts Language Arts Council is doing?" Doris set a plate of sliced bread on the table.

"So help me God, Doris. I'm not coming down with a cold. And I'm not explaining the goddamn meeting again." Charlie seated himself at the table, where a pot roast steamed on a plate in the center. He couldn't catch his breath, and coughed again. He knew this feeling of sponginess in his windpipe meant that he was going to lose his temper in a bad way, that slivered images would arrive in his head, small Filipino soldiers eating the horses they had shot, the jungle on fire, smoke so black when those ammunitions dumps got hit, all that horror swirling around in the back of his head as he stared at his older son now, who had taken a piece of bread and was eating it furtively, ducking his head, the bulbous end of his nose red. Charlie found the sight so repulsive he could have thrown the pot roast across the table, smacked his hand against the poor kid's head. He seemed to shake with the effort it took not to do this, and when the kid looked up at him, frightened, despair filled Charlie.

"Your man Caskey sounded like a damn fool today," he said to Doris. His voice was thick with disgust because of wanting to yell at his son. "Halfway through that puke of a sermon he starts acting like he hates us all—did you notice?"

"He's not my man." Doris placed a bowl of cooked carrots on the table.

"I thought you loved Reverend Caskey, Mom." Lisa was feeling pretty today; she pulled herself back as her little brother squeezed by, her breasts like small funnels beneath her white sweater.

"I do not love Reverend Caskey."

"You don't?"

Doris didn't answer. Her mouth was in a straight line.

"She doesn't?" Lisa looked at Charlie. He shrugged.

"Well, his kid was crying today," Lisa said, folding the paper napkins into triangles. "Not Jeannie, who's cute. But Katie spit at Mrs. Chase and I heard some mother say Martha Watson was so scared of Katie Caskey she didn't want to come to kinderkirk anymore."

"Lisa, you should be careful what you repeat."

"No, Mom, it's true. Katie ripped Mrs. Chase's scarf, too."

"Oh," said Doris. "This is sad."

"Sad," said Charlie. "I'll tell you one thing, Doris. If you died, I wouldn't let these kids go around spitting at people."

"Charlie, stop." Doris sat down at the table.

"I'm not going to stop. I told you from the very beginning, when everyone was so gung ho—Tyler Caskey's not the man he appears to be." He saw his kids watching him with some uncertainty. "Lisa, hand me your plate." Charlie felt all snarled up—he wanted, right now, an alliance with Doris. Knowing he would see the woman in Boston next week, knowing that Tyler might view Doris as some beaten-up housewife, made Doris, and the pot roast steaming before her, appear pathetic and touching; he felt oddly protective of her.

"The trouble with Tyler Caskey," he said, handing Lisa a plate of pot roast and sliced carrots, "is that he wanted to be a big frog in a big puddle, but he could only be a big frog in a little puddle."

"I don't like to think of West Annett as a little puddle," said Doris.

"It's not a little puddle. It's not little enough. That's my point. He needs a congregation of about three people who will sit there and adore him. Oh come let us adore him. And he doesn't give a damn if you get an organ you can play," Charlie added. "And he can't even take care of his kids."

"Goodness, Charlie. That's pretty severe."

"Ah," said Charlie, putting a slice of pot roast on a plate and handing it to his wife, "he's just an ordinary guy. Who isn't as great as he thinks he is."

This might have done the trick, calling him ordinary, for Doris had not thought of Tyler as ordinary. She seemed to ruminate on this, and nodded slightly. "Well, it's a shame. No matter what the circumstances, it's never a happy thing when your child goes around screaming and hitting."

"It wasn't only Martha Watson who started to cry; some other kid said she was scared of Katherine." Lisa tossed back her hair.

"That's dumb," said her older brother. "How can you be scared of a kid that weighs six pounds?"

"Easily." Lisa scowled at him. "If you're only six pounds yourself, she can be really scary. And you should talk. Just a few years ago you'd whimper every time you saw Toby Dunlop on the playground."

"Stop," said Charlie. But they finished the meal like they were a family, and Charlie had stopped coughing.

TYLER REMINDED HIMSELF that he had simply invited a guest home for dinner, but he couldn't stop thinking they were auditioning for parts. Susan Bradford was dressed for the part—in her navy-blue turtleneck and a navy-blue skirt that widened over her expansive hips. She wore a string of pearls and a wristwatch with a thin black leather band. Politely, she offered to help Margaret Caskey in the kitchen, was politely refused.

"I hope you don't object to instant mashed potatoes," Tyler's mother said.

"I eat them all the time. And I love ham with pineapple. At least let me help set the table." She gave Jeannie the spoons to carry into the dining room, and when Jeannie banged them on the oak leg, Susan looked at Tyler and laughed.

He said, "Katherine draws wonderful pictures."

Susan said, "Oh, I'd love to see some," but Katherine shook her head once, moving away. "I'll see your pictures another time, then," Susan said.

As they settled themselves at the table, Tyler just about to say grace, the telephone in his study began to ring. "Excuse me a moment," he said.

"Tyler. We're eating. It can wait." His mother looked at him with a quick look of severity.

"Excuse me a moment," he repeated, rising, smiling at Susan, putting his napkin down by his plate.

He heard his mother say, "He's very conscientious, I'm afraid."

Adrian Hatch was calling to say that Connie had disappeared. Did Tyler have any idea where she might be? Tyler held the phone, staring down at his desk. "But have you called the police?" he finally asked.

No point in that, Adrian answered. It was the police who were after her.

*Book Two*

## SIX

Lauren's home was brick, three floors high, in a neighborhood south of Boston where the houses were not small and the lawns looked as though they had been brushed and combed. Standing in the foyer that first time, Tyler had felt a shadow of loneliness fold over his heart as he gazed at the ornate furniture, the Persian rugs, the tall windows with their long pale-green drapes, the dark stillness of a huge hallway table. But Lauren, rushing down the large central staircase, throwing her plump arms around him, was a shower of sun. "You're here!" she cried, and Mrs. Slatin stepped back as Lauren kissed him on the mouth. "I love you!" Lauren said.

"Let him get his coat off," her mother said. "Would you like a drink, Tyler, after your long ride? A martini, perhaps?" It was one o'clock in the afternoon. Tyler sipped a Coke in the family room, seated on a rose-colored sofa, answering politely when Mrs. Slatin asked him about his studies, his year in the navy, his sister. "And what does her husband do?" the woman asked, fingering her pearls, leaning forward with a kind of exaggerated enthusiasm, as though talking to a child.

"Tom drives a bus," Tyler said.

"I see."

Lauren had slipped off her shoes and was sitting next to Tyler with her feet tucked under her. "We took a field trip once when I was in elementary school, on a bus," Lauren said. "Remember, Mommy? And I threw up."

"You were always throwing up," her mother said. "You were always an easily excitable child. Tyler, enjoy your pistachios. Then I thought we'd drive into Boston for lunch."

Lauren's sister, a tall, slim young woman, joined them. She said hello to Tyler, and then said nothing else, but sat in the front seat while her mother drove, looking out the window. Lauren held Tyler's hand in the backseat. He thought Mrs. Slatin's perfume smelled like bug spray mixed with baby powder, but he was not used to perfume. They ate in the restaurant of a large department store, and, except for the waiters, Tyler was the only man there. He had not been in such a place before.

"Lauren said your father was an accountant. Your mother must be a brave woman to soldier on, losing her husband early."

"Tyler took care of her," Lauren said.

"We all took care of one another," Tyler answered. He closed the large menu. "The way families do," he added. He ordered a turkey club sandwich, and the waiter brought it to him with a silver covering. The women ate fruit salads, Lauren reaching over to his plate to help herself to bits of his sandwich.

"You have no manners," the sister told her.

"Oh, it's quite all right," Tyler said. "I can't eat this whole thing." He had lost his appetite. Nearby, a woman his mother's age with very blond hair was applying lipstick while gesturing with her free hand for the waiter to take her plate away.

"Somehow I doubt that," Mrs. Slatin said, smiling at him with those warm brown eyes. "You're a big man. Just like my husband. We like our men big, don't we, Lauren?"

"Don't forget you said we'd get those earrings, Mommy," Lauren said.

"Jim Bearce wasn't big." The sister announced this slowly, placing an accent on the word "big," and giving Lauren a heavy-lidded gaze while touching her fork to her fruit salad.

"Maybe you could shut up," Lauren said lightly. "Or maybe not. Maybe you and I could sit here and talk our pretty little heads off."

Discomfort touched Tyler like a fine dust on his face. Mrs. Slatin kept smiling. "Tyler has big shoulders just like your father, girls."

That Tyler resembled Mr. Slatin was mentioned more than once in the year to come, though he could not see it himself. Only that they were both, as Mrs. Slatin had said, large men. But Mr. Slatin had a somber fierceness to him, a darkness like the sister. Lauren was all light. Tyler had never met anyone from whom such light shone. When she left the room, the house loomed large and strange once again to him, seated before the fireplace with his future father-in-law.

"Why," said Mr. Slatin, a martini held in his big hand, "did you not go to Andover Newton for your seminary training? It's an excellent school."

"It is. But my mother needed me nearby." Tyler had not applied to Andover; he would not have gotten in. His grades were nothing special. He felt the man looking at him, taking this in.

"That was an erudite sermon you gave, however, young man, the first time we clapped eyes on you in that little seacoast church." Mr. Slatin dipped his head to drink from his martini. "Cheap grace and costly grace. I'm afraid I got left behind. Cheap grace means forgiving yourself? Did I get that point right?"

"Yes, sir." Tyler felt himself flush. "Essentially."

"Essentially."

Tyler studied his fingernails. Never defend your sermon, George Atwood had said. Never, ever get involved in that.

"Well," Mr. Slatin said, "I'm sure you'll be very successful. We preferred Lauren go to Simmons." Tyler looked up and nodded. "An all-girls' school was best for her," the man said. He leaned back, stretched his beefy legs before him, stared at the fire. "You'll have to stay on your toes with her, Tyler. She has a recklessness. You may or may not have noticed." He looked at Tyler sideways, and there seemed to Tyler to be some element of pride and some vague unsavoriness wrapped around the remark.

"Lauren is wonderful," Tyler said.

A round table, twinkling with plates and silverware and crystal goblets, sat waiting in the dining room. He had never seen so much silverware, and watched carefully to see which of the three spoons was used for the soup, which fork for the salad, which knife to tackle the lamb chops with. Mr. Slatin used his fingers to eat the lamb chops, but Tyler did not. The napkins were a nylon, gauzy material that could not possibly, he thought, absorb anything.

"It's a goddamn mess over there in the Middle East," Mr. Slatin said. He ate with his head bent over his food. "Don't you think so, son?" He glanced toward Tyler.

"Leave him alone, Daddy."

Mr. Slatin ignored his daughter. "What's your feeling about Truman telling the Brits to let in all those Jews to Palestine just so he could capture the vote? And did you see that picture?" Mr. Slatin reached for the plate of lamb chops. "Counterrevolutionaries in China being set for execution while the crowds cheered?"

"No," Tyler said. "I didn't see that."

"It's a corrupt world," the man said. "It always has been. Human beings aren't worth much." He wiped the gauzy napkin across his lips vigorously. "Don't you think so, son?"

"I think human beings are worth a great deal," Tyler said.

The sister smirked and rolled her eyes, but Lauren said, "Stop it, stop it, stop it—why don't you leave Tyler *alone?*"

"No one's bothering me, Lauren."

"I thought I'd get new curtains for the sitting room," Mrs. Slatin said, smiling at the maid who came to clear the plates. Tyler was light-headed by the time the peach cobbler had been taken away. Mrs. Slatin said, her brown eyes sparkling, "Why don't you and Lauren take your coffee into the living room, have a few moments to yourselves?"

Lauren closed the French doors to the room and whispered, "I *hate* him."

"He's your father, Lauren. You can't hate him."

"I can so, and I do. And I hate my sister, too. She's always been jealous of me 'cause I'm prettier." She took the cup and saucer from Tyler's hand and kissed him. On the couch beside her, his arm around her, Tyler said quietly, "Lauren, I can't offer you any of this, you know," nodding around the room.

"I don't want any of this. I want you. And I don't want to be married in the stupid old Anglican church here. I want to be married up at Brockmorton. I want to get *out* of here."

"There's no stopping Lauren when she's put her mind to something," Mrs. Slatin said later, when this had been disclosed. "Get married wherever you want to, dear."

"You'll save me some money," her father said. "Our friends aren't going to want to drive all the way up there."

"So it will be small," Lauren said, thrusting her chin up. "And sweet as can be."

But there was a reception held at the Slatin home a month before the wedding. "This will give our friends a chance to meet you," Mrs. Slatin explained. Tyler drove down with his mother, and Belle and Tom arrived later. Mrs. Slatin asked Mrs. Caskey to help tie a small ribbon around each napkin that would be placed on the long hallway table when the guests arrived the next day.

"Tyler, old boy," said Mr. Slatin. "How about you and I go into town and buy a new suit?"

Margaret Caskey's mouth, as she arranged the napkins, stayed closed, but Tyler saw her jaw drop, making her thin face elongated. "Oh," Tyler said, "I guess I'm fine with this one, thanks."

"Do this as a favor to your new mother-in-law and me," the man said. "A wedding present from us. A new suit."

"Is there anything wrong with Tyler's suit?" Margaret Caskey asked quietly.

"No, no. I just never had a son, you see," the man said to her. "It will be an experience for me."

"Let Daddy buy you a new suit," Lauren said. "Even though your mother and I know you don't need one. You are the handsomest man in the world."

"I have a little present for you, Lauren," his mother said. And she gave Lauren a book, *The Pastor's Wife*.

"Oh, what fun!" Lauren said. "Tyler, look!"

The next afternoon Tyler stood in his new suit next to Lauren, outside on the combed-looking lawn. Lauren's sister held a camera to her face, aimed it at them. There was a picture of just the two of them, a picture with just his mother, then a picture with Belle and Tom, then a picture with all of them. Tyler smiled and smiled, his arm around Lauren. Lauren's sister, squinting through the camera, said, "Everyone say, *'Shit'*!"

Mr. Slatin laughed, and yelled, "Shit!" Tyler, shocked with the horror of having his mother hear the use of such language, kept smiling, but after the picture was taken, he could not look at her.

As the guests arrived, Tyler shook hands again and again, finding what he had always found to be generally true: If you are friendly to people, they are friendly to you. He said to his mother afterward, as they sat in the big living room, "That was nice, don't you think?" He glanced at her, but she did not look up from the tissue she held clenched on her lap.

"Very nice," she said.

Belle and Tom said their good-byes and drove home, and Margaret Caskey went off to bed. As Tyler sat with his arm around Lauren, his future in-laws resting across the room with drinks in their hands, Mrs. Slatin said, "Oh, that was so rude of the Tibbetses."

"What, Mommy?" said Lauren, yawning.

"I've always hated the Tibbetses," Mrs. Slatin explained to Tyler. "Well, not always. We used to be good friends. But they went on to a different crowd, joined a different country club. I only invited them out of respect for old times."

"What did they do?" Lauren asked.

"Oh, they were rude."

"They stood in line at the buffet table," said her father, "watching your new sister-in-law, what's her name, there? Belle. Looking at Belle and Tom, looking them up and down, and then they said to each other, not softly, 'What rubes.' "

"You just ignore them," Mrs. Slatin said to Tyler. "Goodness, I am one hundred and twenty percent wrung out. I'm going to turn in." She stood up, and Tyler stood.

"Thank you," he said. "And good night." He turned to see Mr. Slatin's eyes following Lauren's hips as she walked with her mother across the room.

THEY LIVED, THAT FIRST YEAR, in an apartment on the top floor of an old wooden house near Brockmorton while Tyler finished his studies. Lauren, who said she had never cooked a meal, bought a cookbook and made lists, bought groceries, and fussed in the kitchen at night, presenting Tyler with plates of fish and beef, and showing the delight of a child when Tyler praised the food. The next day, when Tyler came home for lunch, they would sit on the couch and eat leftovers. "Tell me everything," Lauren said. "And don't leave anything out."

He told her of the recent excavations that proved King Solomon had been as rich as the Bible said. They had discovered stables for four hundred and fifty horses, and sheds for a hundred and fifty chariots. "They say that horses were treated better than humans."

Lauren tucked her feet under her. "Even better than his seven hundred wives? Tyler, what would you do with seven hundred wives?"

"Be busy, I expect."

"You would do nothing, because I would kill you."

"Then perhaps you should be the Queen of Sheba."

"Yes, yes, yes, I am a queen." Lauren took their plates back to the kitchen, twirling around.

Every part of her was dear to him. The sight of her full hips as she walked back and forth in the kitchen stirred him with longing. The wet footprints left on the floor after she bathed gave him a sense of sweet fortune. She giggled at his astonishment the first time she danced for him unclothed. "You're a wonder," he said. "The inhibitory section of your brain is missing."

"No." She stopped her dancing and looked at him with serious innocence. "No, Tyler. It's just that I love you so much."

"Well, then," he said as seriously, "I praise God."

She laughed and clapped her hands. "Oh, let's praise Him!" she cried, and came and sat on his lap.

On Saturday mornings, Lauren slept late and Tyler would go to the bakery at the bottom of the hill and buy doughnuts and the newspaper. Lauren would just be stirring when he arrived back, the blankets piled over her head. He would undress and get back into bed. "Let's do this when we're eighty," he said one morning, smoothing back her hair from her moistened face. "Yes, oh, yes," she said. And why wouldn't they? World without end—their happiness.

He walked across campus with the sure steps of someone possessed with a sense of rightness. If, at times, the picture of his mother's worried face floated across his mind, he was able to dismiss it. He was living and loving as God had chosen him to do. And there were times, as he walked down the steps of a classroom building, and felt the sharp, cold winter air stab into his nostrils, that The Feeling would come to him. Life, he would think. How mysterious and magnificent! Such abundance! With all his heart he praised God. His own specific history was unfolding.

"Oh, I missed you!" Lauren would say, even if he had been gone only for the afternoon.

"Are you restless?" he asked. "Because I'm sure you could work in one of the offices."

"I'm not restless. I missed you because I love you so much. No, I don't want to work in any office. Tell me everything."

He told of a discussion in Calvinism class regarding the notion of sin and depravity in man, the Atonement of Christ, the notion of predestination. "Get to the good part," Lauren said, eating a cookie. He told how a man's stomach had growled so loudly during a lecture on Christian ethics that the professor had stopped and demanded the poor red-faced fellow go get something to eat.

"But I thought you were all supposed to be nice," Lauren said, eating another cookie.

"I know. But they're not. Some professors are dried up and

stingy. That fellow whose stomach growled is very sharp in systemic theology, by the way."

"And *you* are good at homilies!" she said. "You are the best speaker on this campus. Even Daddy knows that."

She left the bathroom door open, talking even as she urinated. She called him a prude when he closed the door when using the bathroom himself. "I may be," he admitted.

At night they lay in bed while she read to him from *The Pastor's Wife*, the book that his mother had given her. " 'Chapter One,' " Lauren said. "Oh, I love this, Tyler. 'As a Worthy Woman. The girl who marries a minister must expect to be a marked woman.' Marked with what, Tyler?"

"Beauty." He leaned over to kiss her.

" 'Chapter Five. As a Financier. She looketh well to the ways of her household, And eateth not the bread of idleness.' " Lauren was silent for a moment, reading. "Wait, Tyler," she said with some alarm. " 'First set aside a tenth for the Lord.' Do we have to do that?"

"Don't worry," he said.

"It says we should always have a can of fruit cocktail in the pantry in case someone stops by."

"That's easy enough."

"I get scared."

"Oh, no," Tyler said. "Lauren, you'll make a beautiful minister's wife."

"Look at the picture on the back of the book. She looks like a horrible lesbian. Am I going to end up looking that grim?"

"Never." Tyler reached over and turned out the light.

"Daddy said Mrs. Tibbets is a lesbian."

"Why?"

"Because she was the first one to complain about him."

"Complain about what, Lauren?"

"That our house wasn't a nice one for girls to come to. Because Daddy would give us baths."

"How old were you?"

"Oh, I really don't remember."

"Honey, what are you saying?"

In the dark she snuggled close to him. "I'm saying this: I hate everyone but you."

EARLIER THAN PLANNED, she became pregnant. Lauren went to Boston to shop for maternity clothes with her mother, and came back with so many boxes that the bus driver raised his eyebrows at Tyler as he pulled one after another from the storage compartment in the bottom of the bus. An uneasiness rolled through Tyler that he ignored, and when she tried on all the new clothes for him that night, he told her again and again that she looked beautiful.

He was ordained in a service that made his mother's eyes glisten. His in-laws did not attend. Offered the job at West Annett, he and Lauren prepared their move, and drove one morning to see the farmhouse on Stepping Stone Road. They stopped at a diner, where Lauren ate two fried eggs and a piece of pie. "I'm hungry as a bear," she said to the waitress, who didn't seem to care.

Back in the car Lauren sang. "Two little honey bears, happy as can be. Two little honey bears about to be three." She fell silent, though, as Tyler drove slowly along Upper Main Street, past the Academy, the road becoming narrow, up the hill past the lake, back down around Ringrose Pond, and then along the stretch of road where the trees grew close enough to block the sun on the road before them. But back out into the sun, and there was the old Locke place.

"Gosh," said Lauren. "It's kind of far from anyone."

"Don't worry," Tyler said, turning in to the driveway, the tires crunching.

"I guess it's better," said Lauren. "I guess I don't want to be plunk in the middle of the ladies in town."

The house sat. It was not welcoming or unwelcoming, just old and silent, with its broken front railing and tilting porch steps. The Caskeys got out of the car slowly. Lauren hung back as Tyler fiddled with the keys, and then he realized the kitchen door was unlocked, and he pushed it open. "You have to carry me," Lauren cried, holding out her arms.

"Then I wish you hadn't had pie for breakfast." Tyler picked his bride up in his arms and stepped or, rather, stumbled, over the threshold into the little mudroom.

"It smells," Lauren said softly, as he set her down.

"Let's open the windows," Tyler said, and he moved into the kitchen and opened the window that looked out onto the driveway. The window was old and rattled in its casing.

"It smells like death," Lauren said. "Tyler, I don't like it." She began to cry.

BUT MRS. SLATIN arrived for a visit, and took Lauren shopping for curtains, a bathroom rug, a crib, dishes with apples painted on them. And when Mrs. Slatin left, saying, "Well, you won't be here for long, dear. This is just temporary," Lauren said she wanted the horrid old place painted pink, she couldn't stand it, and so Tyler asked the church, and then painted the walls of the living room and the dining room pink. "Perfect!" Lauren said. "I love you!"

Joy filled him, and trepidation, for the job of being pastor of this church was, for Tyler, an assignment of great seriousness. He was moved by the kindness of his parish, how they sometimes left notes for him by his office in the church, saying how his sermon had touched them. He was moved by the Ladies' Aid inviting him to one of their meetings; he stood, the only man among them that day in the activities room, singing with them "What a Friend We Have in Jesus," then eating sugar cookies from a paper napkin on his knee. When he suggested to Lauren that it would be good if she started a prayer group, her eyes grew very round, and she said, "Oh, dear God, no." And so he let it go. She would be a mother soon. Life had moved up upon him in a wave of seriousness and wondrousness, and he felt he had indeed left childhood behind.

Prayer—his own morning prayer—took place in the church sanctuary, where he sat alone each morning. He loved the slightly musty smell, the simple lines of the tall windows, the rows of white painted pews, the air seeming to hold within its quietude all the prayers and hopes and fears of those who for the last century and a half had sat humbled on these benches before God. If someone happened to enter, Tyler would look up and nod, and if they wanted, he would pray with them. He felt immensely blessed to have this job.

He had tried, at first, to pray at home in his study with Lauren. She did not pray with him, as he had hoped. She said she prayed on her own, even though when they lived near Brockmorton, she would go with him sometimes into the chapel and sit with him in prayer. But in West Annett, when he tried to pray in his study at home, he was aware of her in the kitchen, wondering why she was making so much noise with the pots and pans, and when he stepped into the kitchen to say, "Lauren, is everything all right?" she said, "Yes, go away. Go back in there and pray. Or whatever it is you do."

He had a great deal to do. It was a small parish, but he needed to acquaint himself with the board and the deacons and the various committees; he went over the membership files, the records of pledges, the church school enrollment, old reports to area ministers. He spent time with the secretary, Matilda Gowen, a pleasant, elderly woman who came to the church two mornings a week to mimeograph the programs and send out letters and make calls to a plumber if something leaked, though the sexton, Bruce Gilgore, did a good job of keeping the building in shape. Tyler wrote sermons, rewrote them, committed them to memory, made sure to be available to anyone who needed his pastoral counseling. And people did. His first month there, a tractor turned over on the Taylor boy, crushing his leg, and Tyler spent hours in the hospital waiting room, praying and talking with the boy's parents. The woman who ran the small post office came by one day and said when she was in high school she had given birth to a baby boy and put him up for adoption. Did Tyler think she ought to tell her husband?

He was daunted by these responsibilities. But he found that through careful listening, the answers came to him. A good doctor knows the patient holds the diagnosis, George Atwood had said to him, and the postmistress, as it turned out, wanted to tell her husband, and did. It had a happy ending.

Another woman came into his office to say that her neighbor, the widow Dorothy, was wandering the back roads at all hours. Tyler paid the widow a call, and found her daughter was there, spending the day with her small children running about the yard. "Oh, upstairs," he was told casually, when he inquired about Dorothy. He found the old woman tied to a chair in her bedroom. She looked at Tyler with the complacency of a young schoolgirl. "My wrist hurts," she said simply. And so Tyler telephoned the woman's other daughter, who lived in Connecticut, and eventually the poor widow was sent to the county farm, which Tyler found to be such a horrible place that he could visit it only infrequently, and even then for a very short stay. This sort of thing troubled him a great deal. Had he done the right thing? Was there really no money from the Connecticut daughter with which to care for her mother?

The postmistress came back to tell him her husband had taken the news well, and she had one other confession: There had been a second child by a different man a year after the first. Should she tell her husband about that as well?

Mostly, he listened. And spoke of God's enduring love.

He and Lauren were invited for dinner a number of times. At Bertha Babcock's house, Lauren sat on a stuffed sofa and said, "Oh, I hated English class," when Bertha spoke of retiring after forty years. "We had this stupid old woman who used to prop her breasts up with the spelling book." Bertha, who was a heavy-breasted old woman herself, flushed deeply, and for a moment Tyler had a sense of things not being real.

"You see," he said to Bertha, "how lucky your students were to have *you*. Nobody would hate English class with you, I'm sure."

"I hope not," said Bertha, "but apparently you never know."

"This blueberry pie is delicious," Tyler said. "I imagine Lauren would like the recipe."

Lauren looked at him, at Bertha. "Okay," Lauren said.

But Bertha's husband helped out. "Lauren, I bet you were a live wire," he said, and smiled broadly, his teeth crooked and stained from years of tea-drinking.

"I suppose I was," Lauren said.

Tyler said nothing to Lauren afterward; he had made the decision he would not censor her. She was who she was, a bright-faced, beautiful girl, and if she said things that seemed the wrong thing to say, well—he was not going to fight about that.

What they fought about was money. He drew up a budget to show Lauren how much could be spent weekly on food and other things, and she was aghast. "But what am I supposed to do if I want something?"

"What do you want? Tell me, and we'll decide together."

"I don't want a budget! I don't want to be told, 'You can only spend this amount.' "

"But, Lauren, we only have this amount."

"The baby will need things!"

"Of course the baby will need things. And we'll get them." He had a small amount of savings from his summer preaching jobs, and from part-time work he had done in the library as a student. But he learned fairly soon that he couldn't talk to Lauren about money without it becoming a fight. And he did not want the money problems to scrape against the sweetness they had shared.

A few times he arrived home from a meeting and found her in tears. "Oh, my dear," he said. "What is it?"

Lauren shook her head. "I don't know," she said. "But I'm bored. You're away all day, or even when you're here, you're in your study working."

They would go sometimes to see friends of theirs whom Tyler had gone to college with, or they would go back to Brockmorton for dinner with the Atwoods. But she needed someone in town with whom she could talk. He understood this, and he was sorry that she could not discuss anyone in town. "A minister's wife can't gossip," he told her.

"But gossip is the only kind of conversation that's fun," she wailed.

"Then gossip with your college friends when you go back to Boston to visit. You just can't gossip about anybody here."

"You mean I can't find out some woman was tied up in the attic and *tell* anyone? Or that Lillian Ashworth had two babies when she was just a kid?"

"Well, no, Lauren. You can't."

She was weeping now. "Tyler, those women in the Ladies' Aid are gruesome. They never *laugh*. They have these coffee klatches and talk about how to freeze blueberries, and their houses are dark and cold, and it's—it's just horrible."

He knelt before her. "We'll go to a movie in Hollywell this weekend. Would you like that?"

She smiled through her tears. "You big old lumpy teddy bear," she said. "Why did I ever marry you?"

He leaned back on his heels. "Why did you?"

"Because I love you, you big old idiot."

"And I love you. And you can gossip with me all you want."

"Okay," she said, brightening. "Tell me what you learned today. Tell me everything and don't leave anything out."

Tyler sat on the couch beside her. "I learned that Matilda Gowen fell in love with a lobster fisherman when she was a young girl, and her parents were against it, and sent her to England to cool her heels. Then she came back and married Skogie."

"Okay," Lauren said. "That's good. Where did you get that?"

"Ora Kendall."

"Oh, I love it," said Lauren, clapping her hands. "Imagine Matilda as a young girl. She must've been pretty. She has nice skin."

"It seems she taught in a one-room schoolhouse on Puckerbrush Island, and I guess this fisherman was hired to take her across to the island every day, and then pick her up when school was over."

"Oh, imagine!" Lauren hugged herself. "Imagine Matilda, young and pretty, and maybe her skirt would have been long, and was whipped around her ankles by the wind as she stepped out of the boat. Teaching a roomful of kids, and then walking back along a path with wild rosebushes, thinking about her fisherman, and there he'd be, with his big rubber boots on, and help her into the boat. I wonder if they did the whole thing."

"That I don't know, but I doubt it."

"Yes, but you can never tell, Tyler. They must have, or her parents wouldn't have sent her off. Maybe she had a baby in England, maybe that's what she was doing there. When did she meet Skogie?"

Tyler shook his head. "I've told you all I know."

"Well, that's good for one day. Not bad, Ty-the-pie." The feel of her arms around him was joyous, as natural as blue sky. And then she found a friend.

CAROL MEADOWS WAS a quiet woman, who had a lambency in her large brown eyes and a creamy luminescence to her skin. She was in her early thirties, though she could have passed for ten years younger, and there was in the soft gentleness of her motions something otherworldly. This may have been the result of what happened a few years before the Caskeys moved to town: Carol Meadows had put her baby down for a nap, and, looking in on her just a little while later, had found the child unbelievably, inexplicably dead. Carol had three more babies in a row, but she tended to keep to herself, her husband and children being almost exclusively her world.

The Meadowses lived in a small red-shingled house far out of town on a hill with a wide sweep of sky, and a view that looked out over pastures and trees. The discreet pleasantness of the place was somewhat marred by the four large lightning rods attached to its roof, their thrust and size and vehemence seeming to say, "We are ready for any attack!" At the Academy, where he taught science, Davis Meadows was thought to be strange. He kept on his desk a human bladder inside a jar of formaldehyde, and spoke obsessively of entropic doom, and also the effects of the hydrogen bomb in Hiroshima. If Carol had known of her husband's reputation, it wouldn't have mattered. Her heart was an open and loving one, and its ache, which had promised to be immutable after such a loss, eased into a consecration of this man; they were bound by this. She took his fear of disaster quietly in stride, saying nothing about the ugliness of the lightning rods, or the expense of having seat belts installed in their old car, and when he had a bomb shelter built behind the house, she took that in stride, too, and bought the cans of food, the cots, the candles, the board games. And during the summer months she agreed to never have the children play in the little plastic pool unless her husband was home to help watch them.

Whatever instinct it was that drew Lauren Caskey to her, it was a good one, for Carol's sense of discretion was natural and deep, and except for her husband, Carol repeated to no one the things she learned.

"Good God, I had no idea you were so far away," said Lauren Caskey that first day, sitting down and pulling off a red high heel, giving it a shake. "I don't want to run my stocking." She had picked her way across the gravel to get to the front door, and Carol, watching through the window, had felt a pang for this young woman so wrongly dressed in a linen maternity suit with red piping, wearing red, shiny high heels, a red pocketbook on her wrist. "I got lost," Lauren said, accepting the coffee poured. "My God. You make one wrong turn out here and you could be lost for days. None of the roads have names. Why in the *world* don't these roads have names?"

"Everyone's lived here so long, they know where the roads go."

Lauren opened her red pocketbook, brought out a compact. "It doesn't seem friendly not to name the roads. Can I use your bathroom? Does it flush right?"

Carol pointed with her coffee spoon. "As far as I know, it should be all right."

"Some of these old houses up here, the toilets scare me to death. Did you know Bertha Babcock has one that's meant to look like an outhouse?"

"Well, Bertha loves history," Carol said.

"What a cute place," Lauren said, when she emerged. "Tyler hates it when I pee with the door open. Does your husband mind? Truthfully? Tyler can make me feel terrible."

"Oh, I'm sure he doesn't mean to."

"I don't know. But I hate that smelly old farmhouse they stuck us in."

The next time Lauren showed up, the sky outside the window had an opalescent quality to it, and because, to Carol, the sky was like a friend, she pointed it out to Lauren. "Oh, lovely," Lauren said, without looking. "I'm so fat I feel like a cow. I could be lying out there in your pasture."

"But you're going to have this baby soon. Really soon," Carol added. Lauren wore a soft-blue maternity dress, and her bulging front had lowered.

"Gosh, he fills that right up," Lauren said, nodding toward the playpen between them. Matt, Carol's youngest, lay sleeping on its floor.

Carol nodded. She didn't say that when he had his nap she could not have him out of her sight.

"Do you mind if I smoke a cigarette?" Lauren was opening her pocketbook, a blue one today. "I don't see any ashtrays."

"I'll get you one."

"Tyler hates it, so you're not to tell. He says it looks very bad for a minister's wife to be smoking."

Carol set an ashtray in front of her. "Tyler's sermon on Sunday was marvelous. People are really impressed, Lauren. And his prayers—"

"He writes those himself," Lauren said, exhaling like a woman who knew how to smoke. "People might not know this, but a lot of ministers aren't original. They have books and magazines filled with published sermons and prayers, but Tyler writes his own."

"He's gifted," Carol said. "And speaking without notes."

Lauren nodded, the hand with the cigarette placed over her huge stomach. "Yeah, people like him. They're coming to him with their problems, you know." She held up a hand. "Don't worry. I'm not going to repeat a thing."

"Oh, no, you mustn't," Carol said.

"Can I say one thing, though?"

"Lauren, someone in your position must be careful."

"I'm only going to say Bertha Babcock's pie crust could break your toes." Lauren flicked an ash into the ashtray. "When you eat it you feel like someone's being mean to you. How come you don't belong to the Historical Society, or any group?"

"I like to be here in the evenings with Davis. And during the day he has the car."

Lauren rubbed her large, tight stomach. "You're lucky, then. Those church women—oh, I'm not going to gossip. But Carol"— and Lauren's eyes seemed to squint in some confusion—"they don't *like* me."

"They just have to get used to you. You're fashionable and pretty—"

"Well, they could be, too, if they tried."

"It's different," Carol said, but she knew these women did not think of themselves as unfashionable, and Carol didn't think of them that way, either.

"You don't find them a little . . . grim?"

"Oh, well. They are who they are, that's all. They're nice women, really."

"You think that Jane Watson woman is nice?" Lauren opened her eyes wide. "Carol, she'd just as soon sell me to the Russians!"

Carol burst into a laugh. "And what does she think the Russians would do with you?"

"I don't know. Make me into a satellite."

"Oh, Lauren," the woman said kindly, "you really are funny. Tyler's very lucky to have you."

"I'm glad you think that," Lauren said. "I really am." She pushed aside her blue pocketbook, gazed down at the sleeping Matt. Then she looked around, out the window, back to Carol. "But can I just ask you?" she said, with seriousness. "What do you *do* all day?"


WITHOUT REALIZING IT, he had expected to have a son, and when the doctor came out to the waiting room to announce he had a daughter, there was a strange moment of confusion in Tyler's mind. But when he was allowed to see the baby through the glass, her perfect, calm, sleeping face filled him with such awe that tears rolled from his eyes. "*You're* the baby," Lauren said, when she saw his wet face. "For crying out loud. Please don't do that again," she said, reaching for the water by the bed stand. "I have never seen a grown man cry, and I don't care to see it again."

Her mother arrived for two weeks, assuring Lauren there was no reason to nurse—it had gone out of fashion, thank God, since it made your breasts so droopy—and Tyler was shooed to the side as the women moved about, heating bottles in a pan of hot water on the stove, running the washing machine all day, diapers chugging away. "You're really roughing it up here in the woods, aren't you?" Mrs. Slatin said to Tyler one day, smiling her smile that he had come to dislike, seeing behind the brown eyes something hard and intractable. He went to the church to stay out of her way.

Once, arriving home, he found Lauren and her mother making fun of a pair of pink knit booties given by a member of the church. "Can you imagine putting such a scratchy thing on a sweet baby's foot?" Mrs. Slatin said.

And Lauren said, "Oh, Mommy, if you could have seen the awful baby shower they gave me. Such grim politeness—no fun at all!"

Mrs. Slatin went home. But then his own mother arrived, and, after two days, Lauren whispered to him fiercely, "I want her out of here. She thinks the baby is *hers*."

"Oh, she'll be gone soon," he said. "I can't just kick her out."

"You certainly can," Lauren said. And then: "Or maybe you can't. God, you are such a scaredy-cat sometimes."

The next morning at breakfast, while Lauren stayed upstairs, he said, "Mother, you're a big help, you really are. But Lauren is anxious now to do the job alone."

His mother said nothing. She put her coffee cup down, rose from the table, and went to pack her things. He followed her out to her car. "Mother, really—please come back quite soon. You know how it is—she needs to get a schedule going on her own."

Without a word, his mother drove away.

He telephoned Belle from the church. Belle said, "Tyler, she did this to us all the time growing up."

"Did what?"

"The silent treatment."

"She did?"

"She sure did. Welcome to the club. Tom'd just as soon take a baseball bat to her head."

"Belle, good Lord."

"Tyler, good-bye."

At the baptism, performed by George Atwood, both families seemed congenial, and Tyler gave great thanks. He thought, watching the child held in Lauren's arms, standing next to the chapel window that said WORSHIP THE LORD IN THE BEAUTY OF HO-LINESS, while George Atwood was bringing his daughter into the community of Christian life, that it might have been the happiest moment of his life.

Still, the baby's crying frightened him. Sometimes she cried for more than an hour, her tiny face wrinkled in a rage that astonished him. "What does she want?" he asked.

"I don't know," Lauren said. "Can't you see I'm trying to fig-ure it out? I've fed her, burped her—I don't *know.*"

In the middle of the night he would walk the floor, holding Katherine, her little head over his shoulder. As soon as she quieted and seemed ready to sleep, he would try placing her back in her crib. She would wake and cry out. Lauren, appearing in her house-coat, would say, "You're doing it wrong, Tyler. Go to bed." He was glad he was not a woman; it seemed to him their job was immeasur-ably more difficult than a man's. But he wanted his wife happy.

And at times, it seemed she was. As Katherine grew and began to sleep at least five hours straight through, Lauren's spirits lifted, and she would coo and tickle and nuzzle her nose in the baby's neck, or kiss her toes one by one. "Who's the most beautiful baby in the world?" she would sing. "Who's Mommy's prettiest baby in the world? Let's go see Carol today. Tyler, I want the car today."

CAROL MEADOWS RETAINED the impression that some deep un-happiness nipped at the heels of Lauren. Lauren showed off her new baby, undressing her completely, saying to Carol, "Did you ever see a child more perfect?" And then wrapping her up again. But the woman could barely sit still. She walked back and forth, the infant held against her, poking her head into the other rooms of the house, saying, "Oh, can I just have a look?" Walking into Carol's bedroom, she said, "What a cute little pot of rouge. I never see you wear makeup."

"Once in a rare while." Davis sometimes liked Carol to make herself up in their private times.

Lauren's voice came through the open bedroom door to where Carol, in the front room, bent over Matt in the playpen. "Tyler said I might want to start a prayer group. Can you imagine?" Lauren stepped back into the living room. "I told him, 'Tyler, I'd rather die.' You don't mind if I smoke again, do you?"

Carol brought out the ashtray. "I'm sure Tyler understands that now is the time for you to be a mother. The prayer group can wait."

"It can wait," Lauren said. "Boy, can it wait."

At night Carol told Davis that the girl had an essentially good heart. Davis said, "And where is your heart? Let me find it." Later, he said, "Is she too much for you, honey? She seems to come here a lot."

"It's all right. She's lonely."

But it was a burden, to hear everything that Carol heard. "My parents didn't want me to marry Tyler," Lauren said a few days later. Her little baby had just fallen asleep on the nest of pillow and quilt Carol arranged for her. Lauren's finger was lightly stroking the baby's head.

"But Tyler's a lovely man," Carol said.

"My father called him a rube." Lauren still stroked her baby, not looking up. "My father said he didn't send me to Simmons to marry a small-time rube minister, but if I wanted to throw my life away, it was up to me." Lauren stretched her legs out, then stood up swiftly. "My father said it's not too late, if I still want to come home."

"Do you want to?" There was a slightly sick feeling in Carol's stomach.

Lauren shook her head slowly. "My father gives me the creeps, and my sister hates me. And my mother is a little bit of an idiot, frankly. I guess I'm staying here."

It was either that night, or close to it, that Carol happened to notice her little pot of rouge was gone. She looked in the bathroom, each bureau drawer, behind the bureau, where it might have fallen. Davis was scared one of the kids had taken it and would eat the stuff, so they asked each child carefully if he or she had seen Mama's pot of rouge. All shook their heads solemnly. It was gone.

TYLER WAS AWARE those days that alongside his sense of joy—of abundance—was a feeling of being left out. The cozy world he had lived in with Lauren, as though the two of them shared a warm cocoon, was no longer there; or if it was, it was the baby, and not he, who shared it with his wife. "Let's go out for dinner," he suggested. "Just the two of us. A date." Lauren shook her head without looking at him.

"And leave this child with a teenage girl? Never."

But his congregation continued to love him. On Sunday mornings he assured them that only what *came from* a man could defile him, not what happened *to him*. He told them how the business of man's life was to seek out and save in his soul that which was perishing. He spoke to his congregation of cheap grace and costly grace. He reminded them of the Doctrine of Justification, of their Covenant with God, and that we must not think that because of these gifts from the Almighty, we could bestow grace upon ourselves. Cheap grace was this—the preaching of forgiveness without requiring repentance. Costly grace was when you paid with your life, as Jesus had paid with his. Costly grace was the gift that must be *asked* for. Oh, Tyler loved this stuff—and because of that, because he loved it, and believed it, and spoke of it with a quiet fervor, they seemed to listen to him; and those who hadn't understood completely might wait and speak to him after coffee hour, or sometimes telephone him in his office. "You've helped me," a parishioner sometimes told him. "You've helped me be more patient with my father." And he would feel enormously glad.

But the gladness did not last. He had an odd relationship with praise. Often it did not seem to do anything but swoop by like a yellow streak of light, bouncing off him. Sometimes, even if he had no reason to, he doubted the person who gave it. And yet he could see, too, that in some cases it was not only sincere but so heartfelt that the person speaking it seemed to experience frustration beneath the taciturn New England countenance, and this caused Tyler unease as well. What was best was when he was safe up on the chancel, speaking to them honestly, letting them take what parts they would, or could.

The child's first Christmas they spent in Massachusetts, where Tyler was appalled by the massive number of gifts beneath a tree that was loaded with tinsel and twinkling lights and enough balls and decorations that the green boughs could barely be seen. Lauren opened one dress box after another, clapping her hands. For the baby, there was a music box, a jack-in-the-box, rattles, dolls, small dresses. For him there was a wallet of nice leather. They drove up to his mother's that night. Her tree was small, and had nothing but a few gold balls on it. Beneath the tree was one gift for each of them. The baby was given blocks made of mahogany. The next morning, driving back to West Annett, Lauren said, "Your mother makes me feel like crap on toast."

"Lauren," he said. He had never heard her speak that way.

"She does. What's wrong with a little fun? What baby wants blocks with no color or letters or anything? And a plain black belt for me. I'd just as soon hang myself with it."

"Lauren, stop. Good Lord."

"And she hates me."

"How can you say that? Lauren, that's not true."

She didn't speak for the rest of the drive, the baby asleep between them. "Anyway," he said, as they pulled up to the farmhouse, "next year we're not going away. The parish shouldn't have a visiting pastor on Christmas day." By night they had made up.

And he marveled at the child. She pulled herself up and held on to the railing of the crib. She let go of the arm of the couch one evening, and took her first step. Soon, he could not even remember her as a baby. "Goggie, goggie!" she would scream happily at the sight of the Carlsons' dog loping alongside the road. "Dama!" she would announce, smooshing a banana between her small fingers. By the time she was three, Lauren had her in church, sitting in the third-row pew with her sock-doll and her blanket. "You are my best friend," Lauren would say to her, rubbing noses. "You are my very dearest friend in the world. And you're such a good girl you can sit in the big people's church. No kinderkirk for you."

Frequently Tyler walked into town in order to let Lauren have the car. "I can't be stuck here all day," she said. He wished she was more active in church affairs, but it was clear they didn't interest her, and he knew she was busy with the child. He was glad she went to visit Carol Meadows, but he worried that she drove the car too much; they seemed always low on gas. And he could not ignore the fact that she bought things more and more. She bought bracelets and barrettes, brassieres and stockings, shoes and blouses. "Lauren," he said, "we simply can't afford all this."

She cried, and then they would have to climb and stumble their way through an argument before they made up. But these scenes left him queasy for days; things were said that stung him bitterly. "You make me live like an animal!" she cried. "No television set, a horrible old washing machine, and I have to look at magazines that show these sweet pink washing machines, and women in pretty dresses, and if Daddy didn't give me money, I'd never even be able to buy myself some perfume!"

He did not want her father giving her money.

"Why?" she demanded. "It takes away your stupid masculinity?"

Later, when they argued about money, she simply said, "I don't want to hear it," and would turn away.

He understood that he would eventually have to move on to a larger parish, where there would be more money and more people for Lauren to be with. But he loved the town of West Annett. He loved being far out in the country, walking to town with his boots squeaking on the packed snow. He loved the faces of his congregation as they looked at him each Sunday. He loved the smell of coffee in the activities room later, moving among the people, asking about their children, their work, their car troubles, for someone was always having trouble with their car.

In the summer he loved swimming in the lake, bicycling for miles on a Sunday afternoon to unwind after his sermon. As he pedaled past farmhouses, large fields of young corn, seeing the winding stone walls that went off into the distance, he would feel The Feeling, and give thanks for God's beautiful, beautiful world. On Sunday evenings they had pancakes for supper, and he would take Lauren in his arms.

But something was gone. When he said to her, "I love you," she would smile and not answer. When he asked if there was something wrong, she would shrug and move away. Uneasiness sat at the table with them, got into bed with them (she no longer wanted him to touch her breasts during lovemaking), uneasiness was there in the morning, when he stood in the bathroom and shaved. But then Lauren became pregnant once more, and he thought he felt happiness sweep through the farmhouse again.

—

CAROL MEADOWS HEARD a great deal about Margaret Caskey. "She's mean," Lauren said, while Katherine and Matt played on the floor with pots and pans, stacking them high until they crashed down, then stacking them again. "Just as cold as a witch's tit."

"That's sad for Tyler," Carol said.

"He doesn't notice. He doesn't notice anything, except how much gas I've used in the car."

Carol did not want to hear this. What Carol wanted to say was that marital happiness, in her opinion, was not so hard to achieve. It was a matter of giving yourself over. One reason that Carol did not involve herself more with the women in town was that she didn't like how they complained about their husbands. "Why, they wipe the floor with them," she had told Davis. Arguments over replacing a toilet-paper roll—this sort of thing did not make sense to Carol. She thought if Lauren was using too much gas, she ought to try to use less. This petty kind of tug-of-war could chip away at married life; could certainly affect how they felt toward each other in bed, and for Carol, all levels of her intimacy with Davis felt to be a gift that she would not think of harming.

After returning from a visit to Massachusetts, Lauren said to Carol, with tears suddenly coming into her large brown eyes, "Tyler got my father very angry." A streak of black mascara very slowly made its way down Lauren's cheek before she rubbed it off with a tissue Carol handed her.

"Oh, dear." Carol sank back into her chair.

"Tyler said . . ." Lauren opened her compact, touching the skin near her eye with the tip of her fourth finger; it was a natural and elegant gesture. "Tyler said he preferred not talking politics, but went ahead anyway." A tiny shiver of pain moved across Lauren's features as she snapped the compact shut.

"Did they have a serious argument, or just one of those blustering times men sometimes have?"

"I don't know. Blustering, I guess. I was trying not to pay attention because it's *boring*, but Tyler, you know, it's embarrassing sometimes, but he talks about religion."

Carol nodded kindly. "Men like to talk about their work."

"But *religion*, Carol. I'm sure it's much more interesting to hear Davis talk about science."

"Religion is interesting. It seems to me it's very interesting."

Lauren ran her hand through her abundant hair, pink nail polish showing through. "And my sister went to bed with Jim Bearce."

Carol waited. "Is Jim her fiancé?" she finally asked.

"No. Jim was supposed to be my fiancé."

Carol reached over to hand the children each a graham cracker. "Jim is someone you loved, then."

"I guess so. Yeah, I did."

"And what happened?"

"My sister—oh, she's such a cretin, Carol—my sister told him I'd had all these other boyfriends."

Carol did not know what to say.

"And it's true. I had a lot of boyfriends. Tyler doesn't know that. Do you think he should know?"

Carol's face grew very warm. "I think what matters is what you and Tyler feel together now."

"So my sister told Jim, this was a few years ago, and Jim said, well, he couldn't marry someone like that, you know. And now she's gone to bed with him."

"How do you know?"

Lauren looked up at Carol, her big eyes glistening. "She *told* me last week, when I went home. As if this horrid scene with Tyler and my father wasn't enough, she told me in the bedroom when I was packing up the baby's things that, oh, by the way, she'd gone to bed with Jim Bearce. And that Jim said now he'd had both Slatin girls he could see what everyone meant."

"Lauren, this is disgusting. Who is this man?"

"A Harvard law graduate." Lauren looked exhausted now, and waved a hand. "Oh, it doesn't matter. Don't tell anyone what I said."

"Of course not."

"And then I had to listen to all that crap—Tyler saying how Karl Marx said all sin was committed in the name of religion, or something, I mean, Carol, who cares, and my father said, 'Tyler, it's not religion that controls the world, it's oil.' "

"Oil?"

"Oil." Lauren was watching Katherine, who was banging Matt on the arm with a stuffed toy. "Petty-pie, stop that, now."

"Oh, they're just playing, they're fine."

"And Tyler said that's talking apples and oranges and my father said no, it was talking oil and vomit."

"Vomit? He was equating religion with vomit?"

"I really don't think so. But he said when we drove back up here, to take a look at the cars on the road, because they all required gasoline, and where did Tyler think that came from? Mostly from Persia. Iran. And Daddy said it's a good thing the Shah replaced that awful fellow over there, or in a few years we wouldn't even be able to drive to visit them, there'd be no oil for gasoline, and Tyler said, 'I don't disagree with anything you're saying,' but he was. He got Daddy worked up somehow. Daddy said people had no idea how much work went into running this country and keeping it safe."

"I can't imagine Tyler would disagree with that."

"No, Tyler wasn't disagreeing. But Tyler doesn't *know* as much as Daddy does."

Carol said, "Goodness. Tyler appears pretty intelligent to me."

"Tyler knows stuff, sure," Lauren said. "All that religious stuff, but that doesn't have anything to do with the real world, and that's Daddy's point—we live in the real world."

"Oh, well. Men. They get talking. I wouldn't worry about it."

Lauren's eyes teared up once more as she stood. "I should get going," she said. "Back to my monk's cell."

"Oh, Lauren. You'll feel better. Your sister's made you feel bad. But you have a family here. And Tyler won't stay here forever, much as we wish he would. He's a talented man. He'll find a bigger church someday, and you'll find more to do."

Lauren nodded, and wiped her eyes carefully with a tissue before she left.


LATER THAT EVENING, as she got ready for bed, Carol noticed that a rayon scarf she usually had draped over a hook on the back of the bedroom door was not there. "Davis," she said, "have you seen that pretty scarf Mother gave me?" Her husband was lying naked on the bed with a *Playboy* magazine. He shook his head. "I can't think where it would be," Carol said, a real uneasiness coming over her.

"You'll find it." Her husband patted the bed. "Come."

She was glad to go lie with him. Carol did not mind the *Playboy* magazines as long as no one knew about them. "Never as beautiful as you," he always said—he was kind that way.


CAROL DID NOT THINK it possible that Lauren would take things from her house. But the woman's unhappiness bothered Carol, and she thought if Lauren *was* taking things secretly, it represented neediness. And so Carol, having thought this through carefully, remembered how Jesus said that if you are asked to walk a mile, offer to walk two, and she thought if Lauren needed things, then she, Carol, in the truest spirit of Christianity, would give her things. And so one day she gave Lauren a small gold ring with a tiny red stone in it that had been intended for her little girl who had died. The ring, a gift from Carol's mother to the little baby girl, should have, by rights, gone later to one of Carol's other children. But she gave it to Lauren that day. "Katherine might want this," she said.

Lauren, enormously pregnant with the second baby, looked both eager and stricken. "It's so sweet," she said. And then handed it back. "I can't take it," she said.

"But why not? It would please me if you had it."

"Tyler wouldn't let me."

"Why is that?"

"Tyler would say I can't take favors from anyone in the parish."

"Oh, it's not a favor. It's a little gift. But if you think Tyler wouldn't be pleased, then I'll keep it—that's okay."

But Lauren said, holding out her hand, "No, I'd love it. I'll give it to Katherine someday. Tyler won't mind, really." Looking at it carefully again. "It's so *sweet*, Carol."

Carol was always glad that Lauren had taken the ring.

NOT LONG BEFORE little Jeannie was born, Tyler, driving back from church one day, having given a sermon on the parable of "A Thief in the Night"—*But know this, that if the goodman of the house had known in what watch the thief would come, he would have watched, and would not have suffered his house to be broken up*—ending, as Tyler always did, with the assurance of God's enduring love, Lauren had turned to him and said easily, "Tyler, do you actually *believe* that stuff you say?"

A crow suddenly swooped so close to the windshield that Tyler made a slight ducking motion as he turned the wheel. "Lauren—"

"Okay, okay, okay." She waved a hand. "I don't want to have any big religious discussion," she added, as they pulled in to the driveway. "And dear God, here is your mother."

His mother had brought them a gift for the new baby. "The Jews say it's bad luck to bring a baby not yet born a gift," Margaret Caskey said. "But I say, have faith in the Lord, and He will deliver. You weren't supposed to be born," she said, nodding toward Tyler. "But you were. The doctors said my nerves couldn't withstand another pregnancy. But with God's help, I did it."

"Yes, you did," said Lauren, unexpectedly leaning over and kissing her mother-in-law. "You did it."

Tyler stood back and let the women go into the house, Katherine holding on to her mother's skirt, chanting, "Mummy's preg-nut, Mummy's preg-nut." He glanced around at the fields; it was autumn and the leaves were starting to glow like a blush emerging from the depths of a young girl's face.

"Little messy in here—you'll have to excuse us," Lauren was saying to his mother.

"Not to worry," Tyler said. "Jane Watson told me at coffee hour the Ladies' Aid was going to give us a gift—Connie Hatch as a housekeeper a few mornings a week. Starting soon, so she can get used to it, and then for a few weeks after the baby is born."

"But I hate housekeepers," Lauren said. "They snoop."

"It's a gift from the church, and you can't refuse it, Lauren. It would seem very unkind." Margaret Caskey began putting dishes in the sink before she even took off her coat.

"Leave them, Mother—it's okay."

"I don't want any housekeeper snooping through our drawers," Lauren cried and, turning to her mother-in-law, said, "And please leave the dishes alone."

Margaret Caskey walked out of the kitchen.

"Lauren," said Tyler, "Mother's just trying to help. And Connie Hatch is not going to go snooping through our drawers."

"You know what, Tyler?" said his big-stomached, beautiful wife. "You are *aggressively* naïve."

Two weeks later, Jeanne Eleanor Caskey was born. Tyler could not believe he had ever wanted a son. "Lauren," he said, bending to kiss her, "let's have another one. Let's have girls, girls, girls."

A swirl of activity. Connie Hatch came three mornings a week, and still there was chaos throughout the house. Kids and diapers and bottles, and Lauren often snappish. But Tyler felt a maturity swelling around him. He and Lauren weren't kids anymore. They were in charge of a family, he was in charge of a church. He gave great thanks, tiredly but deeply, to God. The Ladies' Aid continued the services of Connie for a few more months, and Tyler walked each morning into town, where he prayed first in the sanctuary, and then went downstairs to his office, where Skogie Gowen dropped in sometimes to talk to him about fishing.

And then one morning Lauren called, and didn't know where she was.

DURING HER ILLNESS, he preached every Sunday. He stood up there in his black robe and spoke of large-heartedness, saying one's actions should be in the service to others, so believers and nonbelievers could benefit from loving-kindness and live with the love of God brought to us through Jesus Christ. He said God was to be praised, always. He shook hands after the service, thanking those who murmured to him that Lauren was in their prayers. If his congregation had loved him before, they now thought he was remarkable. "Look how he stands there so straight and strong," they said to one another. "Isn't that amazing?"

But Tyler didn't think Lauren would die.

He should have. His mother knew, her parents knew, the doctors knew. Lauren knew. She made such sounds of wailing that he gave her the sedatives at night that the doctor had provided. But he told her again and again that she would not die. *Just because you don't want me to?* She bit his arm, she grabbed the bottle of pills and tried to swallow them all, and he had to hold her down, push his fingers back over her gums while she tried to bite him. When she became quiet, he bathed her with a facecloth, and sat next to her while she was sleeping, the August light falling through the window. He was filled with The Feeling. God was in the room.

When she woke, she watched him.

If there were people in town who were picturing the minister holding his beautiful wife, whispering final love whispers, they had the picture wrong. Lauren turned away at the sight of him, saying things he would never forget. Her parents came and she told them to go away. She told his mother to stay out of the room. Connie Hatch was sent home. Belle came to take the children away. He sat by her bed, and when she rested, his gratitude was immense, but when she woke and started picking at the bedclothes, it was agony. She seemed to get better; she could sit up again, and speak. Her fierce words to him: *You're such a coward, you know.* And then the unthinkable, unimaginable thing that he did: He left the bottle of pills by her side while she slept. He went downstairs to sit with his mother, listening for any motion above. In a few hours he walked slowly, slowly up the carpeted stairs. His young wife was dead.

*Have mercy, my sin is ever before me. Have mercy upon me, O Lord, for I am in trouble: Mine eye is consumed with grief, yea, my soul and my belly.* He had waited that first year for winter to come, but when it came, he saw it made no difference; she inhabited winter as well. By the time the snows came, he had signed up for many committees and his days were spent driving the child to different babysitters, driving to different outlying towns. Sometimes he arrived for a meeting that had taken place the day before; he mailed a letter and forgot to put on a postage stamp, and when it was returned he went into the barn and threw a hammer against the wall, and then struck the side of his head with his hand so hard that he saw stars. At night, when the child was in bed, he would put on his overcoat and step out onto the porch to smoke his pipe. *Hide not thy face from me in the day when I am in trouble . . . for I have eaten ashes like bread.*

Spring arrived, summer, then fall. These changes took place far away.

Friends from college, from seminary, invited him to dinner. His parishioners invited him to their homes. But it was difficult for him to be anywhere for long, and he used Katherine as an excuse to get home. It was not until his mother said, "Tyler, that child doesn't talk anymore," that he realized this was true. So he began reading to the child, and asking her questions, but she didn't say much, except for the Lord's Prayer, when he said it with her at bedtime. Belle showed up and bought her new shoes, and Tyler and his mother and Belle all tried making a fuss about that. "Red shoes, Katherine. How wonderful. Haven't you always wanted red shoes?" But she hid her face in her father's lap, even when her grandmother admonished, "You might at least say thank you to Aunt Belle."

He had expected an easing of his grief after that first year, but this was not the case. When Doris Austin's desire for a new organ became known to him—the church treasurer, the board, even a deacon had spoken to him on her behalf—it seemed like an ant in the far corner of a room that people were pointing to, while for him the room was spinning. When Mrs. Ingersoll called him in for a conference, saying Rhonda Skillings was ready to apply psychology to Katherine's trauma, a different kind of darkness, fierce and almost welcome, planted itself inside him.

It was only in the presence of Connie Hatch that he seemed to remember some shadow of his previous self. When she told him about Jerry, about Becky, about her own disappointments, when she laughed suddenly at a common agreement about some small difficulty of life, so that her green eyes moistened with merriment, he would recall it all later when she went home, and think: *Thou hast put off my sackcloth, and girded me with gladness.*

*Book Three*

# SEVEN

November arrived, days passed by, and there was no word
about Connie. She had been missing now for almost three
weeks. Tyler called Adrian Hatch, and every time the news was the
same: There was none. The farmhouse seemed huge in its silence
once Katherine went off to school, and Tyler waited, to see if
Connie might arrive. But there was only the quiet, save for a dripping faucet in the kitchen that had begun to leak. Trying to change
its washer, Tyler's hands trembled, and he had to leave it unfixed.
His hand shook as he wrote out the grocery list. His mother was
right—men didn't know how much it took to take care of a child;
sometimes Katherine was sent off to school in the same clothes she
had worn the day before. At night he heated a can of beef stew,
while Katherine sat with a bowl of Alpha-Bits cereal before her,

and he would eat the beef stew straight from the pan, standing by the stove while she swung her feet, watching him.

"Don't worry," he said to her one night. "Mrs. Hatch will be back."

Katherine's feet swung faster, and something crossed her face—was it worry?—that made him go and kneel by her chair. He put his arms around her and hugged her to him, but he sensed in her smallness, a hesitancy. He placed his hand over the back of her head, feeling the snarl in her hair, and while she allowed her head to be pressed to his shoulder, still there was some unyeilding-ness. "Say," he said, standing up. "I just remembered."

He went and got from his desk drawer the small gold ring with its tiny red stone that Connie had presented to him.

"Look," he said to Katherine, who was watching him now with her mouth partly open in an expression of slight hopefulness. "Have you seen this before?"

Katherine stared at the ring; she thought it was the most beautiful thing she had ever seen.

"Mrs. Hatch found it."

Katherine turned her face away, swinging her feet so hard her shoes touched the table underneath.

"Katherine?"

She looked back at the table and with her small hand, pushed the bowl of cereal with such force that milk slipped over its edge.

"Don't you like the ring?"

She squeezed her eyes shut and shook her head.

The next morning Carol Meadows called to see if there was anything she could do. "Bring Katherine over whenever you need to," she said.

Her kindness made him realize that no other church member had called; the Ladies' Aid remained silent—no offer of another house-keeper, and no mention from the board that he could use a raise.

Even Ora Kendall did not call, and he could think of no excuse to call her. *Thy fierce wrath goeth over me; thy terrors have cut me off.*

It rained, and the rain froze. It snowed, and the snow became granular and gritty, and then it rained again. Torrents of the stuff poured from a sky as dark as dusk. Oak leaves were ripped from the trees by the wind, smashed in shreds against the wet, slushy roads, stuck against the windshields of parked cars, tucked into soggy corners of porches up and down the river. The wind shifted, shifted again, blowing the rain in all directions. Umbrellas popped inside out, their skeletons exposed, some squashed into a public trash can, looking like dead bats with broken wings. Women ducking across a parking lot had their coats drenched by the time they stepped inside a grocery store.

(Alison Chase sat in her messy kitchen on the phone to Irma Rand, telling her that she wanted to quit teaching Sunday school. She didn't have the oomph for it anymore. She didn't have the oomph for anything. "Talk to Tyler about it," Irma said, but Alison didn't want to. She hung up, and went back to bed, sleeping so soundly with the quilt over her head that when she woke, she had to lie motionless for many moments remembering where she was. "In less than two months the days will get longer," Jane Watson said, talking to Alison on the phone while she ironed her husband's shirts with a new spray-on starch she had seen advertised on TV. "Perk up." Bertha Babcock, in her house down by the river, wrote a list of refreshments needed for the Historical Society meeting, and then got the Pilgrim costume from the back of the closet; every Thanksgiving she and her husband dressed like Pilgrims and went to schools around the state giving talks on the history of their forefathers. Doris Austin put together facts and figures regarding church organs, typing them up to be presented to the church board. Rhonda Skillings sat in the upholstered wing chair of her living room, reading and taking notes on Wilhelm

Reich—infants did not play in order to survive, but to *engage*. Katherine Caskey did not engage. Rhonda wrote and read, wrote some more.)

IN A FEW DAYS, the rain lightened up, but the sky remained gray, and the temperature rose enough to melt the ice and snow so that water ran in dirty streams down gutters; cars driving by left a spray of filth on windshields or coats of passersby. Roofs leaked, and in some places water seeped through the eaves, staining wallpaper stained before. Then a cold snap came and stayed, settling in so that the lakes froze clear, and there was ice along the edge of the river.

The people of West Annett were used to this: the earth and its seasons revolving together, and if the elements of weather made life difficult—well, that's how it was, is all. People kept right on doing what they had always done. And they were not idle. Women's hands were busy knitting for next month's Christmas bazaar, baking pies for a grange-hall bake sale, getting refreshments for the square-dancing club, washing clothes and ironing, always lots of ironing. And the men, after working all day at their jobs, came home to fix things around the house, for there is always something that needs fixing in a house, and these men were handy, as their fathers had been. The disappearance of Connie Hatch caused confusion and discussion, that for some was faintly delicious, it's true, but it did not cause anyone to become idle.

Except for Tyler Caskey.

Tyler's restiveness increased; his days were long and shapeless. When Katherine left the house for school, he found he had to leave the house, too. Its silence, its emptiness, made him afraid.

And then, praying one morning in the sanctuary, sitting in the back pew—*Lord, I have called daily upon thee, I have stretched out my hands unto thee*—Tyler smelled an odd, rank odor beneath him, and realized it came from the folded blanket he had placed there weeks ago. He put on his gloves before taking hold of it, then found his keys in his pocket, and drove over to Walter Wilcox's house.

The old man shuffled about the kitchen in a pair of pants held up by a belt of clothesline rope. "I was married for fifty-one years," Walter said, placing a wet tea bag onto the counter. "And for the last twenty, we barely spoke. Run out of things to say, I guess."

Tyler took the tea and sipped from it. The place smelled of cat urine, which must be the smell of the blanket that Tyler had put into the trunk of his car.

Walter opened the top of the woodstove, poked at its insides with a stick, then sat in a rocking chair nearby. "We'd still get mad at each other, though." He rocked slowly. "What I hated—what I hated to the heavens—was she'd put a wet spoon into the sugar bowl." Walter rocked awhile longer. "And how she sneezed. Sneezed like a cat." The old man shook his head. "What I found out when she died," and he looked up at Tyler, taking his glasses off, wiping at his eyes with the side of his hand, "is that it don't matter what you hate. You live with someone all that time, you think sometimes, I wish I'd married someone different, and then all the things you hated don't matter a tinker's damn. If I'd known, you see—" He wiped his eyes again, put his glasses back on.

"We all just do the best we can," Tyler said.

"I didn't. I was a hellion till I got too old. I lie awake in that bed upstairs every night, going over in my mind the things I did. But memory's a funny thing. I think, did I do that? She hated me." Walter nodded. "I think she did. What happened to Connie Hatch?"

"Walter. I'm sure your wife didn't hate you."

"You get to be my age, Tyler, and you realize something. People hate to hear the truth. They *hate* it." The old man shook his head. "So, you don't know what happened to Connie?"

"No. But she didn't steal anything, I'm sure."

"It's hard to know about people. I heard it on the radio. She stole some jewelry and embezzled from the business office over there at the county farm."

"I'm sure she didn't. They wanted to question her, and I suspect she got scared."

"You don't run if you're not guilty," Walter said. He waved a hand. "But who's not guilty, I guess."

AT SCHOOL, KATHERINE was drawing pictures. She drew pictures of women with their heads cut off, big red drops of blood spurting out. She drew a picture of a woman in a red dress with a spiked high heel stabbed into her stomach. "My goodness. Who is that?" Mary Ingersoll asked, bending over the little table.

In a clear voice, the child said, "You."

And then, even more amazing, the child looked Mary straight in the eye. What a look it was! As though the child were not five years old at all, but, rather, thirty-five, and full of knowledge of every thought Mary'd ever had that was not beneficent.

"She's evil," Mary said later to Mr. Waterbury, the principal. "I bet you think I'm overreacting, but you know how much I love my kids." Mary gave the man a look that stirred something in him.

"Ah, Mary," the man said, "you're one of the best we have. I hate to see you go through this."

Mary made no attempt to stop the tears that sprang to her eyes. "But God's teeth," she said. "It's only November! How'm I going to make it to June with this creature in my class?"

"When I started out years ago," said Mr. Waterbury, motioning for the young woman to take a seat near his desk, "I had a child who—oh, I know it sounds foolish—but this little fellow scared me to death." Mr. Waterbury opened his desk drawer, brought out a penknife, and started to clean his nails. "Ah, that kid." The man shook his head. "He didn't come from much. You always find that, Mary. When the kid's in trouble, there's trouble at home." He looked at Mary and made an exaggerated grimace with his mouth. "When the kid's in trouble, there's trouble at home."

"But what do I *do*?" Mary leaned forward. She let the tears slip from her eyes. The fact is, she felt something quite pleasurable inside.

"We'll get Rhonda Skillings in on this," Mr. Waterbury assured her. "You're not going to go through this alone." He dropped the penknife into the drawer, pushed the drawer shut. "Not going through this alone. No sirree. I promise you that."

Through the large window of his office, the setting sun had done something marvelous with the sky. The horizon looked as though it had been painted pink and purple with the large brushstrokes of a child. "Look at that," Mr. Waterbury said, though it had been years since he'd commented on a setting sun.

"Oh, would you *look* at that," Mary said.

The sky had gone dark completely by the time Mary left his office. Mr. Waterbury had talked and talked, and she'd had to sit there, her pleasurable feeling sinking with the sun. Since 1945, he told her, the class size had been getting bigger. Even all the way up here in West Annett, there wasn't enough money to pay for an extra teacher like Mary, well qualified, with talent. Did she know that in New York City, a school had painted a picture of the country's map on the playground? It was true. A fine idea. Time to teach these kids about the country, such a wonderful country, and all sorts of crazy things happening. Russia could blow us up in two shakes, and we couldn't even beat them at math. Had Mary seen this report? *The Pursuit of Excellence.* Put out by the finest educators in the country. Said we should separate the gifted and the retarded, and it would be swell to get some funding, if not from the state, then maybe the federal government. Mary nodded and nodded. "I'll give Rhonda Skillings a call," the man finally said.

TYLER PICTURED Connie Hatch returning, how she would simply show up one day, stepping through the back door, and he would hear her from his study and go to the kitchen to find her hanging up her sweater; she'd turn with a smile of apology. "Sorry about that," she'd say. And he would clap his hands together once. "Oh, Connie, I've missed you," he'd say. "It's been unbearable in this house without you."

She did not come.

He took Susan Bradford skating one weekday morning, and she laughed girlishly as she took her first hesitant glides. "Haven't done this in *ages*," she called, her brown ski pants hugging her ample rump. When she almost lost her footing over a root that was bumping up through the ice, she fell against him, and he held her arms for a moment. It was, other than shaking hands, their first touch, and between them flashed the possibility of intimacy. Later, as they skated side by side, he held her elbow, pointing with his other hand at a hawk that was gliding high.

Over hot chocolate at a diner in Hollywell, he watched her gray eyes, and tried to imagine what she would look like were she angry with him.

"Just about broke my heart," Susan was saying, placing her splayed fingers against her sweater's collar. She had been telling him about mittens she had knit for her nieces, how the pom-poms had been cut off by the children's mother. "But it's better than one of them chewing on it and choking, I have to agree."

"Oh, of course," he said. "You can't be too careful."

"I love to knit," she said, dipping her head toward her hot chocolate.

"It's a nice thing, isn't it," Tyler said. "Mother used to knit." He wanted to talk about Connie. He wanted to tell her how Connie was misunderstood—a good person who had never had the children she wanted. He wanted to tell her about Walter Wilcox alone in his cat-smelling house. He wanted to say that Carol Meadows had lost a child years ago. That all of it seemed unbearably sad. That he had no idea what to do about Katherine.

"My mother used to knit, too," she said. "My mother was wonderful."

"I'm sure she was."

"She was so brave during her illness."

"You'll have to come for Sunday dinner again," he said. But something unpleasant was sprouting inside him, and he looked around for the waitress to get the check.


LYING IN BED next to his wife, Charlie Austin said quietly, "He married a tart."

Doris turned her head. "Who are you talking about?"

"Your minister. The woman was a tart."

Doris struggled to sit up, tugging on her flannel nightgown. "Charlie, you can't go speaking ill of the dead. Good heavens!"

"We're all dead," he responded.

She stayed on her elbow, peering at him in the near darkness. The full moon that shone through the gauzy curtain gave a shape to her body, covered in the quilt, rising up like a big sea animal, the flipper of one arm holding her weight. "I'm worried about you," she finally said.

"Oh, for christ's sake." He turned away, saw the blurry shape of the moon beyond the gauzy curtains. "It's supposed to snow to-morrow, but the clouds haven't moved in," he said.

"Why did you say that about the poor dead woman?" Doris lay back down, turned away herself.

"Because she was. And she knew I knew it, too."

"I guess I can't believe you're saying all this, Charlie. The woman was from out of state; she was shy, I think, and now she's *dead*. Do you want people criticizing you when you're dead?"

"I don't give a damn what they do."

Her silence chastised him. He'd been planning on telling her Chris Congdon, at a board meeting, had mentioned Tyler didn't want a new organ—nobody did except Doris, Charlie realized. Nobody gave a hoot.

But he said instead, "Speaking of out-of-staters. I heard there's a developer coming up from New York, wants to build a string of summer houses along the far side of China Lake. Near that Jew camp."

"Oh, Charlie." Doris rolled back toward him. "That's scary."

He didn't like it himself, picturing those goddamn rich people you saw sometimes in the summer, coming into the post office to buy stamps with a hundred-dollar bill. Taking pictures of the grocery store, for christ's sake. Saying to each other, "Isn't this town cute?"

"Phooey," he said to Doris. "There's already cabins over there—what's a few more?"

"But those cabins, Charlie, belong to people who live in Maine—you know that. They come over from Bangor or up from Shirley Falls. These new places, if the fellow's from New York, will be huge. They may very well be Jews, too."

"Go to sleep, Doris."

"What made you say that about Lauren Caskey? That's a horrible thing to say."

"Go to sleep."

He'd said it about Lauren Caskey because he'd been thinking about the woman in Boston, how everything was known in just one look, that you could meet a woman, and before a second had passed, that woman—not many, but some—could look right in your eyes and you could see she liked to get laid. Caskey, blind, arrogant idiot, thought he could marry for lust and nobody would know. But the knowledge of the woman dying in that drawn-out way . . . Charlie closed his eyes, felt ludicrously and suddenly close to tears; he thought of all the snow that would be covering the town throughout the coming winter, the woman's dead body in her grave. *Please,* he thought. That was the only word he ever used anymore to pray.

ON STEWARDSHIP SUNDAY, the morning skies were a clear expanse of pale blue, and the world seemed stark, and bare naked. Bare branches made the river visible from the road, its edges frozen over with crusted blankets of blue-shadowed snow, the middle a dark gray where you could sense the cold, cold water moving underneath. Annett Academy, its three white buildings, seemed reduced, its parking lot bare this morning, the maple trees in front bare, behind it the blue sky and the thin strip of bare road passing by, and Tyler, driving to church to ask his parish to open their hearts (meaning, today, their pocketbooks), perceived in the landscape a barrenness, an astringency to the scene spread out before him, that seemed to seep into his soul.

Perhaps others felt this, too, for the congregation put away the maroon hymnals and sat down, having sung without enthusiasm "Blest Be the Tie That Binds." There was a stifled yawn behind a church program, women adjusting their coats, someone bending to pick up a dropped glove, a feeling that they were settling in for the long haul now. Reverend Caskey said, "Let . . . us . . . *think,*" and remembered a man in seminary who had fainted in front of his first congregation. "We must not allow religion to become a mockery of God." He could not remember if the man had finished his sermon or not, only that a nurse in the front row had come to administer to him. "The religious man," Tyler continued, "is the man who dares to lose himself in loving others, who dares to sympathize with the suffering of others the way God sympathizes with us." He had not cared for the fellow who fainted, but he could not now remember why.

"People ask these days, How can the world continue to arm itself for war after the destruction of the past fifty years? But the Bible itself tells us the cause of war." Tyler paused and ran his finger lightly over his upper lip. The only time he had ever fainted was in fourth grade, during his only piano lesson, when he threw up all over the keys. He had seen spots before his eyes. He was not seeing spots now; it was just that everyone seemed very far away. " 'From whence come wars and fightings among you? Come they not hence—' "

A hymnal dropped with a loud thump up in the choir loft.

"God's capacity for love is endless," Tyler said, his face becoming so warm it seemed lit from behind with candles. "He has shown us directly how it is better to give than to receive. To give is the way we praise God and stand by Him." Perhaps the man who fainted that day became a librarian at the seminary. Tyler did not want to be a librarian. A drop of sweat rolled down his face and landed on the Bible. With his handkerchief he patted his forehead. "Saint Thérèse of Lisieux, as a young girl, was able to write the truth when she said, 'He comes to find another heaven which is infinitely dearer to Him—the heaven of our souls, created in His image.' "

Two wide strips of sunlight fell through the windows and folded across the maroon carpet, the white backs of the pews; an earring twinkled as Rhonda Skillings turned to pick a piece of lint from her husband's sleeve. Tyler, glancing up, believed he saw her whispering, and heat washed through him once more. "Let us pray," he said. Bonhoeffer confessed in prison that he became tired of praying. Perhaps he should say this to his congregation, but he did not want to look up again. "Let us pray," he said again.

By the end of the service, he felt he had been through a month at boot camp. Not the physical stress of running back and forth with a rifle and knapsack, but the dark pinch of being in the company of those with whom he had not one thing in common. In the car, his mother said quietly, "What ails you?"

A FEW DAYS LATER, and it was snack time in the classroom. The children sat at little tables, bringing out crackers with peanut butter, little bags of potato chips, cookies, apples. Mrs. Ingersoll opened a large can of pineapple juice and poured it into tiny Dixie cups. Katherine saw Martha Watson watching her, and so she opened her red plastic lunch box, pretending to look for her snack, but she knew there was nothing in there except a peanut-butter sandwich.

"How come you never have a snack?" Martha asked her.

Katherine closed her lunch box and looked away. In the doorway stood Mrs. Skillings. Mrs. Ingersoll put down the can of juice and went to speak to her quietly. And then Katherine heard—they all heard—Mrs. Ingersoll say, "Katie, could you come here, please?"

The children stopped talking and watched as Katherine, so frightened she felt like her arms were melting, walked to the doorway of the classroom. "You go along with Mrs. Skillings," Mrs. Ingersoll said. "We'll all be here when you get back."

No one else was in the long corridor. Mrs. Skillings seemed so tall as to be walking on stilts. "We think you're a very special girl," said Mrs. Skillings. "And we thought it would be fun if you and I played some games in my office."

When Mrs. Skillings sat down, her dress rustled. She put on a pair of glasses that had sparkly things on the flipped-up edges of them. She looked so different in her glasses that it seemed like she'd become someone else.

"Now, what's the difference between beer and Coke?"

Katherine looked at the woman's big white earrings, which seemed like the tops of small cupcakes. She sat with her tiny shoulders slumped forward, her hands in her lap. Mrs. Skillings had put a big wooden block under Katherine's feet. "So they won't fall asleep," she said.

Katherine looked away and didn't speak.

"Let's try a different question," Mrs. Skillings said. She moved a sheet of paper, and her bracelets made a delicate clinking sound that caused Katherine's whole body to give a quick shiver.

Katherine whispered to her lap. "I know a secret."

Mrs. Skillings was quiet for a moment, and then she said, "Do you, dear?"


THAT EVENING TYLER sat on the couch in his study while moonlight fell through the window. Katherine was next to him, turning the pages of a magazine that she held upside down in her lap. "Do you want to color a picture?" Tyler asked.

She shook her head.

"Tummy feel funny?"

She shrugged.

"Looking forward to seeing Jeannie again in just a few days?"

She nodded.

"Me, too." He pictured Jeannie's eyes laughing, as Lauren's once had. He pictured Susan Bradford's eyes, and thought they re-

vealed nothing—what would it be like to live a lifetime with someone whose eyes revealed nothing? He thought how poor Connie's
eyes would light up with a laugh, and wherever she was now, her
eyes must be filled with anxiety.

Tyler rubbed the spot beneath his collarbone, and imagined
Bonhoeffer in a freezing prison cell writing, "I know only this: you
go away—and all is gone." Bonhoeffer was comforted by writing
his poems. People were comforted by writing things down. Lauren's
letters, now in the attic, letters she had written to herself. *Why do I
feel such loss, when I have Tyler and the baby?* The minister tapped
Katherine's knee. "Let's go, kid. What do you say?" He got his
skates from the mudroom, tucked her in the car beside him, and
drove over the hill to China Lake.

They were the only people there. His skates made wonderful
scraping sounds against the ice. Katherine sat on a log, wrapped in
a blanket and shivering. Back and forth he went, Bonhoeffer's
poem repeating through his head: "I will think and think again,
until I find what I have lost." Tyler's skates dug into the ice, moving him faster and faster, until he slowed down and went back and
picked up the child, and she clung to him, her little legs spread
against his torso, and together they moved around the moonlit
lake; *scrape-scrape-scrape* went the skates. Scape-grace.

He saw the splash of moonlight that fell upon the earth, and
while he knew that through the love of Jesus Christ his life could
come back to him, he felt then a shudder of despair so cavernous
that his legs might have given out from under him, if not for holding Katherine. One thought, shaky and barely formed, seemed like
a dark pile of stones placed along the edge of a crevice, and his mind
would creep toward it, then run back: Could it be he had no self?

Never before had such a thought seemed possible to Tyler. But
he wondered if madness lay beyond that pile of stones, and while
faith should be able to save him, it seemed that faith was a road that

stretched confidently past that pile of stones, wound past the edge of that deep crevice that he seemed compelled to approach and peek over. No, Tyler was not losing his faith—it seemed to have lost him. And it did not help to know that in another poem Bonhoeffer himself had wondered, "Who am I? This or the other? Am I one person today, and tomorrow another?"

It didn't help, because Bonhoeffer was a man of greatness, and he was just Tyler Caskey. He skated over the lake, the small ridges of ice bumping gently under his feet, the shadows of spruce trees pointed and dark in the moonlight. He did not want to go back to his empty house. Walter Wilcox had said he lay in his bed every night thinking of the things he did and did not do.

Tyler stopped skating abruptly, turning a small, quick circle.

If Walter Wilcox was lying in his bed every night, then he wasn't sleeping in the church. The blanket under the pew had been used by someone else. Tyler skated back to the river's edge. He set Katherine down, unlaced his skates.

"Of course," Carol Meadows said on the telephone. "I'll make up the little cot for her right now."


AS THOUGH HE were a fugitive himself, he opened the church door only partway, slipping through. He passed through the vestibule, where old programs lay fanned on a shelf by the door, their whiteness showing in the near dark, and then entered the back of the darkened sanctuary. The moon shone a stream of pale light through the far window. In a loud whisper he said, "Connie?" And waited; there was no sound. Slowly, he walked down the aisle, past the shaft of moonlight. Up near the front, he could see nothing. "Connie? You must be cold. I'm alone," he added.

He stepped up the two steps to the chancel, and sat in his chair. A car drove by on Main Street, the lights coming through the windows briefly, going away again. He closed his eyes, thinking, *Our Father, Who art in Heaven, hallowed be Thy name,* each word seeming a dark, warm space he was too big to crawl into.

Above him in the choir loft was a soft sound of motion. He stood, his heart pounding in the darkness. And then her voice, youthful: "Tyler?"

"Yes. I'm here."

She made her way down the stairs. When she emerged, he saw her tall outline in the soft funnel of light. Her hair was not pinned up; it fell to her shoulders in thin, grayish waves.

"Are they here?" she asked.

"No. No one. Are you all right?" He went to put his arm around her. "I've been worried, Connie." An odor of something rank rose off her like a small, dense cloud. "Come and sit," he said, and led her to the front pew, where he sat beside her. In the pale light, her face was almost unrecognizable. She seemed like an old woman; the skin from her cheeks hung from her high cheekbones, dropped beneath her mouth.

"I. Am. Scared." She said each word carefully.

"Yes, of course you are." He kept an arm around her.

"Can they arrest me in a church?"

"I think they can. But no one's here. Do you need food?"

She shook her head, and he saw there were tears glistening on her cheeks. He brought his handkerchief from his pocket and gave it to her, then placed a hand on the back of her head, as though she were a child, or a lover.

"What'm I going to do?" she asked.

"We'll figure it out. Where have you been?"

"Nowhere. The Littlehales' barn, the back kitchen of a restaurant in Daleville some nights. It's easy enough to sneak into places. You'd be surprised."

"But you're freezing cold, and you must be hungry."

"Mostly I'm scared and tired."

"Yes." He rubbed her shoulder with his hand.

"Can I sit here awhile with you?"

"Of course." He thought of that day, weeks ago, when he had walked into the kitchen and shown her his cuffs, the silly fear he had felt upon discovering his frayed cuffs, her calm encouragement to go buy a new shirt.

Connie burrowed her head against his chest, and he rubbed her back, her hair. He felt the thrust of her shoulder blade through her coat. "Tyler." Her voice was muffled, and she sat partway up, looking straight ahead. "It's the strangest thing, Tyler. But I don't know if I did it. Just my mind goes all funny, and I think, Now, did I really do that, or does it just seem like I did?"

Her breath was so pungent it seemed like a decaying animal sat in front of her face. He had to work not to turn his own face away.

"Do you have to tell them if they ask you what I said?"

"No. You can talk to your minister in confidence."

"Even if I haven't been to church?"

"Oh, yes."

She leaned back against his arm, shaking her head slowly. "The first time—oh, Tyler. I didn't know it would work. Have you seen people in those places? Nobody ever came to see her. She couldn't move. I'd change her diapers—" Connie began to shiver violently.

"Connie, I'd like to get you some food and warm clothes."

"No, I'm just real tired. Let me stay here a minute. I want to tell you this story. I've never told anyone. But it's a stupid story. I'm not bright, Tyler."

"I'd like to get you warmed up, and get a hot drink into you."

"Don't leave," she said, touching the top of his hand.

"I won't leave."

She took a deep breath and looked at him. He had to hold his own breath so as not to breathe her odor. In the darkness his eyes had adjusted, and he could see her eyes, their aliveness. "I don't mean *in* love, but do you love me?" she asked.

"I do. Yes. And I've worried about you."

She nodded, a small, knowledgeable gesture. "I love you, too. Can I tell you the story?"

"Tell me the story. It won't be a stupid story," he added. "Nothing about you is stupid."

Connie tucked her elbows in toward her waist, her arms together, like a child who is hoping to still be held, and he kept his arm around her. "When Adrian came home from the war, he was different. Oh, I know—everybody was. He'd parachuted into Normandy and they expected to die, I think, even though nobody really expects to die, do they. And he brought home a Purple Heart for saving this man's life." She leaned forward as she spoke, and Tyler loosened his arm. "He didn't want to talk about it, so I didn't ask. Adrian was never one to talk. But it was *years* later when finally one night he said, 'Connie, I've got to tell you.' So he told me. He said, 'I can't describe to you what it was like,' but he did a pretty good job describing it. I thought he was going to tell me how he'd killed somebody, but what he told me was how he loved somebody. And I don't mean a French girl running out from a barn happy to be saved, or even some English girl in the pub in Berkshire.

"He told me how he saved this man's life, lugged him four miles into town as dawn broke, lugged him through cow pastures, and they kept resting, lying down, and he told me he loved this man. At first I didn't know what he meant. But then I said, 'Do you mean you had sex with him, did things like that?' I didn't want him to feel bad. People kill themselves because they're fairies, you know, and I wanted to pretend I would be okay. And he said no, they didn't do things like that—the guy was almost dead. And then I said, after a long while, watching Adrian look uncomfortable—he looked awful uncomfortable—I said, 'But you wanted to have sex with him, right?' And he looked away and said, 'Well, yeah, Connie. I did. I wanted to. And it's just been eating me up.' So that was a shock, but he still sat there uncomfortable, and then I began to think, You know, this fellow he saved, he sends Christmas cards from the Midwest every year, he's got a family and kids and the whole nine yards, but then I thought how Adrian would stare at the cards sometimes, and I said, 'Ade, do you still feel that way about him?' My mouth got dry—I remember that—asking him. And Adrian said, 'Yeah, I do, Connie. I can't get over him and it's just eating me up.' "

Connie's shoulders slumped forward, and she hung her head down, as though the telling of this had exhausted her. "Stupid," she murmured.

"What is?"

"For me to care."

"Well, of course you care. But war does strange things to people, Connie. It's—well, it's intimate, saving a life, and it would make Adrian feel close to this fellow. But he feels a heck of a lot closer to you, or he'd never have told you."

"But why did he have to tell me? Why didn't he keep it to himself?"

"Like he said, Connie—it was eating him alive. And by not telling anyone, maybe it stopped feeling real—and that's a feeling that can make you crazy, I think."

"Yes." Connie looked at him. "I guess that's a feeling that can make you crazy, all right." She looked down at her lap. "But it changed things. Maybe it shouldn't have. But it did. It got me lonely. And it was just after Jerry died he told me." She nodded. "Changed things."

"It's not too late. When you get this business straightened out . . ." Tyler waved his hand to indicate her present situation.

"I've got to lie down," she said, and she moved away, and lay on her back on the pew, her feet hanging over the edge.

"Connie, you should probably see a doctor."

"Let me stay here awhile more."

"Here. Put your feet up on the pew—that's right—just put them right up there." She was wearing men's boots.

"I'm tired. Tyler?" She tilted her chin up, so she could see his face above hers. "I hate to think of myself as pathetic."

"Who's pathetic, Connie? You're just trying to do the best you can, like most of us. That's not pathetic."

She sat up, and the movement brought with it another wave of the smell she carried with her. So quietly that he had to tilt his head to hear her, she said: "I was surprised with the first one that it worked. I still don't know it was me. Strange thing. Kind of a little experiment, like when Jerry and I would play in the woods. He had a jackknife once, oh, he was just a tiny tyke, maybe three or four years old, and it was just a small jackknife, and he said, 'What's the inside of that toad look like?' and he sliced right in its soft belly. I remember that toad's eyes staring at us, all bugged out while his belly was cut straight open, brown runny stuff coming out." Connie sniffed hard, patted her eyes with Tyler's handkerchief. "Poor toad. We didn't know what we were doing. Why didn't we know? Tyler? Could you tell God I'm sorry about that toad?"

"God knows that, Connie."

"He knows everything?"

Tyler nodded.

"Oh, Jesus." A shiver ran through Connie's body, and he moved and put his arm once again around her shoulder. "*She* was pathetic, Tyler. Dorothy Aldercott. She was one of my feeders at first. You know what a feeder is? Paralyzed, so you have to feed them. I was in charge of the feeders. Six of them. Rolled into the kitchen on a gurney; that was the easiest way to do it—line them up. We'd crumble graham crackers in little Dixie cups, with milk. When it got smooshy, I had to spoon it into their mouths, and they'd lie there looking at me, but their eyes weren't nice like the toad's. They were horrible, and Dorothy Aldercott'd grown a beard. I don't know why some old women do that—I hope I don't, but I guess it doesn't matter now—and somebody'd shave her once in a while, and when I fed her I'd have to wipe her face with a napkin, and I could feel the scratching of the stubble under the napkin. And she'd lie there and stare, and she got to me—that's the truth of it. I felt pity—I really did. Couldn't stand to think of her going on that way. No one ever came to see her; she couldn't talk or complain—that's how it was with the feeders. And Dorothy Aldercott had two daughters. I looked in her folder. Never came to see her. So that was a pathetic woman."

"The situation was pathetic," Tyler said. "I don't know that you could say she was."

Connie stared down at her foot; she had crossed one leg over the other and was bobbing the man's boot. "One of the cooks said one day—he'd been there for years—he said they could be put out of their misery in two seconds just by overfeeding them. They can't swallow well, so it goes down the wrong pipe and they drown, I guess, in graham-cracker mush. So I kept spooning it into her mouth one day, and she kept looking at me with those eyes, and I touched her face nicely, and said, "It's okay, Dorothy," because I loved her right then, Tyler. You say Adrian saving someone's life is intimate. Well, it's intimate the other way, too. And then—she was gone. The second one, Madge Lubeneaux, she struggled a bit, and that made me feel funny, so I never did it again."

Chills had spread over the left side of Tyler, his back, his thigh, his arm, as though a wave of tiny sea urchins had washed up on him. "Connie. Are you saying you killed these old women?"

She nodded, looking at him in the near darkness with a kind of innocent, but puzzled, matter-of-factness.

Again, the sensation of tiny sea urchins washing over him.

"Do you think I was wrong?" she asked, as though the idea would surprise her.

"Yes. Yes, I do."

"Why? If you could have seen them . . ."

"I've seen things."

"Well, 'course you have," she said tiredly.

He could not stop the chills spreading over him. He took his arm from her shoulder.

"I guess they'll prove I did it on purpose, and then I'll be gone for life."

"Connie, the police are after you for stealing."

"*Stealing?*" She looked at him like he'd said something insane. "I've never stolen anything in my life. Ginny Houseman did the stealing at that place. My God, I'm surprised they didn't catch her. She took stuff from the patients as soon as they came in; she was in admissions, and she stole checks from the business office, too. We were friends for a while, but then I just didn't like her. Tyler, I didn't steal a thing."

"I believe you."

"Will they believe me?"

"I don't know."

"If they don't know about those two feeders, should I tell them? It's a crime, I suppose."

"It is a crime, Connie."

She moved away from him, turning to look at him full on. "You feel different about me now."

"Connie, you need some help."

"But I told you that day."

"Told me what?"

"I told you about Becky, and how she got rid of the baby."

"Yes." His heart was beating quickly.

"And you said, Oh, we're all sinners. Something like that."

"Yes, but, Connie—"

"And now you think I'm a murderer and you see me different, even when I told you my sister did the same thing."

"It's not the same thing, Connie."

"How come?"

"Connie, look. Let's go get you some help."

"Are you going to turn me in? Becky's baby would've had a whole life. These women's lives were over."

"But they weren't over yet."

"You've got me all mixed up, Tyler. Are you going to turn me in?"

"You can stay right here in the church until we figure out what to do." He added, "You're in shock." But he was the one in shock. He stood up. "You need help. I'm going to go get Adrian."

She hung her head, weeping, and he sat back down. But he was really afraid of her. "Come with me," he said. "I won't repeat to anyone what you said, but come with me back to your home."

She shook her head.

He sat, watching her. "This is what I'm going to do," he finally said. "I'm going to go call Adrian to have him come get you. You can't go on sleeping in churches and barns. And whatever conversation you have with him is your business. What you told me is privileged between a minister and his parishioner. I'll leave that to you and Adrian—what to decide."

Across the dark parking lot she walked between the two men with her head down. Tyler helped her into the passenger seat of the truck. "Connie—"

She looked at him and gave him a sad, tired smile.

He stood back while the truck drove away.

CHARLIE AUSTIN STOOD at the phone booth with fingers that were cold and trembling. He dialed the number. On the third ring, there was her voice—oh, her voice. Everything he had survived in life seemed to be so he could hear her voice, coming up through her body that he knew and adored. "It's me," he said.

"Hi, me."

He cleared his throat. "How are you?"

"Okay, good. How are you?"

"Okay," said Charlie. He pinched his nose, looked up at the dark sky. "I'll see you soon, thank God."

"Listen, I need to tell you something. I've thought this through. And I'm not good for you."

A small dark space he stood in. The words like little wires around him.

"And you're not good for me. I slept better last night than I've slept in months, and that says it all, I think. That says a great deal. I'm glad to have come to the decision."

He said nothing, stood in the darkness, holding the phone.

"We're going to take a break in this."

"How long?"

She didn't answer for a moment. "Long, Charlie," she finally said. "It's just not good. It's made me into a person I don't like, and I blame myself, I do. But you've put pressure on me, and I can't handle that."

He opened his mouth, but said nothing.

"Pressure may not be the right word, and I do think it's my fault. I shouldn't have gone so far with this."

The tiny dark space around him got darker; he was closed into a dark barrel. He was dying. "Can you tell me why?" He heard himself say this.

"Sure," she answered. And he sensed in his dimness that she was prepared, and strong. "It makes me feel like two people. One who wants you and one who—well, I can't take the pressure. And we have to stop."

"Have you met someone else?" he said.

"That's not about this. I'm not having that talk with you, Charlie. I'm telling you this is not good for me, and it's not good for you. It's become unhealthy. And I can't handle it. I feel you're pressuring me all the time, and it's not good for me. Or you. I can be your friend, if you need to talk sometime later. Right now we have to stop."

Friend.

"We can't be friends," he said. His voice was low, weak.

"Okay—I'm not having any more of this conversation. I'm sorry, Charlie. This has been my fault. Good-bye."

The final word was diminished as she hung up.

He brought the cigarettes from his pocket and walked through the cold, smoking. Over and over in his stunned mind were the words "I don't know what to do. I don't know what to do." He walked and smoked. He walked past houses where lights were still on in the windows. He walked past houses where the lights were all off. He thought of his own home, and didn't know how he would do it. Go back there. Stay there. Teach tomorrow. I don't know what to do.

# EIGHT

A light was on in the minister's living room. Charlie drove by slowly, peering through the car window. He had smoked and walked for more than an hour after his dismissal at the pay phone, and now he turned the car around at the bottom of Stepping Stone Road, and drove past the minister's house again, then backed the car up and left it near the end of the driveway, closing the door quietly, walking quietly through the cold. He had not thought the place would look so alone. Through the living-room window, he saw Tyler sitting in a rocking chair and, craning his neck above the porch railing, he saw that the man was sitting forward, his elbows on his knees, his head slumped down. For a long time Charlie stood watching, his hands pushed into his coat pockets, his toes so cold they felt like hot stones in his shoes. Tyler did not move. Charlie wondered, without emotion, if the man was dead. He stepped up onto the porch, lit a cigarette, and coughed, dropped the match, and rubbed his boot over it, coughed again. In a moment the door opened, the minister looking out into the moon-lit darkness. "Charlie?"

Moving past him, Charlie thought the man smelled a little; his hair was uncombed and his white shirt so rumpled it looked like he had slept in it. "Come in, Charlie," the minister said politely. "Come right in," and Charlie had a sudden urge to push the man hard, so he would tumble to the floor. Fleetingly, he imagined this—the blankness of stupidity that would cross the man's face as he fell backward, his big limbs hitting the furniture.

"Where's the child?" Charlie asked. Crayons and a coloring book lay on the floor.

"It's past midnight, Charlie. Are you all right? Sit down." The minister gestured toward the couch.

Charlie turned, surveying the room. The only light came from the lamp near the rocking chair, and a creepy darkness seemed to crouch in the corners. The ceiling was so low, he felt like he was a huge mushroom that had just sprouted in the house's dank midst. A sweater and a pair of child's red shoes were on the floor nearby. The melting snow from the tread of his boots was moving toward the sweater, and he walked to the other end of the couch and sat on the very edge, keeping his hands in his pockets. He'd be a lunatic to tell this man about the woman in Boston, crazy to say that he was scared to go home. He said, "Pledges could be down."

Tyler stood with his hands loosely on his hips. "Early to predict, isn't it? We have to the end of the year."

Charlie raised a shoulder in a small shrug. "Maybe so. But there's rumors." When Tyler didn't respond, Charlie said, "I don't give a shit myself. But they say you've got something going on with that Hatch woman."

"That's ridiculous." Tyler said this with little expression.

"They say you gave her a ring."

Tyler said nothing, only took his seat in the rocking chair.

"Where is she?"

"I don't know what Connie's up to right now," Tyler said.

"And what does your good friend Bonhoeffer say about lust?" Charlie pushed his chin up and thought a look of defensiveness passed over the man's face. But Tyler squinted his eyes at him, and Charlie looked away.

"Are you in any trouble, Charlie?"

Charlie sat back, thrusting his feet forward. He looked up at the ceiling. "I'm not. But you may be."

"Why?" Tyler finally asked. "Because of a rumor?"

Charlie closed his eyes. "Sure. People get antsy. They need to go after someone, especially when they sniff weakness under what's supposed to have been strong."

It was some time before Tyler spoke. He finally said, "There's usually a reason to go after someone."

Charlie opened his eyes, gave a snort of disgust. "Well, you've given them one. After being Mr. Wonderful. You've acted stuck-up and standoffish and they hear about a ring you've given your housekeeper—and it's off to the races they go. Whether they believe you've mixed yourself up with Connie Hatch or not, they're just glad to have a reason to go after you." He hoisted himself to his feet. His distress from the phone call to Boston was so great it seemed to be a physical illness that had overtaken him. He walked toward the door.

"How are you in trouble, Charlie?"

Charlie turned and walked back so he stood in front of Tyler. He bent his face down close to the man's. "You haven't noticed, Caskey," he said loudly. "We're talking about you."

Tyler rocked back in the rocking chair.

"Oh," Charlie said, turning away, "you poor son of a gun. You poor fucking turn-the-other-cheek son of a gun." He suddenly turned back and took a step closer to the man, who was looking up at him with an expression of forced equanimity. "I bet I could knock you in the head right now, and you'd just say, 'Okay, Austin, do it again.' *Wouldn't you?*" Charlie walked away, looked down at his boots. "Boy, Caskey, you could drive a person nuts." He looked up. "You drive your wife nuts?"

Tyler's eyes seemed exhausted, tiny pins of light half buried in earth.

Charlie shook his head. "You stink, too. Don't you have hot water in this place?" He looked around. "This is one shithole."

After a moment Tyler said quietly, "To answer your question, Bonhoeffer believed that lust moves us away from God."

Charlie felt too ill to keep standing. He went to sit on the arm of the couch. "Moves us away from God. I see."

"Which is a terrible place to be."

"What is?"

"Away from God."

"Well, I'll let you in on a little secret, Caskey. You can preach until the cows come home, but the whole goddamn world is away from God."

Tyler nodded slowly.

Charlie felt like his windpipe had turned into sponge; in a minute he might stop breathing. He didn't like the dark corners of this room, but he was afraid to go back out into the cold. He didn't want to go home. In his head, dark images exploded, blood poured from the neck of a man. "Who thought up all this religion crap?" he heard himself say. "Oh, I'll tell you why it's good—sure. It lets people feel superior, and boy, people love that." Charlie laughed. "I'm so much better, I'm not even going to *say* I'm better. God, it makes me puke. Goddamn miscreants." Charlie felt a slight buzzing in his head. He peered into the dining room. On the wall was a picture of a baby deer, the spotted hindquarters aimed at him. "So, Caskey. What do you have to say? Thou sapient sir?"

He looked back and saw Tyler resting his arms on the wooden arms of the rocking chair. Tyler gazed at his knees, and finally said in a tired voice, "Only what I've said before. That it's not the fault of Jesus Christ, Charlie, that Christianity, or any religion, can be used to make a mockery of God."

"Fancy words. Fancy Nancy. There's something else I never understood, Caskey. This cheap grace and costly grace crap you're always serving up." Charlie's knee was trembling. He pressed down hard with his foot. "It's gobbledygook, but you carry on about it like it *means* something."

Tyler said with coldness, "It means something if you think how we live our lives means something."

"Yeah, well—I don't get it," Charlie wanted to shout. He said, keeping his teeth together, "Stupid crap," and spray came from his mouth.

Quietly, in a kinder voice, Tyler said, "The question is—how do I live my life? Do I live my life as though it matters? Most of us believe it matters. That our relationship to God, to one another, to ourselves—matters."

Charlie crossed his arms, stared at his boots, shook his head.

"And if it matters, then to say, 'Oh, I've sinned but God loves me, so I'm forgiven,' is cheap."

"Why? What's wrong with that? You know what I think? I think you guys just love to keep our balls pinched."

"It doesn't cost anything, that's why. Costly grace is when you pay with your life."

"Like your friend Bonhoeffer. Mr. Martyr."

"Well, no. Repentance and the cost of discipleship can take many forms." Tyler opened his hands, palms up. "You, for example, teach young people the beauty of language—"

"Oh, no. Leave me out of this friggin' baloney. I just asked. Nothing more."

Tyler nodded, put his hands to his face and rubbed hard.

"The men at that deacons' meeting last night," Charlie said meditatively, "they're sitting around talking about cars and snow tires and Cuba's revolution and how many washing machines Russia's making. And the women, far as I can tell, sit around talking about the minister maybe screwing his housekeeper. Both conversations mean nothing to me."

"What does mean something to you?"

The question seemed confrontational to Charlie. He couldn't remember what he had just said, only that he had talked too much. He gave Caskey a hard, cold stare. "Figuring out why you're such a smug jackass. That would mean something to me." Charlie stood up. "I've got to get out of here before I smack you senseless."


FOR THE FIRST TIME since moving into the farmhouse, Tyler locked both doors. He picked up the sweater that was on the floor of the living room, glanced at the puddles left by Charlie's boots. He switched on another lamp in the living room: The walls glowed in two circles of pink. That he was alone in the house, that Katherine was staying the night at the Meadowses' home, caused an eeriness to swoop through the room like the large wings of an enormous bat. He had not known until now how much he depended on the child, her silent presence, her cautious glances. He would call her in the morning before she left for school with the Meadows kids.

He left a light on in the kitchen and went to lie down on his couch in the study. He did not get out of his clothes, not even his shoes. He could not have said what worried him most: Connie, or Charlie, or his future. He wished Charlie would resign as head deacon; it would make things easier. He'd let the board know that he would support the decision of a new organ; now was certainly not the time to take a stand against that. But it was Connie, her sad presence earlier in the church, which rolled around within him. What should he have done? What should he do tomorrow? When he remembered the comfort he had received from her presence in this house—why, it made his soul shrink in a kind of sickness. When he remembered that first autumn afternoon, returning home after the conference about Katherine at school, he wondered now what it was he had seen when he'd looked into Connie's green eyes. What was that look of recognition?

Tyler sat partway up, his elbows pressed into the couch. Could it have been some dark camaraderie? As though they were joined by a private, deliberate, acquaintanceship with death? Was *that* what had been seen in their glance that day?

No. He would not accept that.

An icicle thundered to the ground outside the window, and Tyler stood up, his heart beating furiously. He walked through the house, peering out the windows, and saw nothing. Seated back on his couch, he watched as daylight spread ever so slowly across the dark, and he had a sense of how there was no beginning and no end, just the ever-turning world. Tyler thought, then, of his thick-chested father-in-law telling him years earlier how he hated to hear someone say, "The sun has set," or, "The sun has risen," because it wasn't true, and the man had looked at Tyler hard, as though Tyler alone were responsible for such an egregious misuse of the language. "It's an *illusion*," the man had said. And Tyler had said, "Well, yes." Remembering now, Tyler felt disgusted and he wished he had said, "Oh, stop it. You're an idiot philistine."

Staring beyond the birdbath, watching the gray become lighter and lighter on the faraway fields, watching the old stone wall emerge, he became acutely aware that it was merely a pile of rocks arranged a hundred years ago; the labor that had gone into it, the quiet beauty it had supplied him for years, seemed now to have disappeared with the starkness of the tiredly increasing morning light. He turned back to his desk, and thought it was not a good thing to stay awake through the night.

"They need to go after someone, especially when they sniff weakness." Charlie's words caused small bubbles of anxiety to rise steadily, and, returning to his couch, Tyler once again lay down.

What did Charlie mean?

He awoke as though from anesthesia, and heard a knocking on the door. It was the Carlson boy, holding a mittened hand up to squint through the window of the door. "I'm so sorry," Tyler said, the cold air causing his breath to be seen right there. "Katherine stayed at the Meadowses'. Tell your mother I'm awful sorry I forgot to call." The boy ran down the steps, and Tyler waved to Mrs. Carlson, mouthing to her the words "I'm sorry." She nodded, the exhaust from the tailpipe swirling forward and partly obscuring her, but it seemed to Tyler she did not look pleased to have been kept waiting.

He called out, "I'm sorry about that," as she backed the car up. The wintry air seemed to be taking little bites of him through his white shirtsleeves. He thought, with a sudden fierceness, I am so sick of saying I'm sorry.

The telephone was ringing. Almost, he said, "Connie?" But it was Mr. Waterbury, wanting to know if he could come in for a conference tomorrow afternoon at the school with Mary Ingersoll and Rhonda Skillings. "Why, of course," Tyler said. "I'd be happy to."


MRS. MEADOWS HAD found one of her girls' old dresses for Katherine to wear to school. Kneeling, straightening the little white collar, Mrs. Meadows said to Katherine, "What a pretty girl you are." Katherine looked into the woman's large brown eyes. "Just like your mother." Mrs. Meadows's cheeks were smooth and a little pink up toward her eyes. She smelled like baby powder. Katherine took a tiny step closer, hoping there was still more stuff to be done to her collar. "Let me brush your hair. You tell me if that hurts. Am I tugging too hard?"

Katherine shook her head.

"Oh, my. Don't you look nice."

The older Meadows girl was walking past, so big she had schoolbooks. She stopped and watched, and smiled at Katherine. "Ma, don't you think Katherine should keep that dress?"

"Yes, I do." Mrs. Meadows smoothed Katherine's hair behind her ear. "If you don't mind a hand-me-down."

Davis Meadows moved by. His gray trousers had cuffs. Katherine watched him open a drawer in the front hall table, take out his gloves, put his hat on. He said, "Katie's a nice-looking girl all on her own. Hand-me-down dresses or not."

Mrs. Meadows had made her a lunch, and found an old lunch box. Katherine held it a little high and forward, because it was one of the prettiest things she had ever seen. There was a picture from *Alice in Wonderland* on its side. As Mrs. Meadows was zipping up her coat for her, she said, "Did your mommy ever give you a little gold ring?"

Katherine lowered the lunch box and stared at her.

"No? Probably Daddy's keeping it for you for when you get a little older. Your mother had a little gold ring with a tiny red stone in it that she was going to give to you."

Katherine whispered, "Mommy's in heaven."

"Yes, honey. Watching you and loving you just like when she was here. And wanting me to give you a real big hug." Mrs.

Meadows put her arms around Katherine and squeezed. Katherine's mouth trembled. It horrified her to think she might cry in front of these wonderful people. She turned her face away.

"Go out and wait in the car with Daddy," Mrs. Meadows said to one of her kids. "Get the others buckled in—we'll be right there." Sounds of clumping, of kisses so close they had to be on Mrs. Meadows's other cheek, and then the house emptied out. Mrs. Meadows stood up. "What do you think, Katie? Would you like to come here more often? It would make us happy."

Katherine nodded.

"I'll speak to your father."

"Could Jeannie come?"

"Oh, yes! Wouldn't that be fun? Run along and get in the car. One of them will show you how to use the seat belt." Briefly, Katherine felt the cupping of a hand on her head.

RHONDA SKILLINGS HAD told both Mr. Waterbury and Mary Ingersoll that her brief conversation with Katherine Caskey indicated there might be something going on between Tyler and his housekeeper, there had even been, apparently, some gift of a ring. And while Rhonda was unsure as to whether the situation was as serious as Katherine might think, she told Mary and Mr. Waterbury that it was certainly important—for the time being—to hold the information in the strictest of confidence. But Mary Ingersoll went home and told her husband, except that didn't count—he was her husband; you can tell your husband anything—and soon she telephoned a friend. *"Don't tell anyone,"* she said, and believed the assurance she heard, because this, after all, was an old and trusted friend. After that, with the sense of facing a box of chocolates and thinking—Oh, just one more—she called another friend. *"Don't tell anyone,"* she said.

Rhonda Skillings herself, having telephoned Alison Chase regarding contaminated cranberries, found it impossible not to let the news slip.

"I just get so tired," Alison had been saying. "Hold on—let me close this door." Alison had a telephone with a cord long enough that she could walk into her kitchen closet and have a private conversation in there, and Rhonda, picturing this, felt a pull toward secrecy. "I don't give a damn if the cranberries are contaminated," Alison said. "I'll use the canned jelly—who cares. I get so *tired* of being a cook and bottle washer, cleaning up after everyone."

"I get tired, too," said Rhonda, who felt the vague rumor about Connie and Tyler was like a piece of cake in her mouth that she had to speak around. "Sometimes I dream of living in an English mansion with a house full of maids."

"I'm the maid," Alison said. "And the house is a mess."

"Oh, I'm sure that's not true," said Rhonda, but she knew it was. "Does Fred complain?"

"He doesn't. But he says nicely, 'Let's see if we can keep the house picked up.' It's a criticism. Picking up doesn't help, anyway. The furniture's all nicked—"

"Here's a trick. Mix instant coffee with just a little water till it's a paste, and rub that over the nicked spots. It works—I swear. And are you making the beds first thing in the morning? Remember how Jane always says that—just make the beds."

Alison, in her dark kitchen closet, made a small noise of disgust. "I wish they'd make their own beds."

"Boys won't," said Rhonda, who had one boy and one girl. "Boys are pigs, Alison. Maybe there's hope for the next generation, but right now they're pigs."

Alison leaned against the closet door. "With Jane, it's floors," she said.

"That's right," Rhonda agreed. "Jane does her floors each day and then she feels better."

"What are you going to do about the cranberries?" Alison asked.

"I don't know. Remember that scientist who said he'd have to eat fifteen thousand pounds of berries a day for years in order to get thyroid cancer?"

"No," Alison said. "Fifteen thousand pounds a day? Then why should we worry?"

"Because the scientist worked for the chemical company producing the chemical. The weed killer. Aminotriazole. Something."

"My God," Alison said. "You can't trust anybody. The world's gotten so corrupt. Try to live a simple, decent life and what happens? Get poisoned by chemical companies on the one hand, and tyrannized by the minister's daughter on the other. I think I'm going to quit the Sunday-school business after Christmas, Rhonda."

"Listen," said Rhonda. "I'm going to tell you something. In confidence."

When she hung up, Alison opened the closet door and whispered, "Fred, Fred! Come here!"

Fred had been watching television with the boys, and, at his wife's call, he went and joined her in the closet. "What is it, Ali?"

Eventually the older boy banged on the door. "What are you two *doing* in there?"

"Leave us alone," Fred called through the door.

"Yuck," the boy said. "Oh, yuck—you two make me sick."


AND SO THE NEWS had gone around that Tyler might be mixed up with his housekeeper. It was the most dramatic news since Lauren's death—more dramatic, in a way, because it wasn't entirely clear. Many dismissed it, saying the child was "not right" and such a thing was simply foolish and unthinkable. Others weren't so sure. In any event, it provided the townspeople with the chance to complain without guilt about their minister, who had increasingly disappointed them. Tyler's behavior was gone over with such enthusiasm that the fact he had told Alison Chase her apple crisp was delicious while he did, in truth, hate apples, took on the sheen of questionable character. Doris Austin told people that he had promised her a new organ—or that he almost had—and then backed away from it. Fred Chase said he had never heard a Congregational minister quote the Catholic saints the way Tyler did. Auggie and Sylvia Dean wondered about that young woman who showed up in the back pew these days—was it true she sold cosmetics in Hollywell? And hadn't he been seen skating with her? Well, then. That was hardly the action of a man who had proposed to his married housekeeper, a woman significantly older than he was, a woman who was wanted by the state police for stealing, no less! But these things happened. You heard about desperate men all the time, men who couldn't live two minutes without a woman under the roof. He was secretive, when you thought about it. And where there's smoke, there's fire.

Bertha Babcock, the retired English teacher, was so distressed by these rumors that she told her husband to put the Pilgrim costumes away—she didn't feel like going around to the schools to lecture on the history of Maine's early settlers, nor did she feel like hosting the Historical Society meeting because she knew it would be an afternoon of gossip. She sat on her tightly upholstered loveseat while her little pug dog, Miles, stood on his tiny feet and shook in a frenzy of need, yapping his small mouth, his eyes bulging. Bertha sat with her hands in her lap, thinking how Tyler had agreed with her years before that Wordsworth's poem "I

Wandered Lonely as a Cloud" was the most beautiful in English verse, and then had shown her one day, chuckling, a parody he had come across: "When all at once I saw a crowd, / A host, of unpaid household bills!"

She sat there half the morning, watching through the old, swirly glass of her living-room window the vitiated view of the river. Finally her small dog stopped yapping and collapsed at her feet.

TYLER, MEANWHILE, after receiving the phone call from Mr. Waterbury, sat in the kitchen listening to the radio. The news mentioned nothing about Connie, and he did not think he should call her home. "On the national front," said the newscaster, "President Eisenhower has not yet responded to Premier Khrushchev's recent claim that Russia is producing two hundred fifty missiles per year, all equipped with hydrogen warheads. Khrushchev insists he will destroy all these weapons, if other powers will follow suit." Tyler looked around: There were dirty dishes on the table, pots in the sink. A pile of laundry sat in a basket by the door to the mudroom. A dish towel by the refrigerator was streaked with the dark juice of the baked beans from days ago. He thought of his mother walking through the door, and he rose to run water in the sink. "This holiday season, do something special for your family," the radio said, and he reached to turn it off.

Squirting dish soap onto a sponge, he thought the sink seemed far below him, and small. The pot he washed would not come clean; the crusted baked beans fell into the sink, leaving the skin of dark, dried, syrupy stuff on the pot. He left it, and moved into the living room. He was not entirely sure that Charlie had come over last night, not entirely sure that he had encountered Connie in the church. He remembered the chaplain in the navy telling him that in a case of shock, a person needed to be told again and again what had occurred. Repetition, the man had said. Tyler did not think he was in shock, but he was frightened by how distant and unreal the furniture seemed, the ridiculous pink walls, the dirty socks by the couch, the hooked rug his mother had made for them—all this puzzled him. Charlie Austin, he remembered now, had survived the Bataan Death March in the Philippines during the war. This is what had been mentioned to Tyler when he first arrived in town, but who had mentioned it, and was it true? Why would Charlie choose this time to come to threaten Tyler?

He did not believe, as Charlie had said, that people had found him "stuck-up and standoffish." The rumor that he was involved with Connie in some nefarious way was not one he thought to dignify with a response. Besides, who would he respond to? He was tempted to call Ora Kendall, but it was not his job to ask what foolishness was being said about him. He tried looking through his old folders for a sermon he could use on Sunday, but even that he could not seem to do. The call from Mr. Waterbury caused a swelling of warm anxiety to pump through his limbs. The man's voice had been eager and polite, assuring Tyler there would just be a "progress report," but as Tyler moved fruitlessly about the house, it began to seem to him that this voice hid unpleasant news.

He sat down with a pad of paper and wrote: *Shirley Falls. The navy. Dad. Orono. Seminary. Lauren. West Annett. Katherine. Jeannie. Lauren—D. Connie.* Then he erased the word "Connie." He spoke each word aloud, trying to connect himself to it. This, apparently, was his life.

The telephone rang and he hurried to answer it. Matilda Gowen, his secretary, spoke with some hesitation, as she explained that she and Skogie had decided to spend the winter in Florida.

They would be leaving right after Christmas, but she wanted Tyler to know, so he could find a replacement. No, she didn't know, off-hand, anyone who might be interested in the job. "You're not to worry about it," Tyler told her. "I'll find someone. You and Skogie deserve a nice rest."

They were renting a house in Key West, Matilda said. It was her idea.

"Wonderful," Tyler said.

When he hung up he could not tell if she had been her usual self. He didn't think she had been. Matilda was not a talkative person, but he thought she sounded different. Perhaps she had been embarrassed to let him down. Perhaps she had heard the foolish rumors about Connie, but she would not have believed them.

He looked at the list in his hand. *Shirley Falls. The navy.* He shook his head. They were just words, and yet around them swirled a universe of colors, scents, and scenes. With his pencil he circled again and again *Katherine* and *Jeannie*.

THE MORNING SEEMED ENDLESS. Through the window the sky was low and gray. He waited. He waited for Connie to call, or Adrian, or Ora Kendall, Doris—he hardly knew. But he felt suspended above his life, as though he were a large man doing the dead man's float in a lake, while below him fish swam through the town of West Annett, busy on their way to do things. And he had nothing to do. He realized that recently his parishioners had not been calling him nearly so often needing visits, prayer, consultation, guidance. He remembered how he had often felt like there was more than he could manage. How he had slipped into his top desk drawer the quote from Henri Nouwen: "My whole life I have been complaining that my work was constantly interrupted, until I discovered that my interruptions were my work."

He called Carol Meadows and thanked her for taking Katherine, apologized for not calling the child first thing this morning before she went to school.

"Oh, she's a sweet little girl," Carol said. "I told her we'd love to have her come back and visit, and bring little Jeannie, too."

"Say, Carol," Tyler said, "I do hate to prevail on you further. But I have a meeting tomorrow afternoon. Could she come back over just for an hour or so then? I'll drop her off after lunch, when she gets out of school."

"Of course," Carol said. "And listen. I put her in one of Tracy's old dresses this morning, and if she likes it, you keep it."

When he hung up, Tyler thought how Davis Meadows was a very lucky man. Even with the death of their first baby so many years back, Davis and Carol gave the appearance of being quietly united. What he felt was envy, as he moved once more about the empty house. The envy was like a gray sea inside him, filled with swells. That others should be wrapped in the quilt of their own worlds, safe within their families . . . pained him. And he did not want to be this way—*filled with unrighteousness, full of envy, murder, deceit, malignity, whisperers . . .*

Whisperers.

He got his coat and hat and walked into town. The sky had become a light white, and tiny snowflakes appeared as he walked, seeming to come not from above, but from the air around him. Stepping into the sanctuary, he heard organ music, and saw the back of Doris up in the choir loft; Doris was playing the organ. Tyler sat in the back pew, looking for the blanket, or any sign of Connie. But apparently she had not been back. The carpet was vacuumed smoothly—there was no smell, there were no crumbs or anything else. He watched through the tall windows as the snow fell with a gentle steadiness now. Already it had begun to line the branches of the maple trees, a small white powder, like someone had sifted confectioners' sugar over the world out there. His coat still on, Tyler listened to the organ in a kind of tired trance, and it seemed as though little snowflakes fell inside him. When the music stopped, the silence was abrupt. He shivered.

"Doris," he called out, "that was beautiful. Play some more, why don't you? How about that wonderful hymn 'Abide with Me.' Gosh, I'd love to hear that one. It's always been my favorite."

He heard a book thump shut, and in a moment Doris walked down the stairs of the choir loft. "I'm not a wind-up jack-in-the-box," she said.

He followed her into the vestibule. "Doris, is everything all right?"

"Oh, *now* you wonder." She was pulling on her coat, and when he stepped to help her with it, she moved away. "I arrived in your office weeping, and could you bother to call to check back with me? No. How many weeks ago was that? I guess you've been very busy."

"I have been busy. But your point is well taken, and I'm sorry."

Doris's cheeks had grown pink, and her braid was pulled up so tightly onto her head that he could see streaks of her scalp. "Yuh," she said. "Well, don't bother with your pity. I'm fine."

"The music is beautiful, Doris. It's nice to stop in here and hear you playing."

"If it's so nice, Tyler, why is it you never called up Chris Congdon to say they should plan in the budget for a new organ? They're starting their preliminary financial meetings for the new year, as you very well know. Or perhaps you have your mind on other things."

Horribly, a sudden pinpoint of fury seemed to explode in his brain, and he said coldly, "What other things are you referring to, Doris? Is there something on your mind? Why don't you speak to me directly?"

She looked at him with eyes that seemed big as nickels. "Oh, I'll speak to you directly," she said, clutching her music scores against her coat. "I'll tell you directly that I will not be spoken to that way. Do you understand?" She went away quickly, snowflakes falling on her braided bun.

OVERNIGHT, SHE SEEMED to have grown taller. Katherine stood in the kitchen holding her borrowed lunch box and waited while her father unzipped her coat. "I missed you," Tyler said. "It's not the same here without you." He thought even her face was older. She watched him with a kind of detachment, and he had a fleeting image of her growing into a teenager, a young woman, looking at him this way, as if she didn't need him. "Did you have a good time with the Meadowses?"

She nodded.

"You can go back there after school tomorrow. I have a meeting."

Her only response seemed a slight intake of breath. "Is that okay? Do you like being there?" She nodded again. "Good." He took the lunch box from her, set it on the table.

Katherine watched it with longing. She hoped he would not make her give it back. The beautiful Alice in Wonderland right there on its tin side. When she'd opened it at snack time, she had discovered crackers and raisins, and a peanut-butter-and-marshmallow sandwich cut into four pieces, and also two cookies.

SHE COLORED AT the dining-room table until evening. She colored a picture of Mrs. Meadows with her pretty pink cheeks, she colored a picture of Alice in Wonderland with her long yellow hair. She colored a picture of Mr. Meadows with his gray trousers and their cuffs, and a hat on his head like the kind her father wore.

For supper, her father opened a can of spaghetti, heated it in a pan. Katherine, because he asked her to, put two forks and paper napkins on the table. "Pumpkin," he said, as the pan began to sizzle, "did Connie Hatch ever hurt you?" She stared at him. "Did she ever spank you, or anything like that?" He turned the burner off, came and sat down at the table. She shook her head, a tiny gesture, watching as her father's lips became orange from the spaghetti clump he pushed into his mouth. He wiped his mouth with a napkin. "Do you know what gossip is?"

Katherine's face got warm. She knew the word, but not really the meaning, and somehow this failure in front of her father caused her pain.

"Gossip is when people talk about one another, saying things that may not be true."

He kept speaking, but a feeling of horror had come over her, and beneath the kitchen table she crossed her fingers. She thought how in Sunday school they had been told how children were kept in caves and then asked if they believed in Jesus. If they said yes, they were taken out and the lions ate them. Katherine knew she would have crossed her fingers and said she didn't believe in Jesus, and knowing this was a deep secret inside her. It made her as bad as the man who denied Jesus three times before the cock crowed, and that was awful. He got hung upside down.

"So if someone says anything to you about Connie or me, you just ignore them, okay? Rumors get started by an ugliness in people. It's sad, Katherine. But some people can't help but be ugly. You just ignore them, understand?"

Katherine nodded, kept her fingers crossed hard, beneath the table.

# NINE

M r. Waterbury's office had three large windows, two looking over the front parking lot and the other looking toward the playground and playing fields in the distance. A weak winter sun shone through this afternoon, making pale washes of light fall over his big wooden desk and across the brown tweed skirt Mary Ingersoll wore. Mr. Waterbury leaned back in his wooden swivel chair, causing it to creak as he hoisted one leg over the other. He was not a large man, but there was a corpulence to him, as though he had been inflated just slightly with a bicycle pump. He held a pen loosely in one hand, which he pointed now toward Rhonda Skillings. "I agree with you," he said. "There's no need to bring up the business with the housekeeper. If he's carrying on with her, that's a separate kettle of fish. We don't want him to think he's been called in to have rumors flung at him."

"Exactly," said Rhonda. She was seated in a big chair that had darkened maroon leather nailed to it with brass upholstery tacks, and she held a pen herself, a folder on her lap. "We're here to help his child. Period. The end. *Concern* is the name of our game today. We'll lay out for him the fears that have sprung from infantile grandiosity, coupled, as it were, with the further developmental stage of castration—"

Mr. Waterbury and Mary Ingersoll exchanged a quick glance. On Mr. Waterbury's face was the momentary expression of someone perplexed, who very much did not want to appear to be. "Concern, absolutely," Mr. Waterbury said, nodding vigorously, then wiping at his shoulders, as though he had just discovered the dandruff there. "Every day, concern is the name of our game."

Rhonda poked the end of the pen into her hair, and said: "My theory is this: When Tyler hears anything negative about Katherine's behavior, he experiences this as a narcissistic wound. Which then results in narcissistic rage. And that's what we want to avoid."

"We sure do," said Mary Ingersoll, seated over by the window. Both Rhonda and Mr. Waterbury smiled at her kindly.

"You're not to worry," Rhonda assured her.

"Is he going to stay minister?" Mary asked. "If he's involved with a married woman? It's really disgusting."

Mr. Waterbury, who attended the Episcopal church in Hollywell, opened his palm toward Rhonda. "Well, we're hardly sure if it's true," Rhonda said. "And that will be up to the church to decide. That's why I think it's important today to simply focus on Katherine. It's hard to imagine it's true," she added.

"Anything's possible when a man's in pain," Mr. Waterbury said. "Why, I knew a man who married his wife's best friend six weeks after his wife had died."

"But was his wife's best friend *married*?" Mary asked.

"No. No, she wasn't." Mr. Waterbury gave a sorrowful look toward his desk.

"I'm just going to run to the washroom," Mary said, rising.

"Of course, dear." Rhonda moved her legs to let the young woman by.

TYLER DID NOT want to park in the main lot, where he imagined he could be seen by those sitting in Mr. Waterbury's office, perhaps watching him as he walked across the lot, and so he drove the long way around so he could park by the back. He entered the side door of the school and found himself accosted at once by the smell of fear—all mixed with the presence of paint? Chalk? Paste? It swept up his throat, as he stood by the stairwell, along with the childhood memory of old Mrs. Lurvy, who used to tape kids' mouths shut with yellow tape if they whispered; it had sat on her desk with the authority of a surgical instrument. She had favored him, though Belle had broken out in hives for months when she'd first had her. Hearing the sharp clack of heels, Tyler turned. A pair of brown pumps emerged above him, the nylon stockings, a tweed skirt—some kind of paralysis kept Tyler standing, looking up, as the tweed skirt turned the corner of the stairwell, showing him a glimpse of stockinged thigh, the flash of a garter. It was Mary Ingersoll, and she might not have seen him—Tyler, in his state, had opened his mouth, but whatever part of him made decisions had decided not to say hello—but she happened to turn, and she did see him there. She stared; he stared.

"Hello," Tyler said.

She nodded, and then kept walking. "I'll be right there," he called after her. She gave no response, and he watched her walk down the corridor. It seemed to him to be a colossal injustice that he should have received a look from her as though he had been caught in some deviant behavior. It was *not his fault*.

He stood in the empty hallway, the smell of paste and paint pressing on him. Through an open classroom door he saw the little chairs, the small desks. Turning, he saw a janitor with a long mop coming toward him. Tyler raised his hand in a greeting and went down the hall to the principal's office.

"Come in, come right in," said Mr. Waterbury, giving Tyler's hand a vigorous shake. "You know Rhonda, I believe. And of course Mary."

Mary Ingersoll, having taken her seat by the window, was subdued, but Rhonda stood up and said, "Hello, Tyler," taking his hand with both her own. "Thank you for coming in, Tyler." She was speaking slowly, as though he might be deaf and needed to read her lips.

"Have a seat, have a seat." Mr. Waterbury indicated a large wooden chair. "Let me take your coat."

Tyler, shaking off his coat and handing over his hat, felt naked without them, and, sitting down, he glanced at Mary Ingersoll and was surprised to realize in her gaze how very much the young woman disliked him.

"Okay, then." Rhonda Skillings smiled. Her hair was crimped over her head, with bangs curled under and so high up on her forehead that it looked as though she could, if she needed to, reach up and peel the whole thing off. She nodded toward Mr. Waterbury, who sat behind his big wooden desk, leaning forward. The lamp on his desk cast a small arc of light over an open folder of papers that apparently contained, Tyler realized with a slight lurch to his heart, various reports on Katherine. Mr. Waterbury put his glasses on, peered at the papers, took his glasses off.

"A number of incidents, you see," he said to Tyler. "I'm afraid. Screaming, spitting, drawing obscene pictures."

"Obscene pictures?"

"Well—"

"Drawing obscene pictures?" Tyler spoke this quietly.

"She drew a picture of a woman defecating, I'm afraid."

"May I see it?"

Mr. Waterbury handed him the drawing, and Tyler glanced at it. "This is not obscene," he said, handing it back. "For heaven's sake. To call that obscene."

"It's disturbed," said Rhonda. "Let's just put it that way."

Mary Ingersoll had blushed as pink as a sunset, and Tyler realized the drawing had been of her.

"But! This is an exciting time in education." Mr. Waterbury's dark eyebrows shot up as he handed Tyler a bound booklet. "Here you go—you might find this to be of some interest." Tyler looked at the cover. *The Pursuit of Excellence.* "A report," Mr. Waterbury explained. "Funded by the Rockefeller Foundation last year, written by the country's leading educators, suggesting gifted children might be dealt with separately."

Tyler nodded slightly—a gesture of conciliation.

"And the retarded."

In the parking lot, a school bus groaned as it pulled away.

Rhonda spoke. "Katherine scored retarded on an I.Q. test, Tyler. Now, we don't believe the child is retarded—not for a minute. But we do think it's necessary she get help."

Mary Ingersoll caught his eye, held his glance before looking away.

"So much has been learned about children," said Mr. Waterbury. "Gosh, when we were kids, no one thought about these things."

Tyler cleared his throat softly. "What things?"

"Here's my theory on Katherine." Rhonda sat up straight, touching her round white earring. "But let me first fill you in on

some background knowledge, Tyler. Now, the same way we"—
and she moved her hand to include the others in the room—"might
need to be taught about the history of religion, I thought you could
be helped by understanding some basic theories of psychology."

He said, "Just don't use too many big words, Rhonda." She
covered for him, laughing, but they knew—it was in the room—
that he was feeling like a big, cornered animal. He placed *The
Pursuit of Excellence* back on Waterbury's desk, laced his fingers
together, and waited for Rhonda to begin.

"Children are sexual beings," she said.

Mary Ingersoll began playing with the chain around her neck
that held the tiny cross; back and forth her fingers went.

"Children come into the world and all they know is Mommy's
breast." Rhonda placed a hand over her own breast for a moment.
"They're hungry, they cry, and Mommy picks them up. They're
*powerful*, you see. They, as far as they see it, control the world.
'Infantile grandiosity,' this is called."

The afternoon light through the tall windows had become the
pale gray of early dusk. The trees behind the front parking lot
seemed far away, twiggy and bare against the sky. Mr. Waterbury
leaned back and switched on the tall lamp behind his desk, so that
a yellow funnel of light suddenly illuminated half his desk and the
lap of Mary Ingersoll. Tyler said slowly, "Infantile grandiosity.
There's a big word."

"Two words." Mary turned partway in her chair, smoothed a
hand over her lap.

"Two. Yes, indeed." A silence followed, and then Tyler's stomach growled loudly. Mr. Waterbury eagerly offered him a Life
Savers candy. "No, thank you," Tyler said.

Rhonda smiled at him. "Okay. But are you with me so far,
Tyler?"

"I seem to be."

Mary Ingersoll stopped playing with her chain. He looked at her, unsmiling.

"All right, then." As Rhonda spoke, her red lipstick began to stick her lips together on the side. Tyler watched as the lipstick, up and down, became gummy, a little white ball of something appearing finally on her lower lip. She spoke of infantile sexuality, of Oedipal desires, Electra desires, a little girl's developing sexual desire for Daddy. "Often you'll hear little girls say to their fathers, 'I wish you'd divorce Mommy so I could marry you.' "

Tyler had never heard any little girl say this. He glanced at Mr. Waterbury, who was watching Rhonda with the exaggeratedly pleased and embarrassed look of a parent witnessing a child perform in a play.

Rhonda spoke then of penis envy, of castration fears, even placing her hand, amazingly, across her crotch area, as she described the fear a little girl feels when she realizes her mother and she appear to have been harmed. And then Rhonda returned to infantile grandiosity, the belief that one can do anything, that the whole world is in their power, that they are God-like. She stopped to smile at Tyler; he looked back at her without smiling.

"Small children are very literal," Rhonda went on. Mary Ingersoll, over by the window, nodded. Rhonda recalled how Toby Dunlop, when he was a little boy, heard Marilyn say, "Gosh, I really have my hands full," and Toby looked puzzled and said, "But Mommy, I don't see anything in your hands."

Mr. Waterbury laughed. "That's just it—isn't it," he said. "That's just it."

Tyler crossed his arms over his chest. Rhonda continued, "Freud was a genius. Why, before Freud we were as clueless to the ways of the self as people were to the stars before the invention of the telescope. Galileo allowed us to explore the outer horizons, and Freud has allowed us to explore our inner horizons."

Tyler felt so sleepy suddenly that his eyelids almost closed.

"Freud was really smart." Mary Ingersoll said this, over by the window. "He knew so much stuff." Tyler roused himself, took in a deep breath, crossed his legs. "Everything that happens to us in life just comes from our childhood," Mary said.

Tyler watched her. "Is that right?" He spoke this condescendingly.

Mary's face flushed, and she said, "We think Katherine thinks she killed her mother."

There was a silence in the room. Tyler looked from face to face.

"We think," Rhonda finally said quietly, "that, considering the stage of Katherine's development, considering the concept of infantile grandiosity, that she may unconsciously blame herself for her mother's death. You know, Tyler, etymologically, *infant* is the one who cannot speak."

Outside on the playing field, a whistle blew.


ON THE HILL past town where the Meadowses' house sat, the sky was now almost the color of the large sweeps of field that unrolled behind; the horizon line was thin and indistinct except for where hackmatack trees grew in a scattering, the bare woodbine twirled through their branches, all of it with a light snow covering from days before. And there were tall clumps of wheat grass closer to the house that had snow in their bent tops. Everything—the lightly covered snow fields and the bare trees and the grasses— held the lightest tint of lavender.

Katherine, bunched inside a winter coat, wearing a woolen hat and thick gloves, gazed around her. She thought maybe the world was built on the boot of a giant, like Paul Bunyan, only the giant was much, much bigger; on his toe was the town of West Annett, and in the summer, moss grew on his boot, little clumps of earth, and houses were built there, like the Meadowses' red house, and like her own house, and in the winter, when the giant went walking in the snow, the houses got covered with the snow, and nobody knew they were living on the boot of a giant, but it could be true. He was a nice giant, meaning no harm, and maybe he didn't even know the world was growing on the toe of his boot, because he would be so tall he couldn't see all that way down.

But her mother would know, because up in heaven you could see far.

Katherine bent her head back, looking straight up at the sky, but the sky was gray and a little whipped-looking, like a messy swirl made from a dirty boot. Maybe at night the giant lay down with his messy boots stuck up in the air and left it smudgy like that. When the giant remembered to wipe up the floor, then it shone a pretty blue. Katherine smiled to think the sky could be the floor; the giant could be upside down and nobody would know. People wouldn't fall off because he was so strong that everything on earth was protected in the little pieces of twigs and soil and ice and snow.

"Hurry!" shouted the older Meadows girl. She had just come out the back door of the house and was clapping her hands. She called to her sister and brother, and to Katherine. "Come on," she called. "Ma said we can go in the shelter for just a little bit before it gets dark!"

This was a regular, but rare, treat. Davis Meadows liked to know that even when there was snow on the ground, the bomb shelter he had constructed so carefully could be opened quickly, and so sometimes he let Carol open it when he wasn't home, and the children were allowed to play in there. He thought the children should be familiar with it, so should there be a nuclear attack and he and his family had to spend days down there, the children would not be frightened.

Katherine could not believe her eyes. There, in the backyard,

Mrs. Meadows bent down in her red coat and snow boots, and pulled up a trap door. "Careful, kids," she said. "Careful. One at a time." The older girl went first, disappearing down into the earth. Then the little boy, helped by his mother, and then the next girl, and then it was Katherine's turn. A ladder went down, down, and there was a light on. "Turn around and go down backward," Mrs. Meadows said to her, and so Katherine went, slowly, feeling someone taking hold of her legs and guiding them down the ladder.

"Just ten minutes," called Mrs. Meadows from up on the earth. "And remember the rules."

Built into the walls were narrow bunk beds, and also two cots along the sides of the little room Katherine found herself in. "Sit," said the older girl, and so Katherine sat on one of the cots. "Look, there's cards. Want to play Go Fish?"

Katherine didn't move. There was a Raggedy Ann doll on one of the bunks, and the younger girl, seeing Katherine look at it, climbed up and tossed it down. "You can play with her," the girl said. "But then it has to be kept here."

"Do you have a bomb shelter?" asked the older girl, flipping down cards.

Katherine shook her head.

"What will you do when it bombs?" asked the younger girl.

Katherine shrugged.

The boy said somberly, "You might die, 'cause of what gets in the air."

"Stop it, Matt," his sister said. "Don't scare her."

Hanging on one wall was a big shovel, a pickax, a flashlight, and a can opener. Katherine turned to look behind her. There were rows of canned food, like they used to have in the mudroom at home. Mrs. Meadows was climbing down the ladder, and she smiled at Katherine, her cheeks pink. "Matthew, get your feet off the cot, honey. Let's make sure the batteries are working in the flashlight and radio." She took the flashlight from the wall and switched it on.

"Let me hold it," said the younger girl, and Mrs. Meadows handed it to her.

"Do you want to play with the doll for a bit?" Mrs. Meadows asked Katherine, picking up Raggedy Ann. Katherine nodded and sat on the cot with the doll sitting beside her, making the doll's feet stick out in front of her. "Okay, let me try the radio. Turn the flashlight off now. We don't want to use up the batteries." A staticky sound filled the small place, and Mrs. Meadows fiddled with the knobs on the radio, which sat next to a table that held two pots.

"We can live in here up to two weeks," the older girl told Katherine. "There's water behind that cabinet."

"Shhh," said her mother, bending her ear to the radio. "Oh, my goodness." Mrs. Meadows stood up straight. The announcer's voice said, ". . . wanted by the police for robberies at the county nursing home, has turned herself in. Police say Constance Hatch hid for almost a month before deciding to—" Mrs. Meadows turned the radio off.

"Ma, what *was* that?" the older girl asked, turning.

"I'm not sure," Mrs. Meadows said. "Let's go back into the house now."

AS HE SAT captive in the office of Mr. Waterbury, Tyler was aware of the pain beneath his collarbone radiating with such intensity that a nail might have been driven through him there. But he sat without moving. Rhonda, if he heard her right, had been saying in a perky tone of voice that everyone experienced the desire to kill his or her parents. That this information was relayed to him with a sense of irreducible truth about it, that Rhonda's perky tone held a restrained, incontrovertible authority, while Mary Ingersoll spread into the air the noxious, invisible cloud of her disdain, and Mr. Waterbury wore the eager smile of someone in befuddled allegiance with all that was being said—all this seemed to Tyler to be sharply offensive, calling upon the deepest part of himself to remain civilized, polite, manly. But anger, like the Red Sea, swirled through his head.

"Original sin, Tyler," Rhonda said, leaning forward, smiling, "answers all this. It's fascinating, really. The story of original sin has risen from man's need to grapple with guilt. We feel guilty, all of us. And we're confused by this guilt. The story of the fall from grace, being booted right out of that Garden of Eden, and the ability to be redeemed, appeals to us so strongly because we *really* feel guilty by our sense of being enraged as infants, by that unconscious desire we have to kill our parents. Our innocence is shattered, you see, before we barely have words to understand it."

Silence.

They were all looking at him. He nodded his head slowly, because he had no idea, really, what Rhonda was talking about, only that he found it ludicrous, as if she had been brainwashed. He wanted to say that she was an idiot, just as his father-in-law had been, that more and more this was a godless world. He looked out the window, dark enough now that it reflected back to him the scene in the office: the lamp behind Mr. Waterbury's desk, the still figure of Mary Ingersoll, legs crossed, leaning forward in her chair. He peered beyond the reflection and saw a small flock of birds move in one short flutter from the top of one bare tree to another. *Why hidest thou thy face from me? . . . I am afflicted and ready to die from my youth up.*

"What are your thoughts, Tyler?" Rhonda asked.

He turned to look at her. "Well," he said, nodding slightly, "certainly everything you say is interesting. And seems to me to be rubbish." He had a sense of being entirely separated from himself;

where his words came from, who was allowing them, he couldn't have said; a vacuum seemed to be around him, but more sentences came from his mouth, a web of strings, a mess of stuff. "How it helps Katherine for you to reinterpret the story of Genesis is beyond me. Interpret anything you like, but to drag Katherine through such foolishness when she has already much on her back to bear, to accuse her of"—and here Tyler turned toward Mr. Waterbury—"drawing obscene pictures . . . I ask you, what's going on here? They used to say when I was young, 'Get your mind out of the gutter,' and—"

"Whoa now," Mr. Waterbury said, his chair creaking as he sat back. "Whoa now. Let's think here, and not speak so rashly. Let's try and be polite."

Undeniably, Mary Ingersoll smirked. He was their dancing bear, their circus fun. And he thought he had spent his entire life trying to be polite. Thinking of the other man first. Probably, he was having a heart attack right now, or a stroke, for the pain beneath his collarbone was almost intolerable.

Rhonda said calmly, "Oh, Tyler. There's really been a grave misunderstanding. In my eagerness, I've overstated the case. I was only trying to help you see what Katherine might be up against, so that we could get her to start talking again."

A dizziness had overtaken him. "I apologize," he said to Mr. Waterbury. "I certainly apologize for the remark about the gutter."

"Oh, sure, sure. Not to worry now." Mr. Waterbury nodded.

There was a rap on his door, and, after a startled moment, Mr. Waterbury went to answer it. "Thank you," he said quietly. "Yes, you're right. Thank you."

He came back and sat down. "Whoa," he said, looking around. "My secretary just heard, and thought it might be relevant because Mr. Caskey was here"—nodding toward Tyler—"that Connie Hatch—"

Heat washed through Tyler.

"Connie Hatch what?" said Mary Ingersoll, sitting forward more.

"Apparently she's given herself in and confessed to the murder of two women." They all looked at Tyler. He closed his eyes slowly, opened them slowly.

"Oh, dear God," he said quietly. "The poor thing."

TELEPHONES RANG THAT NIGHT. They did not ring in Tyler's house, where he waited to hear from Adrian Hatch. But they rang in many other homes there along the river. Mary Ingersoll was describing Tyler Caskey as a "pervert" to a friend. "He was standing *right there,* looking up my dress. These ministers, they're repressed. My gosh—"

It was a good thing that Alison Chase had a party line for her telephone because that way both Rhonda and Jane Watson could talk to her at once. "He didn't act surprised," Rhonda said. "Most people would say, 'What in the world? My housekeeper is a murderer?' But he didn't act that way."

"Tell us again," Jane said, waving her hand to indicate her little girl, Martha, should go away, back upstairs to her room. "Did he have the demeanor of someone who had been, well, you know, intimate with her?"

"No," Rhonda said. "No, really, I think that part's not true. It was just more like he knew."

"If he knew," said Alison Chase, "then he's been harboring a fugitive."

"Not necessarily," said Jane. "If he didn't know where she was, he couldn't be accused of harboring her."

("What's even more ironic," Mary Ingersoll was now telling another friend, "is that he accused Mr. Waterbury of having his mind in the gutter!")

"How did the rest of the conference go?" Jane wanted to know. "Martha said the child actually had some food in her lunch box the other day."

"The conference went poorly," Rhonda said, and her tone disappointed the other women, for she was using a closed-down "professional" tone of voice that they didn't care for.

"Say, Jane," Alison said, standing in her kitchen closet with the long telephone cord. "What are you doing about cranberries this year?"

"Canned," said Jane. "I'm not going near a contaminated cranberry. I'm not having Martha come down with some strange disease twenty years from now."

"Martha eats cranberries?" Alison asked. "My kids won't eat cranberries. Or fish. Or anything green. Anything with color, come to think of it."

"The conference went poorly," Rhonda said, "because, just as I suspected, Tyler can't bear to hear anything negative about his child. He simply cannot bear it. And poor Mary Ingersoll. She's a sweet kid, but awful young, she just wants to be important, you know, and help out, but she rubs him the wrong way, that's for sure."

"Martha likes her all right," said Jane. "She talks about her hair. But I don't know if she loves her, the way some kids do."

"Some kids love Katherine?" asked Alison. "Who?"

"No, no. My goodness. I'm talking about Mary Ingersoll."

"She's a good teacher," Rhonda said. "A little inexperienced, that's all."

"Where is Connie now?" Jane asked.

"I think she's being held over in the county jail," Alison said.

"Isn't it ironic," Rhonda said, "that the county jail is attached to the same building as the county farm, where she did these things?"

"I thought of that," said Alison. "How funny if she ended up being a prisoner right where she did her crime."

"Well, those are county prisoners, and if she's killed these women, she'll be in state prison. Over in Skowhegan at the women's correctional place. I suppose for the rest of her life. How did she kill them—have they said?"

"Drowning them, I think," Jane answered.

"Drowning?" Alison and Rhonda spoke together. Alison said, "How could you drown a poor old sick lady and not have anyone notice?"

"I don't know," said Jane. "But I heard something about exhuming the bodies to check for water in their lungs. Charlie Austin's cousin, you know, works up there in the police department. So Doris heard some of this."

"Gruesome," Rhonda said. "Absolutely gruesome. And so angry! An angry thing to do."

When they hung up, Jane called Alison back. "Do you need a doctorate in psychology to know that killing someone is an angry thing to do?" The two women laughed until tears came to their eyes.

TYLER WAS NOT able to suppress his feelings of rising anxiety, and after they had eaten, he left the dishes in the sink and said, "Kitty-Kat, let's go for a drive."

Wordlessly, the child went to get her coat, and he tucked her in beside him in the front seat. The dark sky had cleared, the stars were visible above the dark fields, and the moon, like half a white button, shone in the sky. He drove all the way out to Connie's place, not sure what he would do. There was no light on in the trailer, but there were lights on in the downstairs of Evelyn's big house. He imagined Evelyn and Adrian speaking earnestly about

Connie, and it nagged him—he should be there. "I'll only be a minute," he said, parking by the barn. But when he walked up the front steps, he saw Adrian and Evelyn were watching television, both staring straight ahead. Evelyn seemed to laugh at something on the television. Tyler waited a long moment, then turned and walked back to the car.

He drove to Hollywell, to the bus station where Lauren had called him that day, not knowing where she was. He drove down Main Street, past the pharmacy, down a side street by the house where Susan Bradford lived; a light was on in the living room, and he was moved to think of her in there alone, but the feeling seemed far away.

He drove home along the back roads, sorry to think of getting back to the farmhouse, for being in motion made the ache and anxiety in him only just bearable; he began to think of his sermon once again. You have no idea, he thought, envisioning his congregation, how offensive it is to come into God's house and soil it with your petty, unkind thoughts.

It seemed Katherine had fallen asleep. Her head was leaning against the back of the seat, her face turned toward the window. The sudden, quiet sound of her voice surprised him. She said, "Daddy, why is the moon following us?"

IT WAS INDEED ironic that the county prisoners were kept in the same building that housed the county farm where Connie had worked, and where Tyler had visited the bewildered Dorothy Aldercott. The jail was not set up for women prisoners because there were so few, and Connie was being kept in a segregated wing, her meals brought to her so that she would not eat with the men.

"Turns out just because you confess something doesn't mean the state right away believes you did it." Adrian spoke toward the windshield, not turning his head to Tyler, even when Tyler turned to him.

"You mean they need corroborating evidence," Tyler said.

Adrian didn't answer.

The road leading to the county farm was long, winding its way off the main road to a section of land that was treeless and barren. The road climbed up a hill that had on both sides only large sweeps of unbroken snow, gray-blue against the cloudy sky. The building itself was of a dirty yellowish brick, with additions that stuck out here and there, graceless and tired-looking, and so seemingly lacking in anything human that the barbed wire rolled along the top of two walls, coming into sight as Adrian downshifted, appeared momentarily and bizarrely to offer an image of liveliness in that half a second before the meaning sank in. *I was in prison and you visited me.*

Because Connie had said Tyler was a minister—her minister— he was allowed to see her alone. Adrian stayed in the small lobby by the reception area, and Tyler, having been greeted politely by the sheriff, was then handed over to a uniformed, expressionless man, who led Tyler through a series of three locked gates, each one locked behind him before the next was unlocked, so that two times he stood, essentially, in a cage while the man unhurriedly found the keys on a key ring the size of a saucer. Tyler held his hat with both hands, sweat forming so completely over him that he felt it even on his wrists as he waited to pass through the yellow painted bars. And then he was in a small, windowless room that had a plain table and three chairs. He waited. A large clock on the wall had its hands showing a time of ten-twenty, and it took Tyler a while to realize the clock was broken; it was not moving forward.

A feeling of calm filled him, but he knew it was not to be trusted, that it signified only that something inside him had shut down, like the clock. Moving just his eyes, he looked about the room. It probably had not been painted since it was first constructed. Two bare lightbulbs shone from fixtures high above him. He thought, with a kind of lassitude, that had he been Dietrich Bonhoeffer, he might have killed himself.

Across from him was a small commotion, the metal door opening, a guard standing back, and there was Connie, wearing a tan shift, her hair down, her eyes reddened and sunken back in the sockets. He would not have recognized her. But her face lit up, and she reached her arms toward him. "Tyler!" she said.

# TEN

Jeannie had learned to say, "Daddy is a mimster. A mimster," she shrieked, clapping her hands, while Margaret Caskey stood behind her, and the old dog, Minnie, wagged her tail before lying down with her head on the rung of the rocking chair.

"Look how she talks, Tyler," said Mrs. Caskey. "All week I pointed to a picture of you and said, 'Daddy is a minister,' and now she's learned it."

Little Jeannie buried her head in a couch cushion, giggling, then threw the cushion into the air. "Daddy, daddy," and then a fit of delighted laughter. Katherine watched, a hand in her mouth.

"Get your hand out of your mouth," said her grandmother. "My word, if you had any idea how many germs lived on a hand. On anything. Do you know what germs are, Katherine?"

"Daddy is a mimster," said Jeannie, who was beginning to look exhausted now; she was fair-skinned, and around her eyes, blue shadows showed quickly when she got tired. For the first time she had not napped in the car ride up, Mrs. Caskey told Tyler. She was at that stage now of going from two naps to one. Tyler did not remember Katherine going from two naps to one.

"Excuse me," he said, for the telephone in his study was ringing.

Ora Kendall was on the phone. "Tyler—what's going on?"

"How nice to hear from you," Tyler said. "It's been a while. How are you, Ora?"

"Oh, stop it. People are saying things, Tyler. You must know that."

On the horizon it looked as though an egg yolk had broken and was seeping along the edge of the earth. "I don't keep up with the local gossip." He felt suddenly breathless and stiff, inside the body of a very old man. He straightened his shoulders. *The mouth of the deceitful are opened against me: they have spoken against me with a lying tongue.*

"Mostly about Connie. I don't believe it myself, but it's said that you went to visit her in prison yesterday."

"And what if I did, Ora? I went with her husband. A minister visits people in trouble."

"What did she say? God, did she *do* it?"

"Ora, you know I don't repeat conversations."

"Right. Well, people are saying you must have been helping to hide her. Oh, they're saying all sorts of things. And in my opinion—do you want my opinion?"

"I do, actually. Yes."

"In my opinion you'd better start going out and talking to your congregants. Let them see you, for heaven's sake. Tell them your concerns, that you understand their concerns."

The sky was a deepening blue with that streaking yellow below it. The trees on the hills were brown and bare and still. "I see," Tyler said, sitting down slowly.

"Jane Watson was even going to—oh, never mind. But get off your high horse and come back down to the little folk, Tyler."

"I see," Tyler said again. His underarms prickled. "Anyone who wants to see their minister, Ora, see who he is, and hear what he has to say, can come to church tomorrow."

He sat in his chair and watched while the yellow faded from the sky. Just when he thought the sun had gone down fully, there was a reflection back up into the sky of a glorious pinkish-purple against the striated clouds. He tried to remember how he had once liked Ora a great deal, but the memory seemed far away. What filled his head was Connie, like a thick, dark moss—the image of her when the guard took her away, how she had turned to look at him when she was at the door, her reddened eyes like a frightened child's; he had raised his hand in a gesture that was meant to convey he would be back, for he had not said so to her directly when they spoke. On his way out, he had passed the men prisoners on their way into the dining hall, the same dining hall used by the residents in the county farm on the other side of the building, and the men had frightened him; their eyes were shiny as they looked him over, the guards telling them to move along, move along. He had asked the sheriff if Connie was safe, and the fellow had said, Yup, nothing was going to happen on his watch. They had brought in that woman guard from the state place in Skowhegan. Tyler did not think he had ever known a prison guard before. Bonhoeffer had made friends with his guards, some of them.

Tyler tapped his fingers to his mouth. For a long time he sat, until the hills in the distance could barely be seen, the birdbath just a gray shape through the window.

—

WHEN THE CHILDREN were in bed, Margaret Caskey sat down with her knitting, her arm jerking in quick motions. "Sit," she directed Tyler, and he sat down in the rocking chair. "As you can imagine," she said, an eyebrow raised, her eyes cast down at the knitting, "I was sick to hear about Connie Hatch saying she'd gone and killed two women. You had a lunatic in this very house, Tyler. What a shock that gave me."

Tyler waited a moment. "I've been to see her," he finally said.

Margaret Caskey stopped knitting. "You went to see her? Where?"

"In jail. Yesterday with Adrian. We drove over together."

"Why, in the name of the good Lord, would you feel compelled to go see that woman?"

"Mother, for heaven's sake. It's my job. She's in trouble."

His mother resumed knitting. "I'll say she's in trouble. I hope to heaven they lock her up and throw away the key."

He watched her, trying to remember the mother of his youth, and he could not. It seemed the woman seated on the couch was made of molecules pressed so tightly together that her face, her long fingers, her small ankles, could all have been made of some metal beneath the skin, and yet she was perishable, he thought. Everyone was.

"I hope you realize," she said, glancing over at him, jerking the yarn, "that merely having her in your home may have harmed your reputation."

"What are you talking about?" he asked. "The church hired her for me."

"Yes, and as I recall, there were some women in the Ladies' Aid not so keen on it from the very get-go. She stopped going to church years ago, and now it makes you wonder why. Even Lauren didn't like her, but you insisted on keeping her. And I don't think, even as a minister doing God's work, it behooves you to stay in contact with her much longer."

He had not wanted to mention it, but a certain anxiety—and something else—caused him to drill forward with the words. "Well, Mother, there seems to be a silly rumor. The kind of thing that happens in a small town, when people are bored with their own lives and needing some excitement."

Margaret Caskey stopped knitting and looked at him.

"That I was somehow mixed up with Connie. That I even, apparently, gave her a ring."

"Tyler. What in the *world*."

Tyler raised his eyebrows in weariness. "People think up things to say. It's not fair to Connie, though. Or to her husband."

"Connie! Who gives a hoot about Connie? What about you? Who's spreading this rumor, and what have you done to stop it?"

"Mother, relax. Keep your voice down. If a pastor responded to every rumor floating around his parish, he'd have no time for anything else."

Mrs. Caskey put her knitting aside, took a hankie from her sweater sleeve, and tapped her mouth. "And what if Susan Bradford should hear this dreadful thing?"

"What if she should? There's nothing I can do. If she believes this, then she doesn't know me very well."

"She *doesn't* know you very well—that's the point! She's been getting to know you bit by bit. Oh, my heavens. This makes me ill. Ill."

"Then I never should have mentioned it to you."

"Don't do that, Tyler Caskey. Don't pretend that you need to keep secrets from me just because you don't like the way I react to them."

He stood up and started to walk out of the room.

"Where are you going?" his mother said.

"I have work to do. Tomorrow is a very important sermon."

"Well, I've invited Susan for Sunday dinner afterward."

Tyler turned. "You did? Without telling me?"

His mother picked up her knitting. "I'm telling you now, aren't I? Do you think it's been easy for me watching you this past year? You have a chance to make things better, and you don't seem to even know it."

He pictured himself picking up the rocking chair, breaking it against the wall, snapping whatever he could of its back rungs, and the image so surprised him that he came and sat back down in it, resting his hands on its arms carefully.

"There's some person out there wanting to *hurt* you, Tyler, and you need to find out who it is. Perhaps Connie started it herself before she ran off to God knows where."

"That's rubbish, Mother." His mouth was dry.

"It's hardly rubbish. This could cost you your job. Sometimes I think our ancestors had the right idea by putting liars in stocks and pillories, right in the center of town, where people could jeer at them."

Katherine, listening to this at the top of the stairs, huddled against the banister, felt black circles of darkness rolling over her. It was like she'd stepped into the picture on the Sunday-school wall—a small child in a dark cave waiting before they came to get her, to have a lion eat her up. Even though she would have crossed her fingers and said she didn't believe in Jesus so they wouldn't take her away, it was like that hadn't worked, it was her time to go, and there was no one in the cave to pray with her; it was like when Connie told her about being locked in the outhouse with her brother when they were young, cobwebs in the stinky dark; but she didn't have a brother—she was alone and it was happening; the darkness of her deceit had rolled up to get her, and she was so frightened she was dizzy, couldn't even stand up, though she tried, clinging to the banister, and then she was tumbling . . . it went on and on, slow and fast together, bump, bump, upside down, one stair after another, her grandmother's scream, her father's big hand. Finally, there she was in his arms. "I did it," she sobbed. "I did it, Daddy. It was me, it was me. I didn't mean to."

She was placed on the couch, her arms and legs checked. "Move this," they said. "Can you move this?" And then her grandmother standing over her. "Did what, Katherine?" Katherine turned her face away, heard her father in a big voice: "Mother, go to bed."

"I am not going to bed."

A bigger voice. "Mother. Go to bed." The silence that followed as Mrs. Caskey walked up the stairs. Katherine turned her head. Her father, so tall, high up, was watching her.

"I did it," she whispered, crying.

He checked her again for bruises and broken bones, then took her into his study and closed the door, which scared her—she had never seen the door closed before. She cried and cried. Her father sat her on his lap behind his desk.

"Tell me, Kitty-Kat," he said.


SUNDAY MORNING THE sky was clear, the air cold. The snow along the edges of the road seemed shrunken and crusty, and the morning sunlight hit the trees at an angle, causing long shadows to fall across the road. It was too cold for the sun to moisten the little patches of ice or soften the scoops of snow caught in the arms of bare trees. In the gully by Upper Main Street, the small creek that fed into the river was a gray, swollen bump of muscular-looking ice. Alongside were frozen ferns, shriveled and broken, as though someone had opened packages of frozen spinach and flung them into the woods.

Tyler's eye took this in; he saw, too, his mother's bony, gloved hand pressed against the dashboard as they turned the corner; he saw the dust on the dashboard, the bump in her glove where she wore her wedding ring. In the backseat Jeannie giggled, as Katherine whispered to her. "I hope you're not telling secrets," her grandmother said.

Tyler spoke quietly. "Leave her alone." Glancing in the rearview mirror, he caught Katherine's eye and winked. She smiled back so widely her mouth opened, and she raised her shoulders inside her coat.

He had stayed up with her way into the night, while she sat sideways in his lap, her small hands moving as she spoke. He had explained to her that answering Mrs. Skillings's question was not gossiping—that she had done nothing wrong in telling her he had given a ring to Mrs. Hatch; she had been mistaken, and people often got mixed up and said mistaken things. "What are stocks and pillories?" she asked. "What Nana was saying."

He drew a sketch. "Awful things," he said. "People don't do that anymore."

"That was in the olden days?"

"That's right."

"Are you going to lose your job, like Nana said?"

"Oh, no."

"There's a Raggedy Ann doll in the Meadowses' backyard. In a house underground. When the bomb comes, will it hurt?"

"There won't be a bomb, Pumpkin."

"How do you know?"

"Because no one wants to destroy this earth. Russia, just like us, wants the world to keep on going."

"Don't the Meadowses know that?"

"Well, sometimes people get frightened."

"I get frightened." She looked up into his face.

"What do you get frightened of?"

"Dying."

He nodded.

"Mummy died because God was ready for her?"

He nodded again.

"Why was he ready for her?"

"We don't know."

"Does God know?"

"God knows everything."

"Does God know once when I was playing in your office Mrs. Gowen came in and showed me how she could take out her teeth?"

"*Did* she?"

Katherine nodded. After a moment she asked, "How come Nana doesn't like me?"

"Pumpkin, Nana loves you."

Katherine kicked her feet, then was still. "She doesn't act like it."

"Well." Tyler put both arms around Katherine's tiny torso, and squeezed her in a hug. "Nana worries a lot," he said, "and sometimes people have so much going on in their heads, they get their wires crossed."

Katherine appeared to think about this for some time. "Connie Hatch got her wires crossed."

"Yes, I think she did."

Again, Katherine pondered this. "Boy," she said, sighing, "God must be awful busy."

Past midnight he put her to bed. A crack of light shone beneath the door of his mother's room, but he went back downstairs to work on his sermon. He kept standing up, putting his hands to his face, sitting back down. Finally, he wrote and wrote. He felt like an athlete who had trained for years, and the race was now here. Strength rose in him, then fell, then rose again. He had never before delivered a sermon of sternness.

The Scripture reading would be from 59 Isaiah, ending with the words *and justice standeth afar off: for truth is fallen on the street, and equity cannot enter.* Then he would pray, saying, "Only the infinite mercy of God can meet the infinite pathos of human life."

Before the offering he would read the 26th Psalm, *Lord, I have loved the habitation of thy house, and the place where thine honor dwelleth. . . . My foot standeth in an even place: in the congregations will I bless the Lord.*

And then he would deliver a sermon unlike any he had delivered before.

"Do you think," Tyler wrote, "that because we have learned the sun does not go down, that in fact we are going around at a dizzying speed, that the sun is not the only star in the heavens—do you think this means we are any less important than we thought we were? Oh, we are far less important than we thought we were, and we are far, far more important than we think we are. Do you imagine that the scientist and the poet are not united? Do you assume you can answer the question of who we are and why we are here by rational thought alone? It is your job, your honor, your birthright, to bear the burden of this mystery. And it is your job to ask, in every thought, word, and deed: How can love best be served?

"God is not served when you speak with relish of rumors about those who are poor in spirit and cannot be defended; God is not served when you ignore the poverty of spirit within yourselves."

The sky was growing light by the time he put his pencil down. Reading the pages over, he saw that he had broken a cardinal rule of homiletics; he had used the word "you" instead of "we." He sat for a long time wondering about this. Then he washed his face and fell asleep on the couch.

When he woke, Katherine was standing before him. She had dressed herself; her red turtleneck was inside out, the tag that said BUSTER BROWN sticking out like a little white tongue at her throat.

"Daddy," she whispered, "are you still not mad at me from what I told you last night?"

He reached to put his arm around her. "I'm the opposite of mad."

"What's opposite of mad?"

He sat up, rubbed his face. "Not mad, I guess."

Her laughter, genuine and sudden, made her seem older. But then she spun around like the little girl she was. "So you still love me," she said in a singsong way.

Now he glanced at her once more in the rearview mirror, and saw she was holding both of Jeannie's hands in her own.

He pulled into the parking lot of the church. There was the Austin car, and the Chase car, and the Gowens'. He drove past them, down the small hill, to park near his office. How many times had he driven here? A pang of nostalgia squeezed at his heart; the scene, in its familiarity, seemed to disorient him. How tired he was came to him as he turned the engine off, a certain aching of his legs, and the sense that a piece of a screen door was implanted behind his eyes. He kissed the girls, and his mother took them off to the classroom. In his study he sat on the edge of his chair. *Consider and hear me, O Lord my God: lighten mine eyes . . . lest mine enemy say, I have prevailed against him; and those that trouble me rejoice when I am moved. But I have trusted in thy mercy.*

*Be with me now.*

ONE AFTER ANOTHER, cars pulled in slowly and parked near the church, their long, smooth hoods nose-to-nose in the middle of the parking lot. Women emerged, tying scarves around their throats, while over one arm they held their pocketbooks, and they waited for their husbands, who were fumbling with keys and wallets, then headed up the walkway, nodding silent greetings to others. More cars arrived, station wagons and sedans low to the ground. There was no room left in the parking lot, and some had to park on the road.

"Like a funeral," Jane Watson murmured to her husband, who raised an eyebrow in response.

Tyler, in his basement study, was only vaguely aware of an increase of commotion overhead as children were taken over to Sunday school, as the women ducked into the kitchen off the activities room to make sure coffee hour would be ready. He was busy reading Bonhoeffer. In a letter from prison, Bonhoeffer had written to his friend Eberhard Bethge that we should not allow psychotherapy and existentialist philosophy to be God's pioneers. "The Word of God is far removed from this revolt of mistrust, this revolt from below." Tyler wrote this in the margin of his sermon. And then, as he started to close the book, his eye fell on a line Bonhoeffer had written to his parents, "Now the dismal autumn days have begun and one has to try and get light from within."

Overhead Tyler heard the organ prelude starting, and he put on his black robe, snapping it closed down the front, and climbed the stairs. As he stepped through the side door to enter the chancel, the prelude seemed very loud to him, and, without looking up directly, he could sense the church was full. He sat on his "throne" waiting, his eyes cast down, but not closed. "One has to get light from within." He pictured how light-filled Katherine was after their talk last night, and how in that way, she had reminded him of Lauren. He shifted his legs, and they felt filled with cement. That these people today in church had been, behind his back, accusing him of foolishness while his daughter had been caught in sadness, his housekeeper caught in her lonely sins, seemed to him to be contemptible.

The organ prelude stopped.

Tyler stood and walked to the pulpit. Never, in his tenure here, had the church been this full. People sat shoulder-to-shoulder in every pew, including the third row. There in the back was Susan

Bradford, her hair combed very neatly, her face carrying a guarded, pleasant look of vague surprise. His mother sat not far from her, pale, erect. His eye caught the figure of Mary Ingersoll sitting beside her young husband. For a moment he had an image of them all dressed in colonial clothes, here to watch a public hanging. He looked down at his sermon, the words from Isaiah. He looked back up. They waited. He walked away from the pulpit to the center of the chancel. He would say, "Why have you come today to the house of the Lord?" But no words came from his mouth.

He walked back to the pulpit. He was angry, but the anger seemed to be not inside him, but rather around him. Nothing was inside him. No light. Nothing. Tyler raised an arm, lowered it. The faces looking up at him appeared oddly unfamiliar, although there was his mother with so much tension on her face that he had to look away. He walked back to the center of the chancel. He heard the church get very quiet. He looked down at the carpet, turned, and looked at the plain wooden cross hanging on the wall. He looked again at his parish. Rhonda Skillings had her mouth partly opened.

Infantile grandiosity. Tyler swallowed. They were waiting. He went back to the pulpit. All he had to do was read the lines from Isaiah, read a prayer, read anything he had written. *Lord, I have loved the habitation of thy house.* But he could not speak. He thought of Katherine: "Why is the moon following us?" Infantile grandiosity. Tyler leaned an arm across the pulpit to steady himself. Oh, Mr. Freud, we are all big-headed babies, and strangely, the image of Khrushchev, red-faced and shaking his fist, came into his mind. He'd been planning to shake his own fist at these people, and yet he could not even speak. *I am shut up, and I cannot come forth.*

In the silence of the church, it arrived. The tiny hut of failure that had sat on the horizon came toward him with a silent certainty. He leaned forward. His mouth tugged down, like a spasm of his heart. He said softly, "Oh, I am sorry. I can't do this anymore."

He heard a gasp from a back pew, then another gasp, and even another. Bertha Babcock put a hand to her throat and cried out, "No." From the choir loft above came a muted sob. Tyler walked to the middle of the chancel, raised his hands just slightly forward, as though to plead with them, but what he saw was fear on people's faces. They did not look angry, Jane Watson, Fred Chase, Rhonda—no, they looked like children who had gone too far with a prank, and they were afraid. He did not want anyone to be afraid.

A tear filled his right eye. He felt it grow, slip down his face. From both eyes now, tears came over his cheeks as he stood there. He wept, and wept, his shoulders shaking slightly. He did not hide his face; it did not occur to him to do so. He felt only the wet splash from his eyes, blurring the faces before him. Every few moments, he held his hands forward, as though trying to say something.

And then the organ burst into sound. Doris Austin was playing "Abide with Me," and Tyler turned to look up at the choir loft, then turned again to his congregation; they were standing now, some of them singing, and here was Charlie Austin walking up the aisle toward him, Charlie looking right at him, nodding his pink head slightly as though to say, It's all right. And Charlie taking his arm, helping him through the chancel's door, helping him down the few steps.

THE MINISTER'S STUDY was surprisingly messy. The books were put in the shelf at odd angles, some piled on top of others, many with pieces of paper sticking out from them. Charlie hated to see a bookshelf like that. The top of the desk was not visible, so many papers were spread across it. The small window looked out directly onto the snow-covered ground; you couldn't even see a tree from down here.

Charlie looked back at the man. He had thought he would not

ever want to watch such a thing, or that he would have kept his gaze turned away out of politeness. But there seemed no shame in watching what was before him. Tyler wept freely and with little sound. His eyes seemed very blue as he looked at Charlie. There was a kind of innocent bafflement on his face, and Charlie would always remember the way the tears jumped from the minister's eyes, little drops of clear water, and how blue his eyes stayed all the while. The man wept, but smiled at Charlie, too. It was an odd smile, with a kind of childlike forthrightness that suggested friend-liness in the midst of all that was happening. Occasionally, Tyler would raise his hand in a gesture, as though to say something—then let his hand fall back on his lap.

Charlie only nodded. He wondered what Tyler would remem-ber of this moment. He put his hand on Tyler's shoulder, over the black draping robe the man still wore. "Listen," Charlie said.

Tyler nodded, smiling, his eyes big and blue and splashing tears.

"Listen," Charlie said again. But he didn't know, really, what to say. He thought if he had done something as naked and public as Tyler had just done, he would want to kill himself from shame. He didn't want Tyler to feel that. He said, "You're not to worry, Tyler."

"How's that?" said Tyler innocently. He sat with his hands folded on his lap, making no attempt to wipe at his face. When Charlie didn't answer, Tyler said, "I don't know as I can go on as a minister, Charlie. I think I'm not well."

"You're tired. There's no shame in being tired."

"No?"

"No."

Tyler stared toward the window with his blue eyes. Then he looked back at Charlie and said, "You've been in some kind of trouble, haven't you, Charlie? You've had a hard time."

"I'm all right. Do you suppose you could do me a favor and blow your nose?"

"Oh, sure."

For a moment Charlie was afraid he'd have to pull out a hand-kerchief and hold it to the man's nose like he was a child, but Tyler rummaged around beneath his robe and pulled out a handkerchief and wiped at his face. "Say," the minister said, his blue eyes still glistening and wide, "Doris played my favorite hymn when I was up there having trouble. Lovely, wasn't it? Lovely how she did that."

Charlie nodded.

A sharp rap was heard on the door, and Charlie rose to open it. Margaret Caskey stood there. "I'm taking him home now," she said. "The children are waiting in the car. I can't leave Jeannie alone for long."

"Certainly," Charlie said, stepping back.


HIS MOTHER DROVE, the children in the back. No one spoke. Tyler sat with his hands in the pockets of his coat, a tear still slipping now and then from his eyes, so that the wide expanse of blue sky seemed to shimmer, as well as the bare trees that grew by the river, whose edges were frozen over with tucked-in blankets of blue-shadowed snow. The weak noonday sun cast a gentle light over the fields they passed by, the crusty covering of sinking snow radiating a soft brightness that stretched to the horizon, or to a barn, or to the woods nearby.

Katherine, whose earlier happiness had made her picture somersaulting down long, grassy hills, now sat holding tightly to Jeannie's hand while she watched her father, whose face she could partly see from where she sat behind her grandmother. Never, ever, had Katherine known that a grown-up man could cry. It was as astonishing as if a tree had suddenly spoken. Little pieces of terror kept pricking her insides.

Once inside the house, her father stood in the living room, not taking off his coat, his head ducked forward as though the ceiling were too low. "Upstairs, girls. Right now." Her grandmother snapped her fingers, and they followed her, but as Katherine glanced up at her father, he gave her a funny kind of surprised-looking smile, and she knew things were wrong, but the dark pinches stopped in her stomach. She sat next to Jeannie on the bed and sang to her, quietly, song after song.

Downstairs, Tyler remained standing. He looked at the couch, the rocking chair, turned and looked into the dining room. He looked at his mother as she came back into the room, shrugging his shoulders and smiling, but her face was gray, her lips had no color. "Mother," he said, "sit down. Are you all right?"

Very slowly she sat on the edge of the couch, and he went to sit next to her. "Take your coat off," she said, almost in a whisper. "For the sake of God in heaven."

He took his coat off without standing up. "Mother, what's wrong?"

She turned her face to him. Her eyes seemed lashless, naked and pink-rimmed. "What's wrong?" she said. Again her voice was low. "I have never been so humiliated. Ever. In my entire life."

Tyler sat back and gazed down at the ends of his feet, thrust before him; they seemed far away in their black leather shoes. The edges of his shoes were wet. He had left his rubbers in his church office. "To be humbled is a good thing," he said.

"Stop it."

He saw that her hand was trembling on her knee.

"I'll tell you one thing, Tyler Richard Caskey. It is not a good thing to see the last of Susan Bradford. And you have. She was so put off, she could barely look at me, and went straight to her car."

Tyler pictured this: Susan getting into her car, putting the blinker on at the end of the parking lot, driving back to Hollywell with distaste all through her. "Okay," said Tyler. "That's okay."

"Now, you tell me what you intend to do. You're having a nervous breakdown, Tyler, and it is an appalling thing to see. I don't know why you couldn't have come to me earlier, prevented the horror of that scene today."

"Am I having a nervous breakdown?" he said.

"A grown man doesn't get up there and behave the way you did unless he's very, very ill."

"Why," he asked, "are you so angry at me?"

"You'll have to come back to Shirley Falls with me," his mother said, and her voice had returned to its normal level. "But I swear to you, Tyler, I can't have that child in my house for long. And you won't be fit to care for her. I'll have to call Belle and see what she can do."

"What child?"

"Katherine, of course."

"I'm not coming back to Shirley Falls, Mother. You don't need either one of us in your house. And in fact I'd like you to leave Jeannie here."

His mother stood up. "You're crazy," she said. "You really have lost your senses. This is the first time since the death of your father that I have absolutely no idea what to do."

Tyler looked around the room. "I don't think I'm crazy."

"Crazy people never do."

The old dog, Minnie, got up and slunk over to the far corner of the room, where she curled up, her nose on her paws, and watched with lugubrious eyes.

"Mother, good heavens. You're acting as though I'm a murderer." Tyler looked once again around the room. "Maybe I am," he murmured, thinking of the pills he left by Lauren's bed. "Maybe I am."

"Okay, that's it. Get your coat back on. I'm going to call Belle, and we're leaving."

Tyler stood up and went over and sat in one of the dining-room chairs. His mother came and watched him, and he looked at her for a long time before speaking. He spoke quietly. "I'm not leaving right now, Mother. I have to tend to my life and to my children. I do not want you taking Jeannie back with you, and I'm not asking, I'm saying."

"I am not leaving that baby with you."

Tyler nodded slowly. "You are. There's no need here for Solomon's ruling to cut the baby in half."

Mrs. Caskey reached for her pocketbook, buttoned her coat furiously. "And just what are you going to *do*, may I ask?"

"I don't know," Tyler said. "I really don't."


TELEPHONES DID NOT RING from house to house that day, or even in the days that followed. People sitting down for their Sunday meal were quiet, except to direct their children to use a napkin, or to help clear the table. It was as though a death had occurred that could not be absorbed, and a New England reticence took hold, a sense of respectful silence—mixed with some level of guilt—regarding what had been witnessed.

Uneasiness took hold of many, and by the time darkness fell, a number of women had spoken quietly to their husbands, asking that they call the farmhouse to make sure Tyler was all right. "Where will he go?" they asked their husbands. "Tell him we don't want him to go." And when Fred Chase, and Skogie Gowen, and Charlie all telephoned, they were surprised to find that Tyler himself answered. Tyler said he was on his way to Brockmorton to arrange for a student minister until more permanent arrangements could be made. He seemed surprised when he was told they didn't want him to go.

And so people prepared for Thanksgiving with little enthusiasm. Silver did not get polished in some houses, the way it usually did. Walter Wilcox was said to be found sleeping in the church once more. People waited with a sorrow in their hearts, and, bumping into one another in the grocery store, the women did not speak of Tyler as the week went by. They spoke of the scandal of the quiz shows on TV, how it seemed nothing in the world could be trusted anymore. They did not speak of Connie Hatch, who, according to the newspaper, was still being held in the county jail, until investigators and the district attorney determined whether the bodies should be exhumed. On Sunday a student pastor arrived, a thick-faced man with dark eyebrows and a stutter. "M-m-may the m-m-ercy of the Lord b-b-be with us all." It was communion Sunday, but Doris did not sing a solo. "The Lord said, 'This is my bl-bl-blood, and dr-dr-drink of me.' "

Mary Ingersoll moved about the classroom slowly, as though she had added ten years to her life. A feeling of shame prevented her from speaking to Rhonda or Mr. Waterbury about what had happened, and they volunteered nothing themselves. Mr. Waterbury only said kindly, "Just carry on, Mary. We don't know yet if the child will be back."

Mary wanted him to say, "You did the best you could," but he didn't say that, and she didn't know if she deserved it. The minute she had seen Tyler Caskey begin to weep, she understood without words forming inside her that her angry thoughts and assumptions about his character had simply not been true. He was a man grieving, and she was ashamed at the kind of pleasure she had experienced in excoriating him to her friends and husband.

And then the Monday after Thanksgiving, the phones began to ring again.

# ELEVEN

He had been staying with George Atwood. After his mother had left on that strange, strange day, Tyler had tucked the children in the car with a quilt and a pillow, and they slept as he drove up the turnpike through the dark, the snow shining a pale light in the night, the sweeps of fields as he passed by, and then the tall evergreens, darker even than the sky, gave way to the small streets of the town as he wound his way up the hill and pulled up in front of the Atwoods' house. Tyler had called ahead, so they were expecting him. A light was on in the living room. George opened the door almost immediately. "Come in, Tyler," he said. "Come in."

Hilda Atwood put the sleeping children to bed upstairs, and left the men to talk in George's study. Tyler, looking around him, remembered how he had sat there as a student, thinking what a sterile life this couple must have. Now the place seemed as warm and safe as a Norman Rockwell painting. "Oh, boy," he said, and George nodded. He told George what had been happening, and nothing in George's expression showed any surprise. Occasionally George asked a question, and when Tyler reached the part about breaking down in front of his congregation, having Charlie Austin come up to the pulpit to rescue him, George nodded slowly. Tyler sat back, exhausted.

"Stay there," George said. "I'm going to make a pot of strong tea."

Hilda came in to say the children were sleeping. "Gosh," said Tyler. "I forgot to tell you. Katherine might wet the bed."

"I know how to wash sheets," Hilda said.

When George returned with the tea, she left the room again.

"I told Mother it was a good thing to be humbled," Tyler said.

"It is, indeed."

"Well, now I'm simply scared."

"Of what?"

Tyler sipped from the teacup George handed him, and sat back. "I guess of not having a center of gravity. The way Bonhoeffer says a grown man has."

George rubbed a white eyebrow slowly, gazed at his hand, spreading his fingers on his trouser leg, looked back at Tyler. "I'm not sure I have a center of gravity." He didn't seem bothered by this.

"Really?" Tyler asked. "But you must."

"Why?" George took off his glasses, held them toward the light. "As a matter of fact, I could argue that none of us has a center of gravity. That we're tugged and pulled by competing forces every minute and we hold on as best we can." He cleaned his glasses with a handkerchief. "I could make that argument," he said, tucking his handkerchief back in his pocket, "if I were so inclined." He put his glasses back on.

Tyler looked at the old man's well-proportioned hands resting on the wooden arms of the chair he sat in. The fingernails were clean and flat, the faintest pink coloring the fingertips. Tyler could have leaned forward, taken the hand. "It's a relief to hear you say that," he admitted. "You know, sometimes Bonhoeffer has this tone. This—" Tyler held his hand out in frustration. "This *tone* like he knows everything."

"He knew a great deal," said George. "But I suspect if he was concerned about his center of gravity it's because his center felt pretty wobbly at times."

"I suppose that's true. But you know what I realized recently? And I admit it riled me a bit." Tyler picked up his teacup again. "He chose a seventeen-year-old girl to love—because she would adore him. She'd lost her father and brother in the war, you know, so Bonhoeffer became both to her."

"Does that make what she felt not love?"

"But for whom? For Bonhoeffer? She barely knew the man. It was love for her father and her brother she was feeling."

"Tyler," said George, slowly stretching his legs out in front of him, "are you irritated with the man because he was human? Because he wrote about courage, but experienced fear? What was it you'd have liked him to do, Tyler? Stayed alive and faced the prison of domestic drudgery where no one would hail him as a hero? Lived long enough for the seventeen-year-old to become a middle-aged wife who was tired of attending to the laundry and meals, who no longer lit up like a Christmas tree every time he walked through the door? Would you prefer he not be marched out naked to be hanged in the woods, but live to face the horrors of old age, to have his wife die, his children move away?"

"Goodness," Tyler said. He put down the teacup and loosened his tie. "Well, both scenarios require a great deal of courage, I think."

George smiled with his mouth closed, but his old eyes were kind as they rested on Tyler. "Most scenarios do."

Tyler closed his eyes, hearing the small hiss from the radiator. He sighed deeply. Finally he opened his eyes, staring at the white painted wainscoting. "I wonder if there's a job here in the library, George. There must be some student apartment I could live in with the girls for a while."

"You indicated on the phone that the deacons and board members don't want you to leave."

Tyler shook his head. "I can't imagine climbing back up behind that pulpit."

"No one ever said being a minister was an easy job."

Tyler looked over at George with earnestness. "It's a very hard job, George. Good Lord, it is a hard job."

Behind the gold-rimmed glasses, George's small eyes watched him. "Why do you think I teach?"

Tyler picked up his teacup. "I couldn't teach."

"I suspect you could." George slowly uncrossed his legs, crossed them back the other way. "But I think you're a minister, Tyler. You have a job waiting for you, I imagine, in West Annett. After a few years you'll find another church and your life will move on, because lives do. But right now—"

"I need to go back?"

"If your congregation wants you, I think you need to go back."

"I was going to resign."

"So you said. Is it because you feel exposed, lost your manliness up there?"

"I think I showed them I wasn't up to the job."

"Don't you think you should let them decide?"

Tyler didn't answer. He had not really thought it possible to preach in West Annett again.

"We'll arrange for a student pastor to go down for the next couple of weeks. That's no problem. And you can stay here with the children as long as you like. Hilda would love to have the girls around. But you need to speak to your parishioners as soon as you're ready. And I think you're up to it."

"You do?"

George shrugged. "You just stood up to your mother, Tyler. I should think now you could take on the world."

ANYONE WHO HAS EVER GRIEVED knows that grieving carries with it a tremendous wear and tear to the body itself, never mind the soul. Loss is an assault; a certain exhaustion, as strong as the pull of the moon on the tides, needs to be allowed for eventually. And Tyler, during the ten days he stayed with the Atwoods, spent an astonishing amount of time sleeping. Waking at daylight, he would feel sleep roll up to him again, almost immediately, and always with the force of anesthesia. When he finally staggered from the bedroom, embarrassed by what he felt was slothfulness, it was Hilda Atwood who said firmly, "Right back in there, Tyler. This is exactly what you need."

Back to bed he went, his body so heavy with weariness it felt as though his weight would push straight through the mattress to the floorboards below. His sleep was deep and dreamless, and, waking again, he would not know where he was right away, but, hearing the children's voices downstairs, he was reassured, and would lie motionless, as though in traction in a hospital. But he was not in a hospital, and his limbs moved, and as he shaved in the bathroom mirror, he gave great thanks.

Every afternoon he went across the street and prayed in the church in which he had been ordained and married, and where he had sat through the funeral of his wife. He prayed now in the front pew, while the sun came through the stained-glass window that said WORSHIP THE LORD IN THE BEAUTY OF HOLINESS. He thought of the translators who, just a few years before, doing the Revised Standard Version of the Bible, had changed the first line, "In the beginning *when* God created the heavens and the earth," and he thought how beautiful that was, that addition of the word "when," to show what they felt the original Hebrew word had shown— God existed before the beginning; how beautiful it was to glimpse the timelessness of God, and he thought when Katherine was older, he would explain this to her.

Meanwhile, he took the girls sledding, and in the Atwoods' backyard helped build a snowman with them.

Katherine, remembering Mrs. Meadows, tucked Jeannie's blond curls under a hat carefully, patted her on the head, and said, "You're a very pretty girl." When Jeannie lost a mitten, Katherine ran after her. "Don't get cold, honey," she called.

Hilda Atwood said, "You have nice children, Tyler."

He made sure to tell Katherine that night: "Mrs. Atwood said I have nice children."

In George's study the men talked. Tyler spoke of his visit to Connie in the county jail. He told George he did not wish to ever go back, but that he had to.

George nodded. "It's not pleasant, but I think you are obliged to go."

What Tyler did not say was that seeing Connie in jail made him feel he belonged there as well, for he had left the bottle of pills by the bedside for Lauren. Tyler thought a great deal about this, awake in the Atwoods' guest room. Over and over he played it out in his mind—the image of Lauren's suffering those final days— and picturing this, he felt that if he'd had the wherewithal and means, he might have slipped a needle into her so that she need not wake up and learn all over again that she was sick and had to leave her babies. He would have ended her life, if he had dared. *She* had dared. He thought about this often. It even came to seem to him that it was their last act of intimacy, his leaving the bottle of pills for her.

It was wrong, but he would do it again. For this reason he never spoke of it; it was their final, private deed. The complexities of this, and of Connie and what she said she'd done, seemed more than he could understand, and he suspected he would never understand, and that he would have to accept this.

But he did say to George one night, "Lauren was not happy being a minister's wife."

"Well," said George, stretching his legs, "it's worse than being a minister."

"No, I'm serious."

"Oh, so am I." George looked up at him, raising his white eyebrows.

"I think she stopped being happy with me."

George took a deep breath, and for a while the men sat silently. Finally, George said, "No one, to my knowledge, has figured out the secret to love. We love imperfectly, Tyler. We all do. Even Jesus wrestled with that. But I think—I think the ability to receive love is as important as the ability to give it. It's one and the same, really. Consider, for example, the physical act of love between a man and his wife. If one holds back, withholds the ability to receive that pleasure, isn't it a withholding of love?"

Tyler, to his great embarrassment, felt his face flush.

"It's just an example, Tyler."

"Yes."

"I suspect the most we can hope for, and it's no small hope, is that we never give up, that we never stop giving ourselves permission to try to love and receive love."

Tyler nodded, gazing at the rug.

"Your congregation, it seems to me, has given you love. And it's your job to receive it. Perhaps before now they gave you an admiring, childlike kind of love, but what happened to you that Sunday—and their response to it—is a mature and compassionate love."

"Yes," said Tyler. "My word."

In the morning he telephoned Charlie Austin and arranged for a meeting the next evening with the deacons and the board. He telephoned his mother, as he had every day, to check on her. "How do you think I am?" she said. He wondered if his mother lacked the ability to receive love. He telephoned Belle. "She'll get over it," Belle said. "She's not going to cut you out of her life. Meanwhile, welcome to grown-up land."

Tyler took a long walk across the campus of the seminary. Grown-up land. He thought how Bonhoeffer had believed mankind was on the threshold of adulthood. That the world was now coming of age and needed a new understanding of God—God not as a problem solver, not a God to be relied upon exclusively to do what man himself could do. Tyler stopped beneath a huge elm tree, and looked down the hill at the river seen in the distance. If the world's relationship to God was changing, well, Tyler's own relationship to God was changing, too. He thought of the words of the hymn he had always loved: *Help of the helpless, O abide with me.* He knew one could say—perhaps Rhonda Skillings might say—that this was merely the plea of a frightened child reaching up in the dark to hold the hand of Parent God.

But Tyler, softly humming the tune as he stood beneath the elm—*fast falls the eventide; The darkness deepens, Lord with me abide*—thought God existed in the hymn itself, in the yearning and sorrowful acknowledgment of the loneliness and fears that arrived in life. The expression of it, the truthfulness of it, was what was beautiful. He thought of William James writing that a solemn state of mind is never crude or simple, that it seems to contain a certain measure of its own opposite in solution. And it was, to Tyler, this mysterious combination of hope and sorrow that was itself a gift from God. Still—it was hard for Tyler to understand what he felt. It was as though in his long, heavy sleeps, many ideas he had previously had were shifting slowly and getting buried beneath new and shapeless ones.

"I have so many thoughts," Tyler told George that night, as they sat in George's study talking. "And I can't articulate them, or get any of them together."

"Good," said George. "Confusion will prevent you from being dogmatic. A dogmatic pastor is useless."

After a moment, Tyler said, "Bonhoeffer thought the world was growing up. But I wonder what he would think of the world today, all grown-up with its nuclear weapons."

George raised an eyebrow. He said quietly, "He'd probably say that it was up to man, not God, to solve this mess." The old man sat back, sighed deeply. "Get back in the pulpit, Tyler, where you belong. And Tyler—putting nuclear weapons aside for the moment—one of these days you're going to have to call the Slatins. They are the grandparents to these girls, no matter how much you may not be able to stand them."

"Yes," said Tyler, tapping his mouth. "A lot to do."


THE NEXT EVENING, in the living room of the Deans' house, where he had eaten the potluck dinner years before with Lauren, he sat with the board members and the deacons and listened while they said they wanted him back. "What is it you need, Tyler?" Fred Chase asked. "Tell us what you need."

Tyler's heart was beating fast. "Well, I guess to speak honestly," he said, "I need to be out of that farmhouse. Away from those pink walls."

"We thought of that." Fred Chase nodded toward Skogie.

Skogie cleared his throat. "We're going south for the winter, you know, Tyler, and we'd like you to take our house. It's big and warm, and closer to town. And we've been thinking that we might, when we get back, summer in one of the new cottages they're building out by China Lake. The house is really too big for us."

"There's money, you know," said Chris Congdon. "We'll work it out, one way or another. You won't be stuck out in that farmhouse."

"I'll need help with the kids," Tyler said.

They had thought of that, too. Carol Meadows and Marilyn Dunlop had already spoken about setting up a schedule where they would take turns with the children.

"And—I'm in debt." Tyler smiled as he said this, for he did not expect any more than what they had already offered, but when they nodded and said they would give him a raise "long overdue," he was amazed, and might have said, "No, no, don't do that." But he thought of George telling him that the ability to receive was as great as the ability to give, and so he simply said thank you.

THAT NIGHT CHARLIE AUSTIN watched Doris get ready for bed. She turned her back before slipping the flannel nightgown over her head; it had been years since she'd stood before him naked and freely, and perhaps she never would again. He understood now that this was not so much a sexual inhibition—for he felt the same shyness—as an accumulation of shame that had come between them over the years, not only from their spoken altercations, but from the secret of their private disappointments and resentments, as well. There hung between them some fabric of dishonesty, and he was pained deeply to know the fault—or so it seemed tonight—was almost fully his. He felt he had soiled himself, and therefore his family, and they would always have to drag some filthy diaper behind them into their advancing years.

Charlie said, "Tyler looked rested. He looks ready to come back."

"I'm glad" was all Doris said. She got into bed beside him, putting lotion on her hands.

"It was nice of you," he said, "to play that hymn for him that day. He appreciated it, Doris, mentioned it in his study after. It wasn't lost on him."

"I'm glad," Doris said again. She added, "It just came to me."

A natural goodness existed in her, he thought. One that had become hidden beneath the dust of domestic worries. She switched out the light beside the bed, and cautiously, he reached for her hand. She allowed him to hold it, moist from the cream, both of them on their backs in the dark. He remembered how Caskey had once, years ago, said in a sermon that the Hebrew word for Satan was "The Accuser," and he felt like Satan lying there, having accused his wife of much over the years—of spending too much money, of being fretful so often that joy seemed impossible, even of serving him food that was not hot enough. He saw no way to recover from the calumny he had brought into the household: Satan now accusing himself. He still thought every day of the woman in Boston, still missed her with a nauseating longing, although there were times the memory of her would suddenly, briefly, repulse him. The memory of himself repulsed him.

"I don't care about a new organ anymore," Doris said calmly.

"Are you sure?" He turned his face toward her in the dark. "There's still money, even with Caskey's expenses."

"Nope," said Doris. "I hope nobody even talks about it. I just lost my appetite for it—that's all."

He didn't know what to say.

"Don't be sad about it," she added. "Maybe sometime in the future. But I just don't care about it now."

"All right, then."

"Charlie?" She was speaking to the ceiling. "Maybe someday you could tell me what you saw in the war. How it was you survived."

"I survived because I was ordered by the Japs to drive a Jeep. They couldn't figure out how to drive it." It surprised him to realize he had never told her that.

"Well, thank God," Doris said, still looking at the ceiling, her hand tightening just slightly on his. "But if you could someday, just *one* day, tell me what you saw, and then we'd never mention it again."

She had asked him this before and always he answered harshly that she was never to ask again.

"I wouldn't tell anyone," she added, turning her face toward him.

He said nothing, and in a minute she squeezed his hand and rolled away from him. "Maybe I'll try," he finally said hoarsely. "Someday, maybe." After a long while, he heard her breathing slow as she fell asleep.

AND SO IT was that during the time between Thanksgiving and Christmas, Reverend Caskey met with all the members of his congregation, one house at a time, much as he had done when he first moved to town. He came in the evenings and spoke quietly, and people could not help remembering when he had made those visits years before, a younger man, broad-shouldered and gregarious, his pretty, distracted wife not appearing the way they had expected her to. Now he sat, leaning forward with his elbows on his knees, still a keen listener, but with a visage revealing the fatigue of the years. He still laughed in a way that made his blue eyes light up, he still tilted his head as he watched someone speak, but he was older, and when he rose to leave, there was not the quick buoyancy of his earlier step.

He paid a visit to Mary Ingersoll and her husband, asking about their families and their college years. He seemed a man very different from the one Mary had encountered in the school, and she felt intimidated in a different way. But he struck the right note, both she and her husband later agreed; he was not deferential and eager to please, just polite and tired and apparently interested in what their needs might be. "Perhaps we could move the service from ten o'clock to eleven, so those of you who work hard during the week could sleep in. But you come whenever you like—that's the point of the church, to be there when you need it."

And so in this way, it was decided by the town, and by Tyler, that he would stay on—at least for the time being. (The woman from the pharmacy did not show up in church anymore, and there were those who still wondered where Tyler would find a wife.) Tyler himself wondered this, but mostly he felt a sense of enormous relief to have the girls together, and a sense of puzzlement that his parish had in fact loved him this way.

He went every week to visit Connie. He took her books and a sweater and some socks, as the sheriff had told him he could do. Sometimes Adrian went with him and other times he went alone. One time she whispered to him—although they were alone in the visiting room—that she had thought of "ending it all," and he had taken her hands and begged her not to. "If you keep visiting me," she said, "I can keep going. And Adrian, too. If he keeps visiting me, too. But it'll be a longer drive when I get moved to Skowhegan."

"Did Adrian say he was going to stop?"

"No."

"Well, then. And neither will I."

The next time he went, Connie said that the woman guard who had been hired to watch her had become friendly, and for the first time, Connie's eyes looked more like they used to. "You see," Tyler said. "Where there are people, there is always the hope of love."

Connie sat back. "Do you think she's a lesbian?" she asked.

"Oh, my goodness, no. I meant love as in friendship, Connie."

"Like us?"

"Like us."

But every time he drove away, he felt he was driving away from death. He felt greedy for every piece of sunlight that twinkled off his dashboard; every branch of a tree seemed to him so sweet he imagined himself running his hands over the rough bark as though it were the flesh of a dear and loving woman. With all his heart he hated that ride up the hill to the county jail and nursing home; it baffled him to think of the sorrow within its walls, and made him guilty to think he was free—each visit reminded him of the bottle of pills left by the side of Lauren's bed. But he could not stop the huge wave of relief as he drove back down into the everyday world, and out on the main roads he sometimes stopped to do an errand just to bump into people. Doris Austin was sometimes in the grocery store, and he would go to her quickly, her quotidian presence seeming splendid, a gift. "Doris," he would say, "how are you? How awfully nice to see you."

"Hello, Tyler." She was shyer now. When he had visited them in their home, thanking them for their help on his day of distress, he had suddenly bent forward and hugged both Doris and Charlie before he went out the door. He was not sure he had ever hugged a man before—when he left for the navy, he and his father had shaken hands. When he pressed Charlie's shoulder, he'd felt beneath his hand both a surprising thinness and a sudden stiffness, as though the gesture had somehow horrified the man. But they had stood together on their front steps in the cold night air, as he walked to his car, as he waved to them as he backed out the driveway, Doris's braided bun shining under their outdoor light, Charlie's shirtsleeve showing white as he raised his arm and left it there.

HE NO LONGER worked in his study at home—for soon he would be moving to the Gowens' house—but, once again, went every morning to the church after Katherine had been picked up by Mrs. Carlson and he had dropped Jeannie at the Meadowses'. He prayed in the sanctuary, and sometimes he didn't pray, but just sat there for many, many minutes, thinking of Lauren and his children and Connie. He thought of Kierkegaard writing that "No one is born devoid of spirit, and no matter how many may go to their death with this spiritlessness, it is not the fault of Life."

One morning, he realized that what he had experienced the day he stood weeping before his congregation, seeing Charlie Austin come to help him, hearing the hymn burst forth from the old organ, was The Feeling. This surprised him: It was very different from the times before, but that's what it had been, The Feeling. *O Lord, truly I am thy servant . . . and the son of thine handmaid; Thou hast loosed my bonds.* He looked through the long window. The sky was the pale, sweet blue of a baby's blanket. He understood again that his relationship to God was changing, as it would have to do. *I will offer to thee the sacrifice of thanksgiving . . .*

On a snowy day in December, a truck came to move the minister's things from the farmhouse to the Gowens'. Tyler had told

Katherine she could stay home from school, because he did not want her leaving one home and coming back to another. He thought it best for her to see the change take place, but Jeannie stayed with Carol Meadows. After the men left with the truck, after Tyler had gone through the house one more time, he took the child's hand and closed the rattly doorknob behind them, walked down the tilting porch steps.

Icicles the size of a man's upper arm hung from the edge of the porch roof. The light snow that had begun at dawn was already making the world whiter, already renewing the surface of things so that the icicles and snow seemed a faint bluish-gray. "Pumpkin," the minister said, and he picked the child up. She put both arms around his neck but turned to look with him back at the house.

"All gone," she said. He kissed her cheek, and she put her head against his neck. And everything seemed remarkable, the familiar scent of his child, the snarl in the back of her hair, the quiet house, the bare birch trunks, the snow on his face. Remarkable.

ABOUT THE AUTHOR

ELIZABETH STROUT's first novel, *Amy and Isabelle,* won the *Los Angeles Times* Award for First Fiction and the *Chicago Tribune* Heartland Award, and was a finalist for the PEN/Faulkner Award, as well as the Orange Prize in England. Her short stories have been published in a number of magazines, including *The New Yorker.* Currently she is on the faculty of the low-residency M.F.A. program at Queens University in Charlotte, North Carolina. She lives in New York City.

This book is set in Fournier, a typeface named for Pierre Simon Fournier, the youngest son of a French printing family. He started out engraving woodblocks and large capitals, then moved on to fonts of type. In 1736 he began his own foundry and made several important contributions in the field of type design; he is said to have cut 147 alphabets of his own creation. Fournier is probably best remembered as the designer of St. Augustine Ordinaire, a face that served as the model for Monotype's Fournier, which was released in 1925.